# Blackmeadow Abbey

# Blackmeadow Abbey

## Jane Glatt

TYCHE BOOKS LTD.

Blackmeadow Abbey
Copyright © 2023 Jane Glatt

Published by Tyche Books Ltd.
Calgary, Alberta, Canada
www.TycheBooks.com

Cover Art by Niken Anindita
Cover Design by Indigo Chick Designs
Editorial by M.L.D. Curelas
Illustration 141368433 © Sana78822 | Dreamstime.com

First Tyche Books Ltd Edition 2023
Print ISBN: 978-1-989407-40-0
Ebook ISBN: 978-1-989407-41-7

Author photograph: Eugene Choi Echo1 Photography

This book was funded in part by a grant from the Alberta Media Fund.

Alberta
Government

To every Jane Austen fan, ever.
I've tried to do her justice.

# I

It's been called early," Father said once they were all seated for dinner. "I heard it myself over the Ansons' speaker."

Caroline's heart skipped a beat. "The Endeavour?" she asked, and her father nodded.

"No!" Becca wailed. "It's not due for another year!" Her younger sister slapped her hand down on the table. "It can't be true!"

"Stop it, Becca," Mother said with a frown. "You'll compete next time."

"That's forever away," Becca grumbled as she crossed her arms, perhaps to stop herself from taking out her frustrations on the table again.

Caroline had sympathy for her sister. Normally the Endeavour occurred every fifteen years and it had only been fourteen since the last one. But that one year meant that Becca wasn't eligible: she'd be almost thirty when it was her chance to compete.

"I'm sorry, Becca," Father said. "It's not what any of us wanted or expected."

"You should have had me right after Caroline was born," Becca pouted. "I'll be wasting so many years waiting for my Endeavour."

"You will not put your life on hold," Mother said. "I won't allow it. Every Endeavour there are children who are one year too young to qualify, and they grow up and make plans and live their lives. And keep in mind that not everyone gets to enter Blackmeadow Abbey."

Caroline's mother, Thea Morris, hadn't actually competed in her Endeavour twenty-nine years ago. It was the Endeavour where the fewest teams entered the Abbey since the competition began over one hundred and twenty years ago. Father's team had been one of the first to go inside, which is why the Morris family had three artifacts.

Becca wisely didn't say anything else, although when Caroline looked at her sister, she was scowling.

"I'll send word to Jack," Father said.

"He probably knew before we did," Caroline replied. Her older brother was at school, and in addition to his studies, he seemed to always find time to investigate Builder-enhanced artifacts. Like the Ansons' speaker.

"Then we should expect him home soon," Mother said. "Now, I know the news is exciting, but dinner is getting cold."

"This does change our plans," Father said to Caroline. "You and Jack must start searching for suitable teammates immediately."

"Yes, Father," Caroline replied. She looked over at Becca again. It was always supposed to be the three of them. Now that Becca wasn't going to compete, who would they get to make up their foursome? Would Jack even want to team up with her? There were only three years between her seventeen and his twenty, but Jack had matured since going off to school. They only had ninety days to figure it out.

Caroline fingered her necklace—the artifact she'd been given on her fifteenth birthday. It was old-fashioned by today's standards—a silver rope chain with a single diamond—and did such a small magic—just a soft glow that could only be seen in the dark—but it would be odd to hand it over after wearing it every day for the past two and a half years.

"When do we hand in our artifacts?" she asked.

"The Administration will send out those details," her father said. "Until then, I don't want it to leave the house."

The Administration—a group made up of past Endeavour competitors—managed the rules and regulations for the Endeavour, including the timing of when it would take place.

"Yes, Father." Artifacts were prized not just for their magical abilities: each competitor was required to submit one in order to enter the Endeavour. Caroline had read all the histories and knew that desperate people without an artifact of their own or the means to buy one might try to steal one in order to compete.

"I can't stress how important having the right teammates is for you and Jack," Father said. "Especially now that Becca is not eligible." He sighed. "I thought we'd have at least another year to recruit a suitable individual and now we need two people."

"Should I wait for Jack to arrive?" Caroline asked. "I'm sure he'll be home in a day or two."

"You can't afford to wait," her father said. "You must begin your search right away. Thankfully, the Ansons have offered to help. They are leaving for Norbarrow tomorrow and have offered to take you with them. Mrs. Anson has promised to help you meet potential teammates and Mr. Anson has high hopes of joining the Administration."

"That's very nice of them to offer to help," Mother said. "Don't you think so, Caroline?"

"I do, Mother." And it *was* nice of them. She wasn't overly fond of Mr. Anson, but Mrs. Anson was interesting and extremely kind. Becca thought she was silly for liking Mrs. Anson but she was the only adult who encouraged Caroline's fascination with the history of the Endeavour. Mostly because she herself was consumed with curiosity about artifacts.

"If we hear from Jack, or if he comes home, we'll send him to the Ansons' in Norbarrow," Father said. "They've agreed to host him as well. I'm not sure how we'll ever thank them for their generosity."

Caroline spent the rest of the meal nodding at the advice her father gave her regarding the Endeavour. Most of what he said she agreed with; she'd spent hundreds of hours reading about Endeavour competitions all the way back to when it all started.

It had been a dreadful fight between two of the most powerful Natural magic wielders ever born. Caroline hadn't been able to discover why they argued but the resulting magical battle took both their lives and all but destroyed the place where they fought.

But their magic had somehow fused and endured beyond their deaths.

One hundred and twenty years later, the magic of Blackmeadow Abbey waxed and waned in mostly a fifteen-year cycle. Magical artifacts placed inside the Abbey were transformed: the magic changed in ways that often made the artifact even more useful—and therefore valuable. Finding as many of those magically enhanced artifacts as possible was the goal of every Endeavour team.

Even artifacts without useful magic had value since one was the price of admission for every would-be competitor. Many were sold or traded in the months following an Endeavour but they were the most dear right now, when the Endeavour had been called.

*Lost* artifacts—ones that had been inside the Abbey for years or decades—were the grand prizes. The longer artifacts were inside, the more magic they seemed to absorb. Only a few were recovered every Endeavour but they could be extremely valuable. Builders spent fortunes for ones they could enhance and splinter to multiply. The Ansons' speaker had been created out of a lost artifact, and Caroline knew from her studies that the families of the team who had recovered that artifact, even generations later, were very comfortable financially.

Caroline and a sullen Becca tidied up after dinner. Her sister ignored any attempts to talk and it hurt to see her so unhappy. It would have been so much better if they'd been competing in the same year, on the same team.

"You'll be able to compete with Miles," Caroline said. "So, you'll have just as much family on your team as I will."

"Don't try to make me feel better," Becca said. "It won't work. Nothing will work. My life is ruined."

"Don't say that." Caroline looked out the kitchen door to the dining room but didn't see their mother. As much as Thea Morris claimed that she hadn't missed anything by not entering the Abbey, Caroline knew it was a sore point. Those who hadn't gone inside weren't considered true competitors and were even excluded from certain occupations, although they were mostly related to the actual Endeavour itself. A non-competitor could not be an Administrator or hold any of the dozens of other roles that dealt with managing the competition. The fact that over seventy-five percent of the teams that year hadn't set foot in the

Abbey hadn't changed any of that.

She had no idea if all Othians worried about this since she'd never been anywhere other than Gaynesford. Her trip with the Ansons would be her first time away from her family and her first time in a city.

"Caroline," her father called. "In my office, please."

Caroline put the last dish away and smoothed her skirt. She tried to catch Becca's eye but her sister ignored her. Hurt, Caroline left the kitchen and headed to the wood-panelled room at the front of the house where her father managed their small estate.

"Yes, Father?" Caroline hovered in the open doorway. Normally being summoned to their father's office led to being disciplined in some way. But this was not a normal day.

"Your artifact, please."

"Of course." Caroline stepped into the office and reached up to unclasp her necklace. She placed it in her father's outstretched hand and watched as he put in the safe. Excitement warred with dread when her father shut and locked the safe.

"There," he said. "It will be ready when the Administration notice comes. You will need to assure your potential teammates that you have one, but it's best to watch what you say about your artifact when you're in Norbarrow. Now I suggest you ask your mother what you need to pack."

"Yes, Father." Caroline turned and left the room. Away from Becca's hurt and disappointment, she felt her excitement start to grow: Norbarrow and then the Endeavour! Even if, like her mother, she never set foot in Blackmeadow Abbey, Norbarrow would be an adventure she would remember her whole life.

"MR. ANSON HAS rented a carrier!" Caroline called out. She had been staring out the window of the front door as she waited to be picked up for the trip to Norbarrow. "How wonderful." She'd never been in a carrier and had only rarely seen them. Gaynesford wasn't on the way to anywhere important so hardly anyone of stature passed through the village.

"Mr. Anson is making a statement," Becca said from her side.

"He has to," Father said. He was standing behind them in the hallway. "If he wants to impress enough people to get a seat on the Administration. Come now, Caroline, let's get your luggage."

"I'll see you soon." Caroline turned to Becca and gave her a hug. "I'll write twice a week."

"No, you won't." Becca was still obviously bitter about having missed the cut-off age. "I wouldn't, not when you'll be able to have so many new adventures."

"I'm not you," Caroline replied. "And I *will* miss you, no matter how many adventures I have."

She hurried down the hall to where Mother was waiting. Father had already taken her two suitcases out to the carrier.

"Of course, I'll miss you most of all," she said to her mother. "I'll write often."

"You must, so you can tell me of all the wonderful events you're attending," her mother said. "And the people you're meeting. Promise me that you will make the most of any opportunities you get to experience the festivities. There will be dozens of events and I want you to take part in as many as you can. At least until your team is settled."

"I promise." Caroline linked arms with her mother and together they walked outside. The carrier appeared to be much like any other carriage, although to her mind the black paint seemed much shinier. The driver, who was dressed all in black to match the carrier, sat up top although in front of him was a series of levers instead of reins and a team of horses.

"The equivalent of five horses," Mr. Anson was saying to Father. "Even the compartment has been enhanced by Builders. We'll make it to Norbarrow just after nightfall and it will be as smooth a ride as you could ever want."

"A single day," Father replied. "That is quick. I want to thank you again for taking Caroline with you and for welcoming Jack when he can get there. With Becca not eligible, it's a great relief to know that they will have an excellent chance to find teammates."

"We're happy to have them both," Mr. Anson said. "My time will be taken with other matters, so it's good to have Caroline as a companion for Mrs. Anson. Ah, Caroline, there you are. Are you excited?"

"Very much," Caroline replied. "Thank you for inviting me and my brother to stay with you."

"It was all my idea," Mrs. Anson said. She was leaning out the side window of the carrier's passenger compartment. "You both deserve a chance to enjoy everything you can during your Endeavour. Besides, we always have such excellent discussions about artifacts. And here we are travelling in a Builder-enhanced one!"

Mr. Anson pulled out his watch and glanced at it. "We must be off if we want to make it to Bridgehaven for midday."

"Be good," Mother said as she hugged Caroline tight. She stepped back and gave her a serious look. "And enjoy yourself."

"Don't enjoy yourself so much that you forget why you're there," her father said. "Your and Jack's priority is to assemble a team. But don't be too hasty. It's far too important a decision to rush. Take your time and make sure you select people you can trust."

"Yes, Father." Caroline wasn't about to forget that part of her trip. Besides, she had little doubt that the Endeavour—and teams—would be a major topic of conversation wherever they went.

Father patted her on the shoulder, and with a nervous smile, Caroline went to the carrier.

"Sit here beside me," Mrs. Anson said. "Oh, I see that you are not wearing your artifact."

"Father put it in his safe," Caroline said as she sat down beside Mrs. Anson. "It would be terrible for it to go missing so close to the Endeavour." She studied the interior of the compartment. She had to admit she was a little disappointed: it wasn't much different than the horse drawn carriages she'd been in before. Although not smelling horses was a great improvement.

"Of course," Mrs. Anson said. "Far too many artifacts have been lost or even stolen in the lead-up to the competition. Did I ever tell you about the artifact that was stolen from a Natural?"

Mr. Anson joined them in the compartment and twisted a knob that was set onto the front panel. "We're ready," he called. The carrier lurched as it started to move, then quickly settled into a gentle motion.

"My goodness," Caroline exclaimed. "This is a smooth ride."

"In part due to the skill of the driver," Mr. Anson replied. "Since it didn't cost more, I insisted on one of their more experienced drivers."

"Well worth asking for, I dare say," Mrs. Anson replied. She turned back to Caroline. "Mr. Anson does think of every detail. Now, as I was saying, about the artifact that was stolen from a Natural."

Mrs. Anson's tale took up most of the morning drive. Caroline wasn't bored, exactly, she usually found Mrs. Anson's stories interesting. However, her companion could have told it in half the time. She spent almost half of the tale describing the artifact— in this case an embroidered wallet that continuously replenished itself with money. She eventually got around to what Caroline thought was the most interesting part—how the thief was found by a tracking spell the Natural cast—but by then the carrier was slowing.

The knob in front of Mr. Anson twisted and clicked. He folded the newspaper he'd been reading and put it on the seat beside him.

"We've arrived in Bridgehaven," he said. He pulled out his watch and nodded. "On schedule. I've arranged for our lunch and allowed for a few minutes to stretch our legs after we eat. Then it's non-stop until Norbarrow."

He opened the door, exited the compartment, and held the door while Caroline and Mrs. Anson got out.

"This is lovely," Caroline said. A small, sun-dappled building— an inn by the sign—nestled amongst a grove of trees. A watermill turned in the stream that ran alongside the inn. Birds chirped and sang in the trees and the wind sighed through the branches.

A couple of horse-drawn carriages were pulled up at the water troughs: other travellers journeying by less magical means.

"The Inn at Bridgehaven is powered by the mill," Mr. Anson said. "They had a Builder design their lighting and running water to use that power."

"They also have a Builder-enhanced artifact that keeps the cooker at an even temperature," Mrs. Anson said. "Come, I'll ask them to show us."

Caroline followed Mrs. Anson into the inn. After a tour of the artifact, they enjoyed a meal of cottage pie and cheese. Despite Mrs. Anson's claims, Caroline couldn't detect anything different about a meal that had been prepared in a Builder-enhanced cooker.

While Mrs. Anson returned to the carrier and Mr. Anson pulled out his watch, Caroline took a very brief walk along the river. She sighed and stood in the sun for a moment before turning and hurrying back to the carrier: she did not want to be the cause of making them late.

"Thank you for such a lovely meal," she said to Mr. Anson. He nodded and she climbed into the compartment and settled herself beside Mrs. Anson.

"We are right on schedule," Mr. Anson said approvingly when he joined them. He twisted the knob and the carrier set off.

"Look at all the lights of Norbarrow," Mrs. Anson said. "I wonder how many of them are powered by artifacts?"

Caroline poked her head out the window. They passed dozens of three- and four-storey buildings that had lights shining in their windows.

"They even light their front steps," Caroline said. No one in Gaynesford did that, not even the Ansons.

"You'll find that nightlife is much different here in the city," Mrs. Anson replied. "One needs to be able to see where to put your feet when returning from a concert or a late supper. I should think that we shall light our front steps from time to time."

"We certainly will," Mr. Anson said. "I must make sure my contacts feel free to visit whenever they pass by."

"Do you have many contacts, Mr. Anson?" Caroline asked. "I fear that I know no one other than yourself and Mrs. Anson." She hadn't really thought about how she would meet people. Father expected her to find teammates but he hadn't suggested how she should do that.

"I have a few," Mr. Anson replied. "I hope they are enough to allow me to make the acquaintance of an Administrator so I can make my petition."

"We'll make our own acquaintances," Mrs. Anson said. "There's a group who gathers to discuss artifacts that I'm ever so eager to meet."

"This is our street," Mr. Anson said as the carrier turned a corner. "It shouldn't be long before we reach the house I hired." He checked his watch. "The staff should have everything prepared."

The knob turned and clanked as the carrier pulled to a stop.

Caroline peered past Mrs. Anson to a grey stone, three-storey building. A man and a woman stood on the well-lit front steps.

The man approached the carrier. "Mr. Anson," he said. "I trust you had a pleasant journey."

"I did. You must be Wooton," Mr. Anson said as he stepped out of the compartment.

"I am. And Mrs. Anson." Wooton extended his hand to help Mrs. Anson out of the carrier.

"This is our young companion," Mr. Anson said. "Caroline Morris."

"Miss Morris." Wooton nodded and held the door while Caroline got out.

Once everyone was on firm ground, Mr. Wooton waved the woman over.

"Mrs. Wooton, my wife, is the housekeeper," he said. "I'll see to the luggage while Mrs. Wooton shows you in. Cook has prepared a light supper, although if you want something more substantial, that can be arranged."

"A light supper should be quite enough," Mr. Anson said. "Thank you. Our journey has been long, but very easy."

"Come along, Caroline," Mrs. Anson said, and Caroline followed her up the steps and through the door.

The entry hall was as large as her family's dining room, and although Caroline was no expert, everything in it, from the side table to the chandelier overhead, seemed expensive.

"Supper is in the dining room," Mrs. Wooton said when all three travellers were in the entry hall. "I'll show you where that is before I take you to your rooms. I'm sure you'd like to wash off the dust of your journey."

"Yes, thank you," Mr. Anson said. "Although we came by carrier so we accumulated little in the way of dust on the way."

"Of course," the housekeeper said.

The dining room was the second door along the hall, just past a proper parlour. After allowing them a quick peek inside to see a large table laid with three place settings, Mrs. Wooton led them up the stairs. Caroline waited on the landing at the top of the stairs while Mr. and Mrs. Anson were shown to their quarters.

Wooton slipped past her, followed by a young man loaded down with luggage.

"Your luggage will be up shortly," Mrs. Wooton said when she returned to Caroline. "Your room is this way."

Caroline was led to a large room at the front of the house.

"The bathing room is through that door," Mrs. Wooton said. "If you need anything else, just ask Wooton or Sally, the housemaid."

"Thank you," Caroline said, although Mrs. Wooton had already left the room. She crossed the room—which was larger than even her parents' bedchamber at home—to the window. She pulled back the curtain and looked out on the street. The young man she'd seen earlier was out front, pulling her suitcases off the back of the carrier. Once he stepped away from it, the carrier sped off into the night.

The young man climbed the front steps and disappeared from her sight.

The curtains in the houses across the street were drawn and only one had a light illuminating their front steps.

There was a knock on her door.

"Come in," Caroline said, stepping away from the window.

"Your luggage, Miss," Wooton said. He stepped aside to allow the young man to enter and deposit her cases on the luggage racks that stood beside an armoire.

"Thank you." She waited until both men had gone, closing the door as they left, before heading to the bathing room.

She washed her hands and smoothed her hair, before going downstairs in search of the dining room.

AFTER THEY FINISHED their light supper, Mrs. Anson claimed fatigue and Mr. Anson said he had correspondence to write.

Not even the least tired, but not sure if it was appropriate for her to sit in the parlour alone, Caroline went up to her room. She had books to read—she'd finally gotten her hands on a copy of *True Stories of Blackmeadow Abbey* by Samuel Jones—but once in her room she found that she was too keyed up to read.

Instead, she sat by the window and watched the street. Horse-drawn carriages rattled past and even a few carriers glided by. By the time she was yawning, she estimated that more people had passed by her window in a few hours than lived in Gaynesford and the entire surrounding countryside.

# 2

After a sound sleep, Caroline woke up excited to start her new adventure and enjoy every experience on offer.

Even though she arrived downstairs relatively early, when she entered the dining room, Mrs. Wooton told her that Mr. Anson had already breakfasted and left the house.

"The tea should still be hot," Mrs. Wooton said. "And I can bring you some rolls."

"Thank you," Caroline replied. "I will have some tea and wait for Mrs. Anson and eat with her."

"Very well." Mrs. Wooton smiled. "I understand that this is your Endeavour. It's such an exciting time in your life and the whole city comes alive." She paused. "Please don't hesitate to ask if you need anything. There are so many events to enjoy and I dare say you will make some lovely friends."

"I do hope so," Caroline replied. Mrs. Wooton nodded to her and left.

Caroline poured herself a cup of tea, added sugar and a drop of cream, and sat in a chair that faced the window. It wasn't the street view she had from her bedroom. This window looked out onto a small garden at the back of the house.

It was a bright, sunny day and Caroline couldn't help but be impatient to get on with it. Except she had no idea what she should be doing in order to find teammates for herself and her brother.

She was contemplating pouring herself a second cup of tea when Mrs. Anson arrived.

"My dear Caroline," she said. "I hope you're ready to start our adventures."

"I am," Caroline said. "Have you made plans for us?"

"Indeed, I have. Oh, Mrs. Wooton. A fresh pot of tea would be welcome. What are you serving?"

"Currant bread and some rolls," Mrs. Wooton said from the doorway to the dining room. "With jam and heavy cream or butter if you prefer."

"Oh, heavy cream for me," Mrs. Anson said. "Caroline?"

"Heavy cream will suit me as well."

"So, back to plans for our day," Mrs. Anson said once Mrs. Wooton had retreated. "I told you about the artifact group meeting? Well, they meet most days down at Administration Hall. From what I have been told, the artifact group is very informal. I've been corresponding with Mrs. Digby and she has assured me that she will introduce us to the group."

"That sounds promising," Caroline said.

"It does, doesn't it? Oh, there's Mrs. Wooton with our breakfast."

CAROLINE DID HER very best to be patient. After breakfast Mrs. Anson had to go over the household tasks—including planning out their meals—with Mrs. Wooton before they could even think about leaving for Administration Hall.

She wandered in the garden for an hour, trying to enjoy the sun and the scent of the flowers, but she made sure to stay within sight of the back door.

Finally, Mrs. Wooton appeared on the back steps and Caroline hurried over to her.

"Mrs. Anson asked that you be ready to leave in ten minutes, Miss."

"Thank you so much," Caroline said. "I just need to grab a wrap from my room and then I will be ready."

She followed the housekeeper inside and practically ran up the stairs and returned to the front hall, wrap in hand, with eight minutes to spare.

Mrs. Anson finally joined her.

"It's such a fine day for a walk," she said. "Mr. Anson took this house specifically because it is very close to Administration Hall. He says that much of the traffic along the road is either coming or going from the Hall."

"A walk will be lovely," Caroline said. She followed Mrs. Anson out the front door and down the few steps to the sidewalk. A carrier silently swept past.

"See?" Mrs. Anson said. "They are most likely going to the Hall, just as we are." She linked Caroline's arm and the two of them headed off after the carrier.

Caroline was grateful for Mrs. Anson's steady presence as she craned her neck, trying to take in everything at once. She nodded at a couple as they passed them on the sidewalk and almost gasped as a bright red carrier drove past.

"What a beautiful colour," she said to Mrs. Anson.

"It certainly makes a statement," Mrs. Anson replied. "It's sure to belong to someone important."

"It must." How wonderful to be bold enough to drive a carrier like that.

The buildings that lined the street soon switched from houses to shops. All manner of wonderful items were displayed in the large windows.

"You can purchase Builder-enhanced artifacts here!" Caroline exclaimed. She stopped in front of a large, shop window. Small tags had been placed beside the half-dozen items that were arranged on the display shelves.

"*Speaker duplicator,*" she read. "*Listen to your speaker in a second room or even in your carrier.*" She turned to Mrs. Anson. "Have you heard of this?"

"I have not," Mrs. Anson said. She studied the store sign. "They're new enhancements that Builders have devised for existing artifacts. I am very familiar with what the artifacts can do, of course."

"New enhancements," Caroline repeated. "This one here," she pointed, "is for cookers like the one we saw at the inn."

"I don't see any functions that I'm not already familiar with," Mrs. Anson said. "Come now, we mustn't dawdle."

"Sorry, I don't want to make us late," Caroline said, when all she wanted to do was dawdle. Then she remembered that her father expected her to find suitable teammates for the Endeavour, and she relinked arms with Mrs. Anson and determinedly set out towards the Hall.

No one could miss Administration Hall. It was a massive four-storey building that took up an entire block. Groups chatted in the large square in front of it and people streamed through the multiple doors.

"I never even dreamt that such a building could exist," Caroline said. "Which entrance do we use?"

"Why the main one, of course." Mrs. Anson steered them through the crowd to a large arched entrance. Huge wooden doors were open and rested at either side of the entrance. They joined a line of people entering the building, passing a similar line heading in the opposite direction back outside.

Once they were past the entrance area, Mrs. Anson pulled Caroline to one side, and they both stood and stared around. Caroline glanced up and gasped: a coffered ceiling four floors above them was laid in an intricate pattern.

Straight ahead, a wide, wooden staircase rose up to a mezzanine level. Above that, railings lined the half walls of two higher floors.

And people were everywhere. There was so much activity that Caroline had no idea what to look at first.

"That must be the directory Mr. Anson told me about," Mrs. Anson said. She tugged an awestruck Caroline over to a section of wall that was filled with notices. "See if you can find the Artifact Society. I'll start at this end."

It took Caroline three steps to get to the end of the list. She squinted at the lettering, searching for anything that mentioned artifacts.

She was on the third column when she spotted it. "Here's a listing for the Artifact Society," she said, and Mrs. Anson joined her. "It says west corridor, mezzanine level."

"Excellent. Come along." Mrs. Anson led the way through the crowd to the stairs. Once on the mezzanine, she steered them left and then down an interior hallway.

A group of people were scattered along wooden benches that lined the hall.

"Is this the Artifact Society?'" Mrs. Anson asked. "Is there a

Mrs. Digby here? She told me to come here and ask for her."

"She's not here today, I'm afraid," a man said. He rose from his seat on a bench. "She's away for a few days. Was she expecting you?"

"Not specifically today," Mrs. Anson said. "We have been corresponding for some months now, and she said I should visit the next time I came to Norbarrow. I am very interested in artifacts and was assured that this group is as well."

"We are. Are you planning on joining?" the man asked. "We have a very stringent test."

"Only real experts are allowed," a second man said. "Are you an expert?"

"I like to think so," Mrs. Anson replied. "I would welcome your test to determine if I am. What about my friend here? If I pass, is she allowed to attend with me?"

"Is she an expert?"

"In Endeavours, yes," Mrs. Anson replied, and Caroline did her best hide her shock.

She was very interested in Endeavours, but she would not call herself an expert.

"But not artifacts?"

"She's an expert in artifacts that have been retrieved during Endeavours," Mrs. Anson said.

"We can test her too," the second man said. "Although it's not our standard test so we would need at least a full day to devise one."

"We can test you now, if you're ready," the first man said. "That way, if you fail, we don't need to spend time creating another test for your young friend."

"Splendid," Mrs. Anson said. "My name is Mrs. Anson and this is Miss Caroline Morris. I'm ready when you are."

The two men looked at a woman who was sitting on a bench farther down the hall. "Miss Foster will test you. But I'm sorry, Mrs. Anson, Miss Morris can't be present during your test."

"I'll meet you back at the top of the stairs," Caroline said.

"Thank you, dear," Mrs. Anson replied, but Caroline could tell she was already focused on her test.

She walked back along the hallway to the main floor of the mezzanine.

She found a seat on a bench and simply watched people. And there were so many people.

Professional men in suits; women in fashionable dresses; labourers in shirt sleeves; a pair of women with cleaning supplies who were polishing the railing; children running circles around their parents.

And every one of them seemed to be talking. The combined noise from all of those voices was a din like Caroline had never heard before. It was so loud that she could barely hear the conversation between the two young men who were sitting right beside her on the bench.

Not that she wanted to eavesdrop. That would be rude. But both young men appeared very intelligent. The one directly beside her had short dark curls while his companion's hair was cropped close to his head. Both were wearing jackets made of fabric much finer than anything available in Gaynesford.

She heard one mention Samuel Jones and she must have sat up straighter because he looked right at her.

"Miss, are you a fan of Mr. Jones?" he asked.

"I hope to be," Caroline replied. "I have just now acquired *True Stories of Blackmeadow Abbey* but I have not yet had a chance to read it. Are you familiar with it?"

"It's his seminal work," the young man replied. "But he does have a flair for embellishment."

"Are they not true stories? The title clearly implies that they are."

"They are based in truth," he replied.

"But not wholly true. How will I know which elements are not true?" Caroline asked. How could a book of true stories not be true?

"How indeed," the young man replied with a laugh. "If you figure that out, you must tell me. Now, I fear am late for an appointment. I wish you a good day."

"Good day to you as well." Caroline watched the young man and his companion head to the stairs and in moments they were out of sight.

She was confused by his comments. If Mrs. Anson passed her test—and Caroline had no reason to doubt that she would—she was planning to read *True Stories of Blackmeadow Abbey* in order to prepare for her own test. But what if the stories were so embellished that they were wrong? She did not want to disappoint Mrs. Anson by not being allowed to attend the Artifact Society meetings.

"There you are, Caroline."

She looked up to find Mrs. Anson coming towards her, a big smile on her face. "I only got one question wrong and even Miss Foster understood my reasoning. It was about an artifact that became lost, and when it was found decades later, it had a very different major magic. I described the earlier magic, which to my mind was the most useful one. Why anyone released that back to the Endeavour, I will never know."

"Congratulations," Caroline said. "Did they give you more information about my test?"

"We are to come back the day after tomorrow, dear. I did tell them again that you are almost as knowledgeable about Endeavour history as I am about artifacts." Mrs. Anson patted her shoulder. "You should have no trouble. Now come along, we have the rest of the day to take in the sights."

Caroline followed Mrs. Anson through the crowd, down the stairs, and out into the day.

"I hear there's a very nice walk along the river," Mrs. Anson said.

CAROLINE SPENT A whole day reading *True Stories of Blackmeadow Abbey* so on the morning of her test she felt as ready as she could be, given that a stranger had made her doubt how true the true stories were.

Mrs. Anson hadn't interfered with Caroline's plan to study and instead she had insisted that her husband take her to Administration Hall. At dinner she'd told Caroline she'd hoped to run into one of the members of the Artifact Society so that they would know that Mr. Anson would soon be part of the Administration. She felt that it would confirm her very real commitment to the Society.

Caroline had finished reading by lamplight—Mrs. Anson had wanted her to use the Builder-enhanced light but Mr. Anson had needed it for his own reading—and hoped that she'd remember enough.

As she finished getting ready, Caroline resolved to not worry about things she had no control over, like which were the untrue parts of *True Stories of Blackmeadow Abbey*. Besides, she very much doubted that any of the Artifact Society members were better versed in Endeavours than Mr. Samuel Jones.

Mrs. Anson was already at breakfast when Caroline arrived downstairs, which she took as proof that her hostess had much riding on Caroline's success.

"Mr. Anson had an early meeting," Mrs. Anson said. "But I think it's not too soon for us to head to the Hall once you've had some tea and toast. I hope you aren't nervous. I wasn't nervous at all, not one bit, but I suppose that can be said of anyone taking a test on a subject they are expert in."

"I expect you're right," Caroline agreed. She poured herself some tea and picked up a piece of toast.

The truth was, she *was* nervous. The young man she'd met had made her doubt when Mrs. Anson needed her to be absolutely certain of her knowledge. She could not disappoint Mrs. Anson, not when she'd been so kind to her.

Caroline wasn't under the impression that she would find a teammate in the Artifact Society. Miss Foster had appeared to be the youngest of them, and she seemed far older than twenty-nine, the age the oldest Endeavour competitor could be.

But it would be a chance to meet people, and once they knew she was looking for Endeavour teammates, she had no doubt some of them would be willing to help her.

IN THE END it wasn't a very difficult test. It was apparent that Miss Foster had never truly studied Endeavours: the questions she asked were about basic knowledge. Caroline thought that Mrs. Anson would have asked more difficult questions.

But she passed, and so would not hold Mrs. Anson back from attending the Society meetings.

"I will take you out for a celebratory lunch," Mrs. Anson beamed when Miss Foster delivered the news that Caroline had passed. "And tomorrow we shall attend the Society and meet all the members."

"Mrs. Digby might even be here," Miss Foster said. "I think she is due back in town soon."

"Splendid," Mrs. Anson said. "Just all around splendid. Come along, Caroline. I am very excited to tell Mr. Anson our excellent news. This might even help him in his quest for a seat on the Administration."

"I'm sure it will," Caroline said. Once again, she followed Mrs. Anson down the stairs and out of the Hall.

"Yesterday Mr. Anson and I ate at a tea shop not far from here," Mrs. Anson said. "I rather think we should do the same today."

The tea shop was quaint, with tables for two or four set with flowery table coverings.

Mrs. Anson led the way to a table in front of the window. Once they were seated, a woman in an apron approached.

"Tea and soup for us both," Mrs. Anson said. "And a slice of cheese each, as well."

The woman left and Mrs. Anson sighed contentedly.

"You did very well, Caroline, very well."

"Thank you." Caroline had been feeling nothing but relief since Miss Foster told her that she'd passed the test. "I am so glad that I can accompany you to the meetings."

"I am too, my dear."

Their soup arrived: a bowl of creamy white liquid. The tea and cheese arrived a few minutes later.

"We'll need to take care to remember every Society member's name and station," Mrs. Anson said between mouthfuls.

"Do you think any members are Builders?" Caroline asked. "Or even Naturals?" She'd only met a Builder once, when they came to make an adjustment to one of Father's Builder-enhanced artifacts. She'd never knowingly even seen a Natural. Most people born with magic lived on large estates that by all accounts were filled with wonders they'd created using magic: lights that went on the moment you entered a room and running water even for outdoor uses. Why would they ever need to leave them?

As for Builders, they kept to themselves because they were always working on new gadgets. She wasn't sure she would have anything in common with anyone from either social tier.

"I wouldn't expect Naturals to care much about artifacts," Mrs. Anson said. "Not when they can magic up anything they want."

"I'm sure you're right," Caroline said. "After all, only a few Naturals have ever competed in the Endeavour. Hardly any Builders compete, either, although you'd think they would want to find new artifacts."

"Builders don't want to give up an old one to enter," Mrs. Anson said. She set down her spoon and picked at the cheese. "It's a very good rule. Heavens, imagine if everyone else had to compete with Builders and Naturals. No doubt they would find ways to make sure their teams were selected first."

"I never thought of that."

"Excuse me."

Caroline looked up to find a woman staring at Mrs. Anson.

"I am sorry to interrupt," the woman said. "But I am sure I know you. At least I used to know you. Are you Lilian Palmer?"

"I am," Mrs. Anson replied. "I was. Mrs. Anson I am called since I married. Oh my! Mary Newton. It's been almost thirty years since I last saw you."

"Since the Endeavour," was the reply. "And I, too, have a married name. Mrs. Smith, although my dear husband has been gone five years."

"This is my young friend Caroline Morris," Mrs. Anson said. "Mrs. Smith and I were on the same Endeavour team so long ago."

"Like so many teams that year, we didn't see the inside of Blackmeadow Abbey," Mrs. Smith replied. "Are you competing this year, Miss Morris?"

"I am," Caroline replied. "My brother and I are on a team but we will need to find two more teammates."

"My daughter and son are in the same situation," Mrs. Smith said. "You must meet them."

"I would love to." Caroline's heart raced. Was she going to have a team assembled even before her brother arrived? Then she paused. What if Jack had already recruited people? "And when my brother arrives, he shall meet them as well." Father had said to not be too hasty with potential teammates: she intended to follow that advice.

"We must decide on a day and time," Mrs. Anson said. "We have a meeting with the Artifact Society tomorrow morning but perhaps we can meet later in the afternoon."

"That would be delightful," Mrs. Smith replied. "There's an exhibition of flowers in the park. We could meet there."

It was quickly arranged that they would meet in the centre of the park, at a statue that Mrs. Smith said could not be confused with anything else. Once the time was agreed on, Mrs. Smith left.

"What an opportunity this is for you," Mrs. Anson said. "A brother and sister searching for teammates, just like you and Jack. How extraordinary that they are the children of my former teammate."

"It is wonderful," Caroline said. "And it's all due to you." Mrs. Anson smiled. "I do hope Jack hasn't promised to be on a team with anyone else."

"I should think that you would have a say in that," Mrs. Anson replied. "Let's see what the shops carry before we go home."

Caroline rose and followed Mrs. Anson out of the tea shop. She would write Mother and Father tonight and let them know that she was being diligent about assembling a team for the Endeavour. She had gained membership in the Artifact Society and would soon meet the children of Mrs. Anson's former teammate, who also needed two teammates. She doubted even Jack had done so well.

# 3

Caroline handed her letter to Mrs. Wooton to post. It would take two days to reach her parents, but it was possible news of Jack was already on its way. She would meet Mrs. Smith's son and daughter today, and she had to be careful and not promise to team up with them and not just because Father would think it far too early to commit. This was Jack's decision too, and it was entirely possible that he already had one or two people in mind that he wanted her to meet.

She sighed. All of this would be so much faster if Father had taken Mother's advice and bought a speaker, like the Ansons. But Father had claimed the only people he'd be able to call on it were the Ansons and that he was welcome to listen to news and announcements on theirs.

But now that the Ansons were here with her, and Caroline could likely find a speaker to hire, Father didn't have access to one.

"Are you ready, Caroline?" Mrs. Anson asked. "We must hurry or we'll be late."

"I'm ready." Caroline draped her shawl over her shoulders. It was a warm, sunny day and they would be spending much of the afternoon outdoors at the flower exhibition. But before that they were attending their very first meeting of the Artifact Society.

CAROLINE SMILED AND nodded. Mr. Stanford was reading from a

list of books that he thought she should study in order to get a better understanding of artifacts. Mr. Hobson hovered over his shoulder, peering down at the list and either smiling or scowling at each title.

"All of these are available in the records room, of course," Mr. Stanford said. "How long are you staying in Norbarrow?"

"I'm not sure," Caroline replied. She peered beyond the men to where Mrs. Anson was holding court over a group of women, including her contact, Mrs. Digby, and Miss Foster. "Much depends on the success of Mr. Anson's petition to join the Administration. I'm in search of teammates for the Endeavour so if it works with the Ansons' plans, I hope to be here until the competition." She still hadn't seen anyone in the Society who looked young enough to compete in this year's Endeavour, but perhaps these two older gentlemen knew some younger people.

"Ah, the Endeavour," Mr. Hobson said. "I was older than you when I competed, what, forty-four years ago now. Remember that, Stanford?"

"Of course, I remember it," Mr. Stanford replied. "We were on the same team," he said to Caroline.

"We were best friends for years before that," Mr. Hobson added. "Although I think the Endeavour cemented our relationship. It can be a challenge."

"Forty-four years ago," Caroline said. "That was the year a Builder used the artifact for flight to enter."

"That was such a scandal," Mr. Hobson said. "He was in a team that started just ahead of us. Apparently, he never told his family that he was even competing. They only heard about it when the starting positions were drawn, and let me tell you, they were furious."

"By the time they knew, it was far too late, of course," Mr. Stanford added. "The artifact had been inside Blackmeadow Abbey for almost a month. And worse, the Builder lad came out empty-handed. His family was livid. Apparently, they had recently determined that the artifact could be used for flying, and since it was such an extraordinary function, they hadn't told anyone, not even their children, including the one who submitted it." He sighed.

"Rumour had it that because the artifact was so common no

one expected it to have such uncommon powers," Mr. Hobson said. "Who would think a pewter candlestick would hold the key to flying?"

"I heard it was brass," Mr. Stanford replied. "Who said it was pewter?"

"Brass, pewter," Mr. Hobson said. "I am certain it was a candlestick. No artifact since has shown any capabilities for flight."

"Which is why only Naturals can fly today," Caroline said.

"That's right," Mr. Hobson agreed. "And why Builders hardly ever enter the Endeavour." He shrugged and smiled. "But who knows? Maybe you'll retrieve that artifact and it will still allow flight?"

"It would be considered a lost artifact now," Mr. Stanford said. "And no doubt even more powerful, since it's been inside for forty-four years."

"I would settle for anything that is more useful than the artifact I will submit," Caroline said. "Although even a non-useful one is better than none."

"I didn't retrieve an artifact," Mr. Stanford said sadly.

"I found one that whistled," Mr. Hobson said. "The only thing it was good for was gaining entry into the next Endeavour. Since I had no children, I gave it to Stanford's son."

"Not that it did him any good," Mr. Stanford said. "He didn't even get to enter the Abbey."

"Nor did my mother," Caroline said.

"Nor did a lot of people," Mr. Stanford replied. "Let's hope you have better luck this year."

"From my studies," Caroline said. "I believe that an early Endeavour call is a good sign. The last time one was called after just fourteen years almost every team was able to enter Blackmeadow Abbey."

"Ah, that was the one just before us," Mr. Hobson said. "However, the artifacts that were retrieved were of an inferior quality."

"Except for the one for flight," Mr. Stanford said. "It wasn't even documented as a lost artifact."

"Not all of the lost artifacts are documented?" Caroline asked. "I thought they'd all been catalogued."

"The ones we are aware of have been," Mr. Stanford said with a shrug. "But the records from the earlier Endeavours aren't necessarily complete. Look, your Mrs. Anson is coming our way."

"Are you ready to leave?" Mrs. Anson asked Caroline when she joined them. "We don't want to be late." She turned to the two men. "I am meeting my former teammate at the flower exhibition. Can you imagine? We haven't seen each other since our Endeavour."

"Remarkable," Mr. Hobson said. "I hope you have a nice visit." He nodded and headed down the hall towards Miss Foster, Mr. Stanford in his wake.

"Did you enjoy your first meeting?" Caroline asked.

"I did," was the reply. "It's so good to talk to people with such an interest in artifacts and who are close to my expertise. And Mrs. Digby is just as welcoming as I expected. But we must be off. Miss Foster assures me that tea and a small meal will be available at the flower exhibition."

Caroline's nerves fluttered as she and Mrs. Anson walked down the stairs and out of the Hall. She really hoped she liked Mrs. Smith's children and that they liked her. She wanted Father to be proud of her and finding teammates would surely impress him. Especially since she'd only been in Norbarrow for a few days.

A TABLE HAD been set up at the entrance to the park, and a sign that hung off the table said *Norbarrow Garden Club Flower Exhibition*.

"Welcome," said one of the two women who sat behind the table. "Are you here to compete or judge?"

"Goodness, neither," Mrs. Anson said. "We're here to enjoy the blooms."

"It's a lovely day for it," was the reply. "I have a map that shows what flowers are where in the park, if you have something specific you want to see."

"Caroline, will you be in charge of that?" Mrs. Anson asked.

Caroline took the map from the woman and followed Mrs. Anson along the path to just past the table.

"We still have an hour before we're to meet Mrs. Smith, so I think the tea house should be our first goal," Mrs. Anson said.

She stopped where the path branched out into two paths. "Which way do we go to find that?"

Caroline frowned as she studied the map. The entrance was clearly marked, as was the place where the path branched. "Oh, I see it." A spot on the map was marked with a cup. "We go right, then straight for a bit and then left. The tea house is in the middle of the park but there isn't a direct path to it."

"You lead the way," Mrs. Anson said. "And concentrate on where we're going and I'll keep an eye out for Mrs. Smith."

Caroline hesitated. She wasn't used to leading, nor had anyone ever expected her to. Certainly not Father, or Jack either, for that matter.

She straightened her shoulders and stepped past Mrs. Anson. She was going to compete in the Endeavour: if she wanted to be a contributing member of the team, she needed to be able to take charge.

The path wound through trees and bushes; every few feet punctuated by colourful flowers. The farther from the entrance they went, the more crowded the path was. She passed the first intersecting path but kept going. That one went left, leading farther away from the centre of the park. At the second intersecting path, she turned right. "We go straight for a while and take the next left," she said to Mrs. Anson, who was a half-step behind her. "That path leads right to the tea house. Perhaps we'll even find Mrs. Smith and her children there."

"I hope so," Mrs. Anson replied. "I'm not sure I would know how to find our rendezvous point. The park is much larger and busier than I had thought."

"There's a statue marked on the map," Caroline said. "And it's very close to the tea house so I hope it's the one we're to meet at." She studied the map again. "I don't see another statue so it must be the one."

She led the way to the next intersection and went left. A few minutes later they rounded a hedge and stepped out into a small courtyard. A fountain splashed in the centre, a statue of a winged horse standing over it. Along the far side was a small building with a dozen tables and chairs set out in front.

"We've found the tea house," Caroline said. "And the statue." She was quite proud to have navigated them here. True, the map was accurate and the park layout was fairly straightforward, but she'd never done anything like this before.

"Ooh, I see Mrs. Smith!" Mrs. Anson said and hurried forward. "Mrs. Smith," she called out. "We've found you!"

Caroline folded the map and, excited and nervous, followed Mrs. Anson across the courtyard. Mrs. Smith was sitting at a table with two others: no doubt her son and daughter. She waved at Mrs. Anson.

"We didn't need to find the rendezvous point after all," Mrs. Anson said as she reached the table. "Caroline did a splendid job reading the map to get us here. This must be your son and daughter."

"Mrs. Anson, Miss Morris, allow me to introduce you to my children; Mr. Sean Smith and Miss Iona Smith."

The Smith siblings both had delicate features that Caroline thought must have come from their father; only Sean seemed to have inherited Mrs. Smith's rather square jaw. Iona's blonde curls framed her very pretty face, while Sean's tousled hair was certainly longer than Caroline was used to. She assumed it was a newer fashion since Iona's rose print dress and Sean's jacket and vest were both considerably more up-to-date than her own outfit.

Pleasantries were exchanged and Sean Smith found chairs for Caroline and Mrs. Anson. Soon the five of them were seated around a small round table, a pot and cups of tea arranged on it, along with a plate of sandwiches.

"I am so very happy that Caroline now has acquaintances her own age," Mrs. Anson said. "She's a delightful companion but no doubt she will welcome time away from me." She leaned over to Mrs. Smith. "She's too polite to say it but I'm sure she finds Mr. Anson and me boring."

"That's not true," Caroline replied.

"See what I mean?" Mrs. Anson said.

"Are you visiting for long?" Sean asked.

"Oh, we have no idea," Mrs. Anson said. "Mr. Anson has business to attend to and it's of a nature with no firm timelines. So, we must amuse ourselves. Why, just this morning we attended our first meeting of the Artifact Society right in the Administration Building."

"How impressive," Sean said. "Are you members of this

society?"

"We are now," Mrs. Anson said. "We both had to take very difficult tests in order to secure membership." She turned to Mrs. Smith and started detailing the questions she'd had to answer.

"Did you take the same test, Miss Morris?" Iona asked, fixing her startling blue eyes on her.

"No," Caroline replied. "Mrs. Anson is an expert on artifacts while I . . ." she paused. "I hesitate to call myself an expert, but I am endlessly fascinated by the Endeavour and read every history I can find."

"I think that's a worthy pastime," Sean said. "I have often thought about doing the same but my studies keep me busy."

"My brother attends school as well," Caroline said. "At Linley Academy."

"That's the school I attend," Sean replied. "Morris. Your brother must be Jack Morris. We have a class together."

"I feel as though we were fated to meet," Iona said with a laugh. "Sean has mentioned his friend Jack from school, but how extraordinary that he should be your brother."

"What's this?" Mrs. Anson asked. "You are already acquainted with Jack Morris? He's due to arrive in a few days."

"What a happy coincidence," Mrs. Smith said.

Caroline beamed at Mrs. Anson. It was looking very much like both she and Jack would be willing to form a team with Sean and Iona Smith. Father would be so pleased. Although not if he felt they were too hasty.

They finished their tea and decided that they must take in some of the splendours of the flower exhibition.

Mrs. Anson and Mrs. Smith paired up while Caroline fell in step with Iona and Sean.

"Have you been to Norbarrow before?" Iona asked.

"Never," Caroline replied. "I have not even travelled far from my village of Gaynesford."

"It can be rather overwhelming," Sean said. "As Iona has said to me many times. Linley isn't as large as Norbarrow of course, but I am used to crowds as well as amenities."

"I'm afraid I'm not even used to meeting strangers," Caroline said. "They are so rare in my village."

"We are not strangers," Iona said, linking her arm with

Caroline's. "We are friends who have just met. After all, your brother and mine are classmates."

"I so wish to be friends with you," Caroline said. She smiled shyly and was rewarded when Iona returned her smile with a brilliant one of her own.

"I am feeling rather left out," Sean complained. Then he grinned and the three of them laughed.

"What's so amusing?" Mrs. Anson said.

"Caroline and I have decided that we are good friends who have just met," Iona said.

"That's very sweet," Mrs. Anson replied. "Are either of you interested in artifacts? Caroline and I will be attending society meetings as often as possible. Any or all of you could join if you were to pass the test."

"This close to the Endeavour," Mrs. Smith said, "I think that everyone is interested in artifacts. But will Caroline attend every meeting? Surely, she can spend some time with Iona and Sean?"

"Of course, she can," Mrs. Anson said. "And most especially when Jack arrives. I am perfectly capable of attending the Artifact Society meetings myself. Mrs. Digby and I are now well acquainted, and I have been made to feel welcome by the other members. Even though I dare say I am more of an expert than many of them." Mrs. Anson and Mrs. Smith walked ahead, and Iona, her arm still linked companionably with Caroline's, slowed.

"We must plan to meet again," Iona said. "There is to be a concert tomorrow night. Perhaps we can persuade you to attend?"

"I would love to," Caroline replied. "I've never been to a concert but I have listened to one on Mr. and Mrs. Ansons' speaker." That had been last year and Caroline had been humming those songs ever since.

"Then we shall all go together," Iona said. "Mother, Mrs. Anson and Caroline simply must come to the concert with us."

"Yes," Mrs. Smith said. She turned to Mrs. Anson. "Mr. Anson might like to attend as well. It's an official event to mark the Endeavour."

"I'm sure we would very much like to go," Mrs. Anson replied. "Whatever should I wear?"

Mrs. Anson and Mrs. Smith walked with their heads together

as they discussed wardrobe options. Caroline heard Mrs. Anson profess to having just the thing before they were out of hearing.

Iona met Caroline's eyes and smiled. "That's settled then. The concert starts at 7:00 in the theatre directly across from Administration Hall. Sean will ensure that we have tickets for us all and we can meet out front a few minutes before the start. Sean?"

"I will be happy to get tickets," Sean replied.

"Jack might arrive tomorrow," Caroline said. "Could you get a ticket for him as well, just in case?" She was anxious for Jack to meet the Smiths: if they both approved, they would be able to complete the task of creating a team. After a suitable period of time, of course.

"One more ticket should not be a problem," Sean said. "But I think I should go and do that now."

"Yes," Iona agreed. "Caroline and I will become even better friends without you around to interfere."

"I'll see you tomorrow," Sean said to Caroline. "Until then." He did a quick bow before catching up with his mother and Mrs. Anson. After a brief discussion, he took a side path and disappeared from view.

"Sean will manage the tickets," Iona said. "He's quite resourceful."

"And kind," Caroline said. "He's forgoing a lovely walk with views of spectacular flowers in order to secure our plans for tomorrow evening."

Iona's bright laugh drew looks from Mrs. Anson and Mrs. Smith.

"My brother is kind," she said. "But he will not be sad to miss the flower exhibition. He much prefers fast-paced action to a leisurely stroll."

"I see," Caroline said, when she didn't actually understand the comment. What was a fast-paced action? She was sure it must be a college activity since she couldn't think of any pastime in Gaynesford that would be described that way.

The rest of the afternoon was spent wandering the park, although none of them paid very much attention to the flowers.

Mrs. Anson and Mrs. Smith spent their time remembering their shared history before detailing the events of the years since then.

Caroline was completely enchanted with her new friend, who not once left her side or even unhooked arms with her. She was ever so attentive to Caroline's observations and comments and very forgiving about Caroline's lack of world experiences.

Iona Smith, while not having travelled as often nor seen as much as she credited her brother with, had nonetheless seen more of the world than Caroline had.

This was Iona's fifth trip to Norbarrow, and she'd visited her brother in Linley twice, although she said she'd not met any of Sean's friends while there.

All too soon, Mrs. Anson declared it time to return home.

"We will be meeting with the Artifact Society in the morning," Mrs. Anson said when Iona protested. "And will see you in the evening. Perhaps at that time we can decide on another outing?"

They all agreed that this was a good plan and Caroline said goodbye to Mrs. Smith and Iona.

"How fortunate we met up with them," Mrs. Anson said as they left the park. "And to think that poor Mrs. Smith has been widowed for five years. She did not complain, but it can't have been easy raising two children on her own. They seem properly raised, too, with excellent manners."

"I agree completely," Caroline said. "Iona was so nice to invite us to the concert and Sean immediately volunteered to secure tickets." She sighed. She didn't think she'd even met anyone as nice, as dear to her, as Iona Smith.

"The concert is a very good plan," Mrs. Anson said. "And since it's an official Endeavour event, I have no doubt Mr. Anson will want to attend. He will be so impressed that we have it all arranged."

WHEN THEY ARRIVED back at the house, Caroline returned to her room to find that Mrs. Wooton had left a letter for her.

It was from Mother. Caroline sat in the chair near the window to read it.

Jack was on his way to Norbarrow, her mother wrote. He had come home in order to put his artifact in the safe, but was leaving early the same day the letter was being posted. Since Mother had paid extra to have the letter go by carrier and Jack would take a horse-drawn carriage, he should be expected in Norbarrow the day after the letter arrived.

Letter in hand, Caroline set off in search of Mrs. Anson. She hoped Jack did not arrive so early that he interfered with Mrs. Anson's plans to meet with the Artifact Society, but surely, he would be here in time to attend the concert.

"Someone should stay home and wait for young Jack," Mr. Anson said. "It's unseemly for us to be out when a guest arrives."

They had just sat down for dinner and Caroline was certain that Mr. Anson's comment meant that he would not be here to greet her brother. She looked over to see Mrs. Anson frowning at her husband: she seemed to have come to the same conclusion.

"I can be here," Caroline said. "If you think that appropriate." The last thing she wanted was for Jack's arrival to cause discord between the Ansons, and she knew Mrs. Anson planned to attend the Artifact Society meeting in the morning.

"I think that would be satisfactory," Mrs. Anson said quickly. "That way you and Jack will have privacy for your reunion."

"I will agree this once," Mr. Anson said. "Normally having a guest greet another guest would not do, however, since this is an Endeavour year, and it's imperative that you and your brother discuss your plans for assembling a team as soon as possible, I will allow it. Make sure Jack knows about the concert tomorrow. I do believe that it will help my case with the Administration to have some active Endeavour competitors attend with me, especially when I am hosting two of them."

"I certainly will, Mr. Anson," Caroline said. "I'm sure Jack will agree that it's an honour to attend such a significant Endeavour event with you and Mrs. Anson."

"My dear," her husband said. "Is there a way to confirm the tickets have been procured? We can't leave that to chance."

"Yes," Mrs. Anson replied. "Mrs. Smith told me where her family is lodging. I'll have Wooton send someone in the morning."

"Ask Mrs. Smith and her family to come here before the concert. We can have a quick supper and then set off as a group."

"Oh, how lovely," Mrs. Anson said. "Not even a week here and already we are entertaining. I'll talk to Mrs. Wooton about what to serve. Something not too heavy, I imagine. We'll need to leave the light on out front because I dare say it will be dark when we return."

"We certainly shall leave the light on," Mr. Anson agreed.

Caroline spent the rest of the meal vacillating between excitement over attending her first dinner party in the city and nervousness about what to wear.

Mrs. Anson talked through the meal, describing all of the day's events to her husband. At times Caroline was called on to agree or interject a brief observation, but Mr. Anson made very few comments.

Caroline took his silence as approval. And didn't his wish to entertain the Smiths mean he was pleased? Once Jack arrived, they could discuss formally teaming up with Iona and Sean, after a suitable period of time had passed, of course. Then Father would also be pleased.

It would be such a relief to have their team settled. What a stroke of luck for Mrs. Anson to reunite with Mrs. Smith just before the Endeavour, and with two sets of siblings with the same goal of creating a team of four.

Already, Caroline was terribly fond of Iona and could imagine years of friendship much like Mr. Stanford had with Mr. Hobson. Oh, to make a lifelong friend in someone as utterly charming as Iona Smith. Even her dullest days in Gaynesford would be brightened by letters from someone as travelled, as sophisticated, as wonderful, as her.

After dinner Mr. Anson retired to his study to attend to some correspondence. Mrs. Anson went in search of Mrs. Wooton, claiming that she had much to do to plan the next day's dinner.

Caroline headed up to her room, where she reread her letter from her mother. Besides news of her brother, her mother had said very little else, but Caroline imagined Becca was still unhappy.

She took out her writing supplies. She would write her sister a letter and do her very best to be kind and not create more unhappiness. She concentrated on the Artifact Society and the test she'd had to pass in order to join. She made a brief mention of Mrs. Smith and Iona and Sean: if they did indeed team up with her and Jack, Becca would want to know why she hadn't thought them important enough to write about.

Caroline yawned as she addressed the envelope.

She'd write her mother after Jack had arrived and they'd all attended the concert.

She spent a few minutes staring out the window, but there was only a single porch lit across the street. After two horse drawn carriages went past, she got ready for bed.

Despite being tired after an exciting day, it took her a long time to fall asleep.

# 4

**M**rs. Anson was already downstairs when Caroline arrived for breakfast.

"I am sorry that I can't attend the Artifact Society meeting with you," Caroline said as she sat down at the dining table. "I know you wanted me to join so we could attend together."

"Don't you worry," Mrs. Anson said. "I am perfectly capable of walking there on my own today. And it's far better for you to be here when Jack arrives than for me. Besides, I already have numerous connections in the society, including Mrs. Digby, who I have not spent nearly enough time with to claim that we are fully acquainted. Perhaps today will allow me to do that."

"I am relieved," Caroline said. "I do not wish either Jack or myself to interfere with your plans." She helped herself to a sweet roll and jam.

"Nonsense," Mrs. Anson replied. "Mr. Anson has already stated that arriving at the concert with Endeavour competitors will help him in his quest to become an Administrator, so it is all working out wonderfully. Now, Mrs. Wooton has sent a message off to Mrs. Smith asking that they come to dinner as well as to confirm that tickets were acquired for us all. If for some reason there is an issue with the tickets, I've instructed Mrs. Wooton to let you know, and you are to come and fetch me."

"Sean was very confident that he could get the tickets,"

Caroline said.

"Yes, but there could have been some confusion over exactly how many tickets are required," Mrs. Anson said. "Mr. Anson is counting on us to secure tickets for both him and Jack, along with you, me, and the Smiths. I do not wish to disappoint him."

"Of course not." Caroline put her roll down on her plate. Disappointing Mr. Anson was not something she wanted to do, either. "I'll ask Mrs. Wooton to let me know immediately when Mrs. Smith's answer arrives."

"Thank you. Now, I must be off if I am to have time for a meaningful conversation with Mrs. Digby. Enjoy your reunion with your brother and remember that you must focus on the Endeavour."

"I couldn't possibly forget that," Caroline replied. "I hope you have a pleasant time at the meeting and that my company is not missed."

Mrs. Anson left, and Caroline stared down at her breakfast, a knot forming in her stomach.

She hadn't been worried about the number of concert tickets since Sean had promised to get tickets for both Jack and Mr. Anson. But now, until she knew he had successfully acquired them, she wasn't sure she'd be able to concentrate on her reading.

She'd planned to spend more time with *True Stories of Blackmeadow Abbey*, in case she could determine which parts of the tales had been embellished. The comments from the young man she'd met that first day at Administration Hall still bothered her.

Her appetite gone, she returned to her room to retrieve the book. Then she sat in the parlour, trying to read, when in fact she was waiting for a reply from Mrs. Smith.

AN HOUR LATER, the front doorbell rang, and Caroline resisted the urge to jump up and answer it herself.

She heard Mrs. Wooton greet whoever was there, and a moment later, the door to the parlour opened.

"A reply has come from Mrs. Smith," Mrs. Wooton said. "And the gentleman has asked to speak to you. A Mr. Sean Smith."

"Oh, of course, send him in." Caroline stood up and smoothed her skirt. She wasn't entirely sure Mr. Anson would approve of her entertaining Sean alone in his home, but on the other hand, if he became her Endeavour teammate, they would no doubt spend enough time together to make them almost as close as family.

"Caroline," Sean said when he entered the room. "I am happy to find you at home."

"I am waiting for Jack to arrive," Caroline said. "Although I expect he won't be here until after noon. Mrs. Anson has gone to the Artifact Society meeting alone since there was no need for us both to wait for him. Please, sit down. You have a reply to Mrs. Anson's note?" She sat back down and closed her book.

"My mother, sister, and I would be delighted to dine here with you tonight," Sean said. He took the chair opposite her and reached into his coat pocket. "And I have tickets for all of us—seven in total. I will leave them all here so they are ready when we have dined."

"Thank you. There was some concern that Mrs. Anson and I had not been very clear on the precise number of tickets required. Mr. Anson is quite interested in joining us tonight, as it's an official Endeavour event and the four of us are competing this year." She wished she hadn't said that last bit: now she felt awkward not bringing up the issue of teaming up. "It seems to be a lovely day," Caroline added, moving to a safer subject.

"It is rather nice," Sean replied. He looked around the room before settling on her. "We should take advantage of it and go for a walk."

"I'm sorry but I can't. I'm to be here when Jack arrives." Mr. Anson would not be impressed if she was absent for her brother's arrival, even if she was in the company of a potential teammate.

"You said he wasn't likely to come before this afternoon," Sean said. "That's hours away. Come on, we have time for a quick walk. I'm meeting my sister at a shop. She has her eye on a shawl to wear tonight, and I'm certain she would prefer your opinion over mine."

Caroline smiled. How she would love to meet Iona and discuss a shawl. "I am sorry, but Mr. Anson was very clear that someone should be here, and we all agreed that it would be me. We could take a quick stroll in the garden. Mrs. Wooton will let me know if Jack arrives."

"Another time," Sean said. "As I said, I am meeting Iona." He stood up and Caroline got the impression he was angry at her.

"We'll see each other tonight," Caroline said, following Sean to the door that led out into the hall. She paused, not sure if she should see him to the front door. Thankfully, Mrs. Wooton was there and she ushered Sean to the front door.

"We'll see each other tonight," Sean repeated.

"Thank you for bringing the tickets," Caroline said. "I very much look forward to attending the concert with you and your family."

When Sean had gone, Caroline retreated into the parlour. She was very much afraid that she'd disappointed Sean Smith, and through him, Iona.

But what else could she have done? Mr. Anson was very clear that someone had to be on hand to greet Jack and had only reluctantly agreed it could be her, despite thinking that it was not completely proper.

Although Sean was probably right and Jack wouldn't arrive for hours. What would it have hurt to visit his sister with him? She desperately wanted to get better acquainted with Iona and shopping for a shawl was such an intimate thing to do.

She sighed. She might have just ruined her and Jack's chances of teaming up with Sean and Iona. Why would they trust someone who couldn't even make her own decision about going for a walk?

She picked up the tickets and counted them: seven in total, so at least something had gone right.

She placed them on the tray on the sideboard and went to confirm with Mrs. Wooton that the Smiths were dining with them. Then she grabbed up her book and went out into the garden.

But even the sunny day couldn't ease her doubts.

"Is THAT HOW you're preparing for the Endeavour?"

Caroline glanced up from her book. "Jack! You're here already!" It was a good thing she hadn't gone out with Sean: it was well before noon and lunch hadn't even been served. She closed her book and set it aside and smiled at her brother. His dark hair was slightly shaggier, but the crooked grin was the same.

"I was able to get an early start this morning," Jack replied. He joined her on the bench and gave a gentle punch to her shoulder. "Father said you came by carrier so you must tell me all about it."

"It took us a single day," Caroline replied. Of course, Jack's first concern was about her trip in a Builder-enhanced carrier. "And it was as smooth as Mr. Anson predicted."

"How are the Ansons?"

"Very well. Mr. Anson has been busy lobbying to get a seat on the Administration. Oh, and we are all going to a concert tonight. Mr. Anson thinks that attending with four Endeavour competitors will help his cause."

"Four?" Jack asked. "I know Father is keen on us getting a team together but I hope you haven't committed to anything without me."

"Of course not," Caroline replied. "Just as I assume you haven't." It wasn't a question but her brother shook his head anyway. "Mrs. Anson ran into her former Endeavour teammate, Mrs. Smith, who has two children eligible to compete. You already know one: Sean Smith attends Linley and says he and you have a class together. The other is his sister Iona. We haven't discussed anything but they are also trying to create a team."

"Sean Smith," Jack said. "I do have a class with him but I can't say I really know him well. Our interests outside of school vary wildly."

"Yes, you are fascinated by Builder enhancements. What are Sean's interests?"

"Fast carriages and carriers from what I can tell," Jack said. He shrugged. "I have very few leads for teammates. Most of my friend's parents have long-standing commitments for them, which is what Father should have done."

"It wouldn't have been enough," Caroline said. "We all assumed Becca would be competing with us."

"True." Jack sighed. "Becca is so angry I fear that she may never get over it."

"I worry that you are right." Caroline sighed too. She hated the thought of her sister being so unhappy.

"Beside meeting Sean Smith and his sister," Jack said. "What else have you been up to?"

"Mrs. Anson and I have both joined the Artifact Society," Caroline said. "They meet in the Administration Hall. That's where she went this morning. We each had to pass a test in order to join, so they are very serious."

"That doesn't sound like it's any fun."

"It's interesting," Caroline said. She didn't think Mrs. Anson had been looking for fun when joining the society. "None of the members seem younger than thirty."

"Ah, so there is no one who is competing this year," Jack said. "Have you met anyone besides the Smiths?"

"No, although tonight's concert will be an opportunity to meet other people." She'd thought she was doing well for being in Norbarrow for just a few days, but Jack's questions made her doubt herself.

"Jack Morris, there you are."

Mrs. Anson stood on the back step, waving.

"It's very good that you made it here safely. Mrs. Wooton tells me she has shown you to your room. She also advises that lunch is ready."

"It's very good to see you, Mrs. Anson," Jack said. He rose and strode towards her, Caroline following. "And I am ever so grateful for your hospitality. You know how important Caroline's and my task is."

"Indeed, Mr. Anson and I are happy to help. Come in for lunch and tell me all your news."

By the time they were seated, Jack had given a brief account of his journey. Once Mrs. Wooton brought in the platter of sandwiches, Mrs. Anson took over the conversation, telling Jack in detail everything that had happened since they'd set out from Gaynesford. She spent a lot of time on the artifacts they'd crossed paths with, as well as the test she'd taken to gain entrance to the Artifact Society.

Jack made polite comments and a few times Caroline was asked to confirm a detail. Finally, lunch was over and the three headed to the parlour.

"Mrs. Wooton said that Sean Smith delivered the reply to my note personally," Mrs. Anson said. "And that he and his mother and sister have agreed to dine with us."

"Yes. He also brought the tickets to the concert," Caroline said. She picked them up off the tray and handed them to Mrs. Anson. "Seven in all."

"Wonderful," Mrs. Anson beamed. She counted the tickets. "I'll just leave these in Mr. Anson's study."

"Are you enjoying you time with Mrs. Anson?" Jack asked once she'd left the room. "At the Artifact Society?"

Caroline smiled. "Yes. Mrs. Anson's interests are very close to mine. I have even decided to investigate something that came up in conversation at the Artifact society."

"Let me guess. It's something to do with Endeavours?"

"Of course." Caroline laughed. It was a running joke between her and Jack that her interest in Endeavours was as singular as his interest in Builder enhancements. "Apparently in the past when an Endeavour was called early, it resulted in very few powerful artifacts. Between mine and Mrs. Anson's expertise, I'm sure we can figure out if that's true."

"What is my expertise required for?" Mrs. Anson said as she rejoined them.

"Mr. Stanford and Mr. Hobson mentioned that the last time there was a short interval between Endeavours that—except for lost artifacts—the artifacts recovered were inferior," Caroline said. "I was hoping that between us we could figure out if that's true."

"I'd be happy to help," Mrs. Anson said, beaming. "Would that be useful information?"

"It might be," Jack said. "If artifacts newly added to the Abbey are less powerful, we'd want to concentrate our efforts on finding lost artifacts."

"Of course," Mrs. Anson replied. "But how would you do that?"

"I'm not sure," Jack replied. "We'd have to figure that out. And if we can't, we might decide not to take too many risks while inside the Abbey." He met Caroline's eyes and she nodded solemnly.

Most years at least a few competitors were hurt, but deaths also occurred. The Endeavour their father had competed in was one of the worst: four people died, including three from a single team. It was deemed so dangerous that the competition was stopped early and several teams, including their mother's—and Mrs. Anson's—hadn't even entered the Abbey. Only nineteen of the one-hundred-and-thirty-five teams had set foot inside, and four people had died.

As someone interested in Endeavour history, Caroline was well aware of the risks. She hadn't thought of her research as anything more than curiosity, but Jack was right. If there was little chance of gaining a powerful artifact, they might not want to take great risks. Unless they could concentrate on lost artifacts: those would always be worth some risk.

JACK TOLD HER that she was worrying over nothing, but Caroline still wished she had something nicer to wear for dinner and the concert.

She sighed as she left her room. She only had two suitable dresses to choose from and neither Mother nor Father had thought to supply her with enough money to buy anything new. She'd chosen her blue silk, since this would be her best chance to impress someone new. Her other formal dress would have to do for the next event, assuming there was one.

"Any little bit of knowledge that gives you an advantage would be worthwhile," Mr. Anson was saying as Caroline entered the parlour.

"My thought as well," Jack replied. He looked up at Caroline. "Mr. Anson and I have been discussing how we can concentrate on lost artifacts."

"Every team has always searched for them," Mr. Anson said. "But I've never heard anyone say that there was a way to ensure you find them. I suppose that the longer you're in the Abbey the better chance you have."

"But the longer you're in, the more likely you'll encounter some dangerous magic," Jack said.

Caroline joined her brother on the sofa. "We need to research," she said. "Maybe there's a list of teams that found lost artifacts and we can figure out where they found them?"

"The records room at Administration Hall has some Endeavour team accounts," Mr. Anson said. "I've spent some time there studying the history of the Endeavour rules. You can't access the records unless you have been—or are currently—on a team."

"We should do that as soon as we can," Caroline said to Jack, who nodded.

"That's dinner all sorted out and ready," Mrs. Anson said when she joined them. "Mrs. Wooton has hired a man to serve and clear the table." The doorbell rang out. "Oh, that must be our guests now." Mrs. Anson stood near the door to the hallway.

Mrs. Wooton entered, followed by Mrs. Smith and her children.

"Mrs. Smith, Mr. Sean Smith, and Miss Iona Smith," Mrs. Wooton said and stepped aside so the three guests could enter the parlour.

"My dear," Mrs. Anson said. "How lovely that you could join us. Allow me to present my husband, Mr. Anson. This is Mrs. Smith and her son Sean and daughter Iona."

Iona's shawl was a striking blue, making Caroline's blue silk dress seem dowdy in comparison.

"I am very pleased to meet my dear wife's Endeavour teammate," Mr. Anson said, coming to stand at his wife's side. "As well as her children. Especially at such an exciting time in your lives, when you will be competing in your own Endeavour."

"Mr. Anson," Mrs. Smith said. "It was so very thoughtful for you and your wife to invite us to dine. And yes, the excitement in the air reminds me of my own Endeavour, although I'm sure you know that we did not enter Blackmeadow Abbey."

"But we all have high hopes for our young competitors, don't we?" Mr. Anson said. "Please, sit." He took out his watch. "We have a few minutes before dinner. I am afraid we are on a tight schedule if we are to make the concert on time."

"Oh, I am forgetting myself," Mrs. Anson said. "Here is Jack Morris. Caroline's brother arrived earlier today. Jack, meet Mrs. Smith and Miss Iona Smith. I believe you know Sean."

"Yes, from classes at Linley Academy," Jack said. "Mrs. Smith, Miss Smith. It's a pleasure to meet you."

Caroline was thrilled when Iona found a seat between her and Jack. Mrs. Anson took charge of Mrs. Smith and Sean settled across from Mr. Anson.

"I was sorry you could not come to the shops with me today," Iona said. She held out her shawl. "I will ask for your approval of my choice now."

"It's very pretty," Caroline said. Up close she could see that it was fine cotton and that the blue matched Iona's eyes. "I was sorry too, but it was good that I was here. Jack arrived earlier than all expectations." She glanced at Mr. Anson. She had no doubt he would disapprove that she'd even entertained the notion of leaving the house this morning.

"I suppose I shall have to forgive you," Iona said, and smiled. She turned to Jack. "Although I'm not sure I will forgive you. I, too, have a brother, so I know how unpredictable they can be and how we poor sisters are ever dependent on their actions."

Caroline was distracted by Mrs. Anson's laugh and didn't hear Jack's reply, but he was smiling at Iona. She was relieved that her brother seemed to like her new friend.

A moment later Mrs. Wooton was standing in the doorway.

"Dinner is ready," Mrs. Anson said.

Her husband glanced at his watch and stood up. "Right on time," he said and led the way to the dining room.

Mrs. Anson directed everyone to their seats. Mr. and Mrs. Anson were each at an end of the table while Sean sat to Mr. Anson's right. Caroline was in between Sean and his mother, who was beside Mrs. Anson at the other end of the table. Jack sat opposite Caroline, next to Iona and Mrs. Anson.

Even though she was disappointed to not be sitting next to her dear friend, Caroline was excited to be at her first real dinner party. Real in that some of the guests were practically strangers: not like at home where anyone invited to dine was someone she'd been acquainted with for years.

The dishes were passed around by the hired man and Caroline made sure to sample every one of them.

"I am still sorry that you did not come out with me this morning," Sean said to her. "Iona would have much preferred your opinion to mine in regards to her shawl."

"She made an excellent choice," Caroline said. "It's very lovely."

"In spite of me, you mean," Sean said.

"Oh no, I did not mean that."

"I am not offended," Sean replied. "Besides, my sister gave very little weight to my opinion." He leaned closer. "That shawl was not my choice. Mine was, as Iona told me, not suitable."

"I'm sure it would have been," Caroline said. "Perhaps your choice would have been mine as well?"

"I doubt you would have such poor taste," Sean replied. "You were missed."

"It was good that I did not go," Caroline said. "Jack arrived well before noon. Mr. Anson would not have been pleased if I hadn't been here to greet him."

"Are you afraid of displeasing Mr. Anson?"

"Afraid?" Caroline asked. "Why would you ask that? Both Jack and I are here at Mr. and Mrs. Anson's pleasure. I would very much like to not upset either of them and make them regret inviting us. They are good friends of my parents and that would greatly disappoint them, especially Father." She was confused. Why would she ever want to go against Mr. Anson's direct wishes? What would be the benefit?

"I suppose it would," Sean said. "I'm not sure anything I did would ever disappoint my mother, but I suspect my father would have been of a very different mind, if he were alive today."

Caroline didn't know what to say to that so she concentrated on her dinner. Mr. Anson was not a very talkative man and hosting a dinner didn't seem to change that. She did see him glance at his watch a few times, but he didn't frown, so she assumed they still were on schedule.

Jack was in conversation with Iona and Caroline wished she was on that side of the table. Mrs. Anson, of course, was having a loud conversation with Mrs. Smith.

"We must all of us plan a daytime outing," Mrs. Anson said. "Mr. Anson, what do you say to that? Should we take a picnic in the park? Or perhaps a river cruise?"

"I cannot spare the time during the day," Mr. Anson said. "But you should go. Perhaps Jack could arrange it on my behalf?"

"I would be happy to, Mr. Anson," Jack replied. He smiled at Iona. "What would be your preference?"

"A river cruise sounds lovely," Iona said and sighed. "I've never been on one. Caroline, would that do for you?"

"That sounds splendid." Caroline was inordinately pleased that Iona had asked for her opinion. "I've never been on one either."

"That's settled then," Mrs. Anson said. "We shall pick a day for our river cruise and Mr. Jack Morris will arrange it on behalf of Mr. Anson."

"An outing," Sean said to her. "That sounds very fine."

"It does, doesn't it?" Caroline smiled at him. Out of the corner of her eye she saw Mr. Anson take out his watch again and frown. She gently set her cutlery on her plate. "Mr. Anson, Mrs. Anson, thank you so much for the lovely dinner," she said.

"Yes," Mrs. Smith said. She, too, set her cutlery on her plate. "On behalf of myself and Sean and Iona, I thank you both."

"You are all very welcome," Mr. Anson said. He put his watch away. "We do not want to be late for the concert. Shall we get ready to go?"

They all agreed and left the dining room for the parlour while Mr. Anson retrieved the tickets from his office.

When everyone was ready, they filed out the front door. Mrs. Anson remarked on the light as she went down the front steps.

IONA LINKED HER arm through Caroline's as they set out for the short walk to the concert hall.

Mr. Anson took the lead, along with Jack and Sean, while Mrs. Anson and Mrs. Smith trailed the small group.

Mrs. Anson's voice carried in the still night: a tale about an artifact that had two different magics, depending on who wielded it. It was a story she'd told Caroline more than once.

"Mother is ever so happy to have rekindled her friendship with Mrs. Anson," Iona said.

"I believe Mrs. Anson is just as pleased," Caroline replied. "As am I since it led to me meeting you."

"And Sean," Iona said. "And now I have met your brother Jack. All in all, a very happy circumstance."

"It is, isn't it?" Caroline said. "For here we are going to a concert, an event I have never attended, and planning a river cruise, another new thing for me. My mother told me to enjoy my time in Norbarrow but I don't think even she expected me to have so many wonderful experiences."

"It is wonderful," Iona said. She tilted her head and grinned at Caroline. "And the atmosphere is all the more intense because it's an Endeavour year. Are you nervous about competing?"

"Yes." Caroline sighed. "I have read extensively about Endeavours so I know exactly how many things can go wrong. Starting with not even setting foot inside Blackmeadow Abbey."

"Like my mother and Mrs. Anson," Iona said.

"And my mother as well," Caroline agreed. "Although my father entered and did rather well. At least, well enough to have artifacts for me, Jack, and our sister Becca, who has missed the cut-off age by less than a year."

"Artifacts for all three?" Iona asked. "You were planning on all three competing on the same team?"

"Yes. But the early call for the Endeavour has ended that plan, and Becca will have to wait until the next Endeavour."

"She will be one of the oldest competitors then," Iona said. "That might be an advantage. Her artifact will be kept for her?"

"Oh, yes. Father has already locked them all in his safe," Caroline replied. "He felt it too risky to do anything else." She looked over at Iona with wide eyes. "I have read stories of the terrible things people will do to get their hands on an artifact. I trust that yours and Sean's are equally safe."

"Of course," Iona said. "Mother is very cautious. Look, Administration Hall is fully lit. How beautiful. The concert hall is across the street."

"I don't think I've ever seen anything more beautiful," Caroline said. She paused in awe and stared at the Hall. Lights ran along the top of the building and highlighted every window and door. "Do you think Naturals used their magic to do that?" Surely Naturals were excited about the Endeavour even if they didn't compete.

"It was most likely done by Builders," Mrs. Smith said as she and Mrs. Anson caught up to them.

"I doubt even Naturals could make it any prettier," Mrs. Anson said. "It is a sight. Oh, Mr. Anson and the gentlemen are already at the concert hall. We mustn't keep them waiting."

# 5

Caroline sighed happily and sat back down. Her hands tingled from clapping. The music had been wonderful: so much more impressive in person than hearing it over the Ansons' speaker.

"The sound had to have been Builder enhanced," Jack said. He was sitting behind her with Mr. Anson and Sean.

"I expect so," Mrs. Anson said from her side. "An artifact would be needed to project sound so clearly."

Caroline didn't really care what made the sound carry, just that it had carried to her. The performers were packing up their instruments, and the lights—Builder-enhanced artifacts, according to Mrs. Anson—went on in the hall.

"There's a reception across at Administration Hall," Mr. Anson said. "I arranged the invitation for us."

"Oh, Mr. Anson, what a lovely surprise," Mrs. Smith said from Caroline's other side.

"It is," Mrs. Anson said. "I knew before dinner but Mr. Anson swore me to secrecy. Now come along, let's all of us get organized."

Caroline followed Mrs. Smith into the aisle, where Iona caught up to her and linked arms.

"Wasn't that marvellous?" she asked.

"The most marvellous music I've ever heard," Caroline agreed. "I do hope there's another concert. Would you attend one with me?"

"Of course," Iona said. "I'm sure Jack and Sean would like to go to another one as well. Now, about this reception, do you know who is organizing it?"

"I have no idea," Caroline replied. "Truly."

"I am astonished," Iona said, leaning close, "that Mrs. Anson kept it a secret."

"It sounds like it was important to Mr. Anson," Caroline said. "Mrs. Anson hates to disappoint her husband." Mr. Anson generally indulged his wife, but he expected her to follow his wishes the few times he made specific requests.

The two of them finally made it outside. Other concertgoers were heading off in all directions, and Caroline craned her neck looking for the Ansons or Mrs. Smith.

"Well, the reception is an excellent surprise," Iona said. "I am not ready for this wonderful evening to end. Who do you think will be there?"

"Other competitors," Sean said as he and Jack joined them. "And some of the Administrators. At least that's what Mr. Anson told us."

"We can size up our competition," Jack said, and Caroline suppressed a frown. The way Jack had spoken, it sounded as though he meant that the four of them were a team. It wasn't that Caroline was against it, but surely, they should all have a conversation first. Not to mention, Father would not approve of such a quick decision. Jack had only just met Iona.

"The reception has started," Mr. Anson said, pocketing his watch. "Let's not dawdle." He set out across the street, Mrs. Anson and Mrs. Smith right behind him. Caroline was about to fall into step with her brother, but Iona grabbed his arm, leaving Caroline to follow with Sean.

"Did you enjoy the concert?" Sean asked.

"Very much. I was saying to Iona that if there is another concert, I would love to attend. If you both are interested."

"I am very much interested in spending more time with you and your brother," Sean replied.

"Do you attend a lot of concerts?" Caroline asked. "This was my first and I adored it."

"Linley Academy regularly holds concerts," Sean said. "With

student musicians." He grinned. "Some are not very good, but they need to practice playing for an audience, and for the rest of us, it's a night out."

"It sounds lovely." Caroline sighed. To be able to regularly hear music played live, even by students, would be such a treat.

There was a crowd in front of Administration Hall: people waiting to get in, Caroline assumed. She and Sean joined the rest of their party at the edge of the crowd.

"Stay together," Mr. Anson said. "We need to enter as a group."

Caroline edged closer to Iona and Jack, who were having a quiet conversation. Iona laughed and touched Jack's arm.

"What do you think is so amusing?" Sean asked her, leaning close to her.

"I don't know," Caroline replied. "My brother is not usually funny." Jack had always been very serious and studious, traits their father prized. Iona laughed again and Jack grinned at her.

"Well, hello," someone said.

Caroline turned to find the young man she'd spoken to at Administration Hall peering at her with dark eyes. His elaborately tied cravat framed a handsome face and warm smile.

"It is you," he said. "I worried that I was mistaken. Have you read Samuel Jones yet?"

"I have," Caroline replied. "Twice. And I confess that although I rather enjoyed it, I still have no idea which parts of *True Stories of Blackmeadow Abbey* are embellished."

"I never said Jones wasn't a good writer. I assume that you are competing this year?" He gestured to the crowd. "The reception is for competitors and their supporters."

"Ah, that explains it," Sean said. "My name is Sean Smith, and as you guessed, an Endeavour competitor. This is Caroline Morris."

"I'm Harry Townsend." He gave a quick bow. "It's an exciting time, isn't it?" His eyes met Caroline's gaze.

"It certainly is," Caroline said. "None of the reading I've done has captured even the tiniest sense of the excitement. We were just at a concert across the road and now we're attending a reception. Either one of these events back at home would have been the highlight of the season, and here we are, attending both in the same night."

"Indeed," Harry replied with a smile. "There are many events scheduled until teams are selected and artifacts are handed in. Oh, there's my sister. I hope to see you inside." Harry nodded at her before heading towards the front of the line.

"Who was that?" Mrs. Anson said, stepping over.

"He introduced himself as Harry Townsend," Caroline replied. "We had a conversation about a book when you were taking your test for the Artifact Society. I forgot to mention him in the excitement of you passing your test."

"Oh, I remember that day very well," Mrs. Anson said. She turned to Sean. "I'm sure taking tests is something you do all the time at Linley Academy, but even though I'm not used to them, I wasn't nervous at all."

Caroline only half listened as Mrs. Anson told Sean how well she did on her test. She scanned the people ahead for another glimpse of Harry Townsend. She would like to talk to him more about Mr. Samuel Jones.

She didn't see him before her group arrived in the entrance to the hall. Mr. Anson dealt with a couple of people who were seated behind a table and soon they were all waved in.

"There is a refreshment table set up under the staircase," Mr. Anson said. "The mezzanine is reserved for competitors. Caroline, Jack, I would appreciate it if you went upstairs to investigate what is happening and then came back to let me know what you see." He pulled out his watch. "I suggest we meet back here in one hour."

Jack grabbed her arm. "Let's go up now and report back to Mr. Anson as soon as possible."

"Yes," Caroline agreed. Mr. Anson didn't like waiting once he'd given his instructions.

She followed Jack to the stairs along with Iona and Sean.

Another table was set up at the bottom of the stairs.

"Please write your name, year of birth, and home village or city," a woman said. She pointed at two lists and pens that were on the table.

Jack leaned over one list while Caroline took the other. She scanned the list. There was no Harry Townsend but she did see an Ella Townsend. His sister perhaps? She wrote down her name, her year of birth, and Gaynesford.

She stepped aside to allow Sean to fill out the form. Iona had lined up behind Jack.

When all four had signed the sheets, they were told to go up the stairs.

"You've been here before?" Sean asked her.

"Yes, for the Artifact Society," Caroline replied. "They meet in a hallway up here."

"So, it's not an official group?" Sean asked. "I mean, they don't have a room to meet in?"

"They don't meet in a room," Caroline replied. "But there's a notice on the board downstairs that says where they meet." That seemed official to her.

"But they don't have a room assigned to them," Sean said. "I think that means they are not officially recognized by the Administration."

They were almost at the top of the stairs and Caroline was annoyed by Sean's statements.

"Mrs. Anson considers them official," Caroline said. "She'd heard about them before we arrived in Norbarrow." She stopped at the top of the stairs and gasped. "Look at the lights!"

The entire ceiling was dotted with twinkling lights.

"Isn't it marvellous?" Iona said, linking arms. "It's like they brought the stars inside."

"Marvellous," Caroline repeated, her annoyance with Sean forgotten. "Oh, there's even a moon." As she watched, the moon travelled across the *sky*, waxing and waning as it went.

"There's a refreshment table near the back wall," Jack said. "Iona, can I get you a drink?"

"Yes, please," Iona said, and Jack headed off before Caroline could ask him to get her one as well.

"I'll get you one," Sean said with a smirk, and as he walked away, Caroline's annoyance came back full force.

"I could get my own drink," she said.

"Oh, let the boys take care of it," Iona said. "That way we can enjoy the atmosphere. Look, I think that must be some of the Administrators."

A group of four men reached the top of the stairs and in single file they made their way through the crowd. Caroline strained to see where they were going, but too many competitors fell in behind them, obscuring her view.

"Should we see what's happening?" Iona asked.

"Shouldn't we wait for Jack and Sean?"

Iona pulled her forward. "If I know my brother, he'll be at the front before we get halfway there."

"All right." Caroline still felt odd about leaving when Sean and Jack were getting them drinks, but she and her brother did have to report to Mr. Anson. One of them had to learn what was happening.

They were at back of the crowd and too far away for them to see anything. Not even a determined Iona was able to squeeze them any farther forward.

Suddenly, the ceiling changed from stars to an image of the four men up front.

"Welcome, competitors," one man said. He appeared to be the oldest one, and Caroline judged him to be the same age as Mr. Stanford and Mr. Hobson, so would have competed in the Endeavour forty-four years ago.

"It's an exciting time for all of us, but most especially for you who are about to compete. You have less than sixty days to form your teams. Once you have your teams, you will bring your artifacts here, to the square in front of Administration Hall, thirty days prior to the start of the Endeavour. At that time your team will be entered into the draw. In the following days, we, the Administrators, will place the surrendered artifacts inside Blackmeadow Abbey."

A second Administrator stepped forward.

"Three days before the start date, starting positions will be drawn," he said. "Starting positions are final. Teams are not allowed to switch positions, and if you are late by more than one hour, your turn is forfeited."

"If you need help assembling a team," a third Administrator said, "a list will be available here, in the Hall, one month from now. If you need team members, or you need a team, you will be allowed to submit your name or contact anyone or any team on the list. I suggest you not wait too long. Teams must consist of four people. If you have any questions, we will make ourselves available for the next hour."

"I'm going to try to talk to one of them," Iona said. "Are you coming?"

Caroline took in the throng of people and stepped back. "You go ahead. I need to report to Mr. Anson." She scanned the crowd, hoping to find her brother. It would be better if they spoke to Mr. Anson together: she was afraid that in her excitement she might get some of the details wrong.

"Suit yourself," Iona said. She pushed forward through the crowd and Caroline turned to head back to the stairs.

"You don't have any questions?"

She looked up to see Harry Townsend watching her.

"I do," she replied. "But my friend is going to ask one. Besides, if everyone ahead of me tries to reach the Administrators, I fear the hour will be up before I get there."

"True," Harry said. "Is your friend your teammate?"

"My brother is my only confirmed teammate," Caroline said. "We were supposed to compete with our younger sister, but the early call means she missed the age cut-off."

"I, too, am in a family team," Harry said. "My sister Ella is downstairs somewhere, and our older brother Cedric lives in town but didn't want to attend the reception tonight." He shrugged. "Like your younger sister, Cedric was a year too young to compete in the last Endeavour."

"Did he ever get over his disappointment and bitterness?" Caroline asked. "I fear my sister never will."

Harry laughed, although Caroline wasn't sure what was funny.

"I'm sorry," Harry said. "But you've just explained much of what has confused me about my brother for my entire life. So, I have to say, no, he never got over it and is bitter to this day."

"I am sorry to hear that." She sighed. Becca might be miserable for years. It was bad for her sister, but also bad for everyone around her, including her.

"There is no chance for me to get a question in," Iona said as she rejoined her. "But I saw Sean up at the front."

"And Jack?" Caroline asked. "Did you see him?"

"Sorry, no." Iona looked at Harry. "I saw you two talking out front."

"Yes," Harry said. "I've met Caroline before on this very floor. I'm Harry Townsend."

"Iona Smith," Iona said. "What business did you have here when you two met?"

"I was meeting a friend," Harry said. He turned to Caroline. "How about you?"

"I was waiting while Mrs. Anson took her test to join the Artifact Society," Caroline said. "She and her husband have been kind enough to host me and my brother Jack."

"And did she pass her test?" Harry asked.

"She did," Caroline replied. "As did I the next day, although my test was more about Endeavours than Artifacts."

"But they are inextricably linked," Harry said.

"They are, although Jack, my brother, might not agree."

"What might I not agree with?" Jack said from behind her.

"That artifacts and Endeavours are linked," Harry said. "Harry Townsend. You must be Caroline's brother."

"I am. Jack Morris," Jack replied. "Caroline, I think one of us should go and find Mr. Anson. Can you do that? I am waiting for Sean."

"I suppose I could." She'd expected them to go together, but really, she was as much a competitor as Jack, wasn't she? "Is there anything you specifically want me to tell him?"

"We all heard the same thing," Jack replied. "Shall I get you that drink now, Iona?"

"I'll catch up with you later, then," Caroline said, but Jack was clearly not paying attention to her. She smiled and nodded to Harry and started making her way through the crowd to the stairs.

She doubted she would come back up here: no doubt it would take some time to find Mr. Anson.

CAROLINE PAUSED ON the lowest stair and scanned the crowd, hoping to spot the Ansons. The large space was packed with people and the din of so many voices made thinking almost impossible. How would she find Mr. Anson?

"I'd try the refreshment table if I were you."

She turned to find Harry Townsend smiling at her.

"I tried to ask you to wait up but you left too quickly," he said. "It's time for me to find my sister and see if she wants to leave. She's not fond of crowds."

"I don't think I am either," Caroline said. "I've never seen so many people in one place before. I think there are three times as many people in this space down here as live in my village." Even major holidays in Gaynesford didn't attract this many people.

"I appreciate country life—and the lack of crowds—myself," Harry said. "Come on. The refreshment table is this way. I am quite sure that at least one of us will be successful in finding our missing companions."

"I hope so," Caroline said. "Although in their minds I'm sure *we* are the missing ones."

Harry laughed. "I am sure that is the case."

Harry held onto her arm as they pushed their way through the crowd. "There she is." He steered them towards the back wall. A young woman, who seemed to be a few years younger than Harry, spotted them and waved.

"Finally," she said when they reached her. "That was the longest hour of my life. I hope this means you are ready to leave?"

"Soon," Harry said. "Once I help Miss Morris find her party. Caroline Morris, meet my sister, Ella Townsend."

"Hello," Caroline said. "I am very pleased to meet you. And honestly, there is no reason for your brother to delay your exit. I am quite sure I am capable of finding Mr. and Mrs. Anson myself." Ella Townsend had her brother's same dark hair and a very infectious smile.

"I wish you luck," Ella said. "This crowd is impossibly large."

"I do hope I can find them sooner rather than later," Caroline replied. "I must update Mr. Anson on the announcement. He's taken a very keen interest in Jack and my Endeavour experience. And Mrs. Anson will want details on how the announcement was made. Harry, do you think a Builder-enhanced artifact was used?"

"I'm certain there was," Harry said. He turned to his sister. "Both Mrs. Anson and Caroline are members of the Artifact Society, although Caroline's main interest is Endeavours."

"Oh my," Ella said. "Watch out, Caroline. My brother will bore you for hours with facts about Endeavours."

"I'm sure I wouldn't be bored," Caroline said, and she meant it. She would love nothing more than to talk about Endeavours, especially with Harry, after his comment on Samuel Jones.

"Caroline has just recently read *True Stories of Blackmeadow Abbey*," Harry said.

"Did you like it?" Ella asked. "I haven't read it but Harry can't seem to make up his mind."

"I did like it," Caroline replied. "Oh . . . there's Mrs. Anson. I am sorry, but I must see if she knows where her husband is."

"Of course," Harry said. "I hope we run into each other again."

"Why don't we plan to?" Ella asked. "Have you been to the flower exhibit?"

"I have, but there is more than enough to see for another visit," Caroline replied.

"Then let's meet there tomorrow at noon," Ella said. "At the centre of the park."

"At the statue? I know exactly where that is." Caroline still had her map in case she got confused.

"Until tomorrow then," Harry said.

"Yes. Now I must say goodbye. Mrs. Anson is on the move."

Caroline hurried through the crowd towards Mrs. Anson who, with Mrs. Smith in tow, was heading towards the back wall and away from the stairs.

"CAROLINE, THERE YOU are," Mrs. Anson said when she finally caught up to her. "Where are the rest of our competitors?"

"They're still up on the mezzanine," Caroline said. "There was an announcement and then some of the Administrators were available for questions but there was no chance that all four of us would get close enough for that. I came down to report back to Mr. Anson. Do you know where he is?"

"He went off that way," Mrs. Anson said, waving a hand towards the back wall. "But don't bother him right now. He's hoping to make a connection with an Administrator."

"You can tell us what was announced," Mrs. Smith said. "I would very much like to know."

"Of course." Caroline knew that whatever Mr. Anson's instructions, she should not interrupt him in his quest to become an Administrator. Besides, this would give her practice reporting what she'd heard.

She had barely started when Mrs. Anson interrupted with a detail about the Builder-enhanced artifact that allowed the scene to be projected on the ceiling. When her hostess was finished, Caroline continued her report.

"That was it?" Mrs. Smith asked. "That sounds like information everyone already knew."

"Well, Sean was near the front," Caroline replied. "We thought it likely he would be able to ask a question or two. Perhaps he will find out more?" Now she worried that she should have waited for Sean's information before reporting to Mr. Anson.

"That is typical of my son." Mrs. Smith beamed. "He is very often in the right place at the right time."

"And there were no other artifacts used?" Mrs. Anson asked. "Just the one that projected the scene?"

"Perhaps a second one amplified the sound?" Caroline couldn't recognize Builder-enhanced artifacts when they were in use the way Mrs. Anson could.

"Oh, yes, that's very likely. To my knowledge there are no artifacts, Builder enhanced or otherwise, that both amplify sound and project a scene."

"Oh look, there's Sean and Iona now," Mrs. Smith said. "Along with your Jack."

When they arrived, Iona linked arms with Caroline.

"Isn't this all so exciting?" she asked. "That presentation made it all so real."

"It did," Caroline agreed. "I have butterflies from the excitement."

"Did you report to Mr. Anson?" Jack asked her.

She shook her head. "I haven't had a chance. Mrs. Anson said that he was making a connection and wasn't to be disturbed."

"I'll do it," Jack said. "Oh, there he is. It looks like he's free now."

Before Caroline could object, Jack was halfway to Mr. Anson. She frowned. She was the one who'd left the excitement upstairs in order to report to their host. It wasn't that she was excited about making the report, but she was determined to be—and be seen as—a fully participating team member.

And yet Jack seemed to be the one in charge. She'd only come downstairs to give the report because he'd told her to, and now she was left behind because he'd decided that he was the one who would inform Mr. Anson.

"Sean was able to speak to two of the Administrators," Iona said, pulling Caroline's attention away from her brother's actions.

"One of them said that my question was good," Sean said, sidling closer. "I didn't hear him say that to anyone else."

"What was this *good* question?" Caroline asked.

"I asked if he thought people with traces of Natural blood had an advantage."

"Isn't that a good question?" Iona said.

"It is," Caroline agreed, when she really didn't think it very good at all. She'd read numerous Endeavour accounts that all agreed that a trace of Natural ability helped. The real question was how did one know if they had Natural blood? Naturals rarely married anyone other than a Natural, and on the rare occasions when they did, any children were considered Naturals. People with Natural blood didn't move to places like Gaynesford or even Norbarrow. No, they stayed on their estates, socializing with each other.

"Can you guess what the answer was?" Iona asked.

Sean crossed his arms, waiting for Caroline to answer.

"Was it yes?" Caroline knew it was yes, but Sean, and Iona especially, seemed to think this was such a huge revelation that she didn't want to deflate them.

"You are correct," Sean said. "The Administrator said that he knew first-hand that Natural blood was an advantage. Do you and Jack have Natural blood?" He looked at his sister. "I don't think we do. At least not any that is known."

"I don't think Jack and I do either," Caroline said, not bothering to add that if any of them did, it would probably be from so long ago that it would be too diluted to matter.

Mr. Anson and Jack joined them.

"It seems that we've had a successful night all around," Mr. Anson said. "Based on Jack's report and my own chance meeting. But I think it's time for us to leave. Mrs. Smith, do you and your son and daughter need assistance getting home? No? Then we must say good night. And I thank you for providing tickets to the concert."

"We thank you and Mrs. Anson for a such lovely dinner," Mrs. Smith said. "And for ensuring we all attended this wonderful reception."

Sean and Iona echoed their mother's thanks.

"My pleasure," Mr. Anson said, beaming. He took out his watch and checked the time. "My dear, shall we go?"

"Of course." Mrs. Anson departed with her husband, leaving Caroline and Jack to say hasty goodbyes.

"We didn't have a chance to make plans with Iona and Sean," Jack complained when they were outside. "We were supposed to pick a day for the river cruise."

"I'm sure we'll see them soon," Caroline said. She wanted to spend more time with Iona, of course, but tomorrow she had plans to meet Harry and his sister Ella.

She briefly wondered if she should bring Jack with her, if they might make a four-person team, but then she remembered that Harry and Ella already had a third teammate in their older brother. The Smiths seemed the most likely pair to compete alongside, which made her wonder why she'd agreed to meet Harry and Ella.

She sighed. Because her mother had told her to take advantage of her time here and she wanted to do that: to enjoy all kinds of people and experiences. And she liked Harry: he took her love of Endeavour history seriously.

# 6

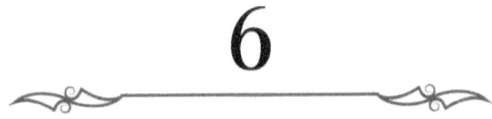

I'm sure the Smiths would welcome a visit," Mrs. Anson said as Caroline entered the dining room.

Jack was seated beside Mrs. Anson, a plate with rolls and jam in front of him. He glanced up at her as she sat across from him.

"You'll come with me," he said.

Caroline raised her eyebrows. When had her brother become so bossy?

"Caroline will be attending the Artifact Society meeting with me this morning," Mrs. Anson said. "Won't you, dear?"

"I'm looking forward to it," Caroline said. Jack might not have any duties, but she had been invited—they *both* had been invited—because Mrs. Anson needed a companion. She took a roll from the serving plate and spooned some jam from the small pot. "This afternoon I am meeting with Harry Townsend and his sister Ella. We are going to investigate the flower exhibition."

"What should I tell Sean and Iona?" Jack asked. "I'm sure they will expect both of us."

"Iona and I had discussed attending another concert," Caroline said. "Perhaps you can find one we can all attend." She met Mrs. Anson's gaze. "I hope you would come with us, as well as Mrs. Smith."

"That sounds lovely," Mrs. Anson said. "Jack, if you could arrange that, I would appreciate it." She frowned. "I'm not sure

Mr. Anson will be available. His efforts last night have paid off and he told me that he expects to have quite a few meetings in the next few days."

"That's settled then," Caroline said. "Jack will approach the Smiths with an eye to sorting out the details for another concert."

Her brother frowned at her, but Caroline ignored him and poured herself a cup of tea. Why should she do Jack's bidding? Weren't they equal Endeavour teammates? And really, she was the one with the knowledge of Endeavours: perhaps they weren't equal because she was in fact the superior one. That made her wonder about Iona and Sean: would she be superior to them as well?

"Caroline, are you ready to go?" Mrs. Anson asked. "We don't want to be late."

Caroline took a last sip of tea and put down her half-eaten roll. Jack smirked at her but she ignored him again. The Artifact Society was something she quite enjoyed.

"I'm ready," she said.

AS SOON AS Mrs. Anson spotted Mrs. Digby, Caroline was left alone. She didn't mind: she was quite certain that independence was an excellent quality for an Endeavour competitor.

Mr. Hobson waved her over.

"Stanford can't make it today," Mr. Hobson said. "But I hear you were at the reception last night. You must tell me all about it."

"How did you know I was at the reception? Did Mrs. Anson tell you?" She didn't know how Mrs. Anson would have had time to give that news: they'd only just arrived.

"They posted the sign-in sheets," Mr. Hobson said. "Miss Foster and I looked this morning. Well, she looked since my eyes aren't good enough to see that high up."

"I didn't realize they were going to post those," Caroline said.

"They only do that for the formal reception," Mr. Hobson said. "Now, tell me everything."

For a second time, Caroline described the evening's presentation. Like Mrs. Anson, Mr. Hobson detailed the artifacts that were used, but unlike Mrs. Anson, his comments were short and did not interfere with her narrative.

"I love hearing about Endeavour activities," Mr. Hobson said when she finished. "I have to admit that when I attended my reception, I was so nervous and excited that I barely recall anything. Mr. Stanford says he recalls it very well, but I cannot confirm that what he remembers actually happened."

"It's all very exciting," Caroline agreed. "We even attended a concert before the reception. I don't think I've ever had a more exhilarating evening."

"Nothing but excitement for the next few weeks," Mr. Hobson said. "Right up until you hand in your artifact. I don't need to ask if you really have one, do I? Not everyone who attends the festivities has an artifact."

"Both mine and my brother's are safely locked up at home," Caroline said. "Do people really attend events like the reception when they know they can't compete?"

"Of course. Even if you didn't have an artifact, would you want to miss any of this? It's your one chance to be a part of the lead-up to the Endeavour. Besides, not everyone gets to enter the Abbey. Your experience—even without an artifact—might not be that much different from that of many others." Mr. Hobson grinned. "And the bonus is it won't have cost you an artifact."

"I suppose," Caroline said. "But it would be sad to attend events knowing that you had no chance to compete."

"Well," Mr. Hobson said. "There are always those who hope to trick someone into giving them an artifact." He leaned closer. "And those desperate enough to steal from someone they pretend to befriend."

Caroline nodded. "My father has warned my brother and me about that." She sighed. She found that sad as well: that someone would lie, cheat, and steal to get what they wanted.

CAROLINE SPENT MOST of the meeting in Mr. Hobson's company, but Mrs. Anson and Mrs. Digby came over for the last few minutes so that Caroline could tell Mrs. Digby about the previous evening.

Well, that was what Mrs. Anson asked Caroline to do, but she ended up simply nodding her head in agreement with Mrs. Anson's version of events.

Finally, Miss Foster came around. "Our time is up," she said.

"The drawing club will be here soon and I have promised that we will not disrupt their lesson."

"Of course," Mrs. Anson said. "We shall make way for them at once. Caroline, since you have plans, Mrs. Digby and I are going to take a walk. Shall we accompany you to the flower exhibition?"

"That would be lovely," Caroline said. "Thank you." The park was only a few blocks away and she was quite sure she could make it there on her own, but it was kind of her to offer.

She trailed the two older women the whole way, listening in as Mrs. Anson described an article that she'd read that described how a Builder had discovered what an artifact's magic did.

At the park entrance, Mrs. Anson and Mrs. Digby stopped at the table.

"We could take our walk here," Mrs. Digby said. "I haven't been yet."

"Brilliant," Mrs. Anson said. "We can accompany Caroline and meet her friends. Mr. Anson is not very fond of young ladies being out on their own."

"I didn't realize that," Caroline replied. "I often go for walks on my own at home." She was mortified: the last thing she wanted to do was disappoint Mr. Anson.

"No need to worry," Mrs. Anson replied. "In a small village like Gaynesford there is little danger, but Norbarrow is a different matter. You are under our care, after all. Now, lead us to your meeting place."

"All right." Caroline led the way along the path, taking the same turnoffs as she had on her previous visit. When she stepped into the centre square, she was quite proud of herself: she hadn't had to consult the map even once.

She spotted Harry and Ella Townsend sitting at the base of the statue, and she waved and they headed towards her.

"I hope I'm not late," Caroline said when they were close. "We were at the Artifact Society meeting. I don't think you met Mrs. Anson last night. Mrs. Anson, this is Mr. Harry Townsend and Miss Ella Townsend. Harry and Ella, this is Mrs. Anson, who has been kind enough to bring me and my brother Jack to Norbarrow, and Mrs. Digby, another member of the Artifact Society."

"Mrs. Anson," Harry said. "I saw you last night, but in the

crowd, introductions were quite impossible. Mrs. Digby, it's very nice to meet you."

"It's a lovely day to visit the park," Ella said. "And for making new acquaintances."

"Indeed," Mrs. Anson agreed. "And don't worry, Mrs. Digby and I are only delivering Caroline into your company. We are very capable of entertaining ourselves."

"I am sure," Mrs. Digby said, "that while we find our conversations fascinating, they would bore you." She paused. "Townsend. Are you any relation to Mr. Patrick Townsend?"

"He is our father," Harry said. "Do you know him?"

"We have met," Mrs. Digby said. "But it was years ago and I am certain he would not remember me."

"Father has a very good memory," Ella said. "So, you might be surprised. Was it in your capacity as a member of the Artifact Society?"

"It was," Mrs. Digby replied.

"Father is fascinated by artifacts," Harry said.

"Aren't we all?" Mrs. Anson said. "Now, if you don't mind, Mrs. Digby, I think you and I should start with a cup of tea and let these young people get on with their visit."

"Of course. A cup of tea is just the thing."

The two women said their goodbyes and strolled towards the tea pavilion.

"Is your father really interested in artifacts?" Caroline asked Harry and Ella. "Because Mrs. Anson will want to discuss them with him if they ever meet."

"Father does love talking about them," Ella said. "But he has little patience for those who claim to be experts when they are not." She glanced over her shoulder at Mrs. Anson and Mrs. Digby. "I know he was not overly impressed with the Artifact Society."

"He called them *interested amateurs*," Harry added. "And since Father is not one to hide his feelings, I believe he said that to them when they met."

"Did they find that disrespectful?" Caroline asked. "I'm not sure Mrs. Anson would be offended by that description because it's true, they are interested amateurs."

Harry laughed. "Father certainly meant it as an insult but did the Artifact Society take it as such? You've caused me to doubt that. Come on, let's go look at some flowers."

THEY SPENT THE next two hours wandering the park. Caroline's map proved to be quite useful for finding the most direct routes to some of the more significant garden beds, and she was happy to be able to navigate using it. After a while, they found a shaded bench and sat down to rest.

"Do you have gardens back home?" Ella asked. "We have grounds and meadows with wildflowers, but not much in the way of formal flower gardens like these. I grow useful plants, like herbs."

"There are no gardens like these in all of Gaynesford," Caroline admitted. "My mother and Mrs. Anson both grow roses with some success."

"Our mother loved roses," Harry said. "Father didn't see the point in them after she died."

"I am sorry you lost your mother," Caroline replied.

"It was years ago," Ella said. "Although I think, as a young woman, I miss her even more now than I did then. Father does his best but . . ."

"He is not Mother," Harry finished. The two siblings shared a sad look and Caroline felt sorry for them.

"I am lucky to have two older brothers to look out for me," Ella said, trying to be cheerful. "Although I often wished for a sister."

"Wish for an older sister," Caroline said. "Younger ones make such annoying demands. At least mine does."

"I can attest to that," Harry said. "Since I also have an annoying younger sister."

Ella stuck her tongue out at him, and he laughed, the sombre mood of a few minutes ago now broken.

"I should get back to the Ansons'," Caroline said. "Before they start to worry. We should plan another outing. I went to my very first concert and I'm quite eager to attend another one."

"I don't get to attend enough concerts," Ella said. "I would be very interested."

"As would I," Harry added.

"Where in town are you staying?" Ella asked. "We can walk you there."

"Thank you. Mr. Anson hired a house not far from Administration Hall." Now that she knew Mr. Anson would frown on her walking out alone, Caroline appreciated their offer. She told them the address and the three of them headed out of the park.

"YOU SHOULD HAVE asked them in," Mrs. Anson said. "After they were kind enough to walk you home."

"I wasn't sure you or Mr. Anson would be here," Caroline said. "I worried that it would not be appropriate for me to act as host since I myself am a guest."

"I'm sure Mr. Anson won't mind you hosting Mr. and Miss Townsend," Mrs. Anson said. "Mrs. Digby tells me their father, Mr. Patrick Townsend, is an Administrator. You must ask them to dinner and include their father in the invitation, of course. Just wait until Mr. Anson learns of this. An Administrator dining in our home!"

"I will certainly ask them when I see them next," Caroline said. "But I am shocked to find out that their father is an Administrator. I was told he had met with the Artifact Society but not in what capacity."

"Yes," Mrs. Anson said. "They needed the approval of an Administrator in order to meet in Administration Hall. Mrs. Digby told me they had hoped to be authorized to use a meeting room, but the hallway was a compromise suggested by Administrator Townsend. When do you see them again?"

"We have made no firm plans," Caroline said. "Although we discussed attending a concert together."

"Another concert," Mrs. Anson said. "That would do nicely. Mr. Anson will be so pleased. Oh, Jack, there you are. I hope you had as fruitful a day as your sister. Now, I must speak to Mrs. Wooton. We'll need a fine menu that can be assembled on short notice." She bustled out of the parlour in search of the housekeeper.

"Fruitful?" Jack asked as he sat down across from Caroline.

"It seems that Harry and Ella Townsend's father is an Administrator," Caroline said. "According to Mrs. Digby."

"They didn't tell you that themselves?"

"No." Caroline sighed. "I'm not sure why. We spent all

afternoon together and they failed to mention it."

"Perhaps they thought you knew," Jack said. "My afternoon was also successful. Iona is truly an impressive young woman and Sean is as trustworthy as anyone I've ever met. We could do worse than teaming up with them for the Endeavour." He paused. "You haven't promised the Townsends, have you?"

"Oh no. They are competing alongside their older brother," Caroline said. "It's long been planned."

"Just as we were to be on a team with Becca," Jack replied.

"Yes. I hope you haven't made any promises to Sean and Iona," Caroline said. "I'm not sure Father would feel we've spent enough time getting to know them." She couldn't think why they wouldn't pair up with the Smiths. She adored Iona and she thought Jack did as well, and Sean seemed like a fine fellow.

"I have not promised anything," Jack said. "I have heard Father's urge for caution more times than you have. It will be up to us to ensure we spend enough time with them to satisfy Father."

"How much time do you think that will be?" Caroline asked.

"Two weeks. I think after that even Father will concede we have been cautious enough."

CAROLINE WAS THE focus of Mr. Anson's attention all during dinner.

"I absolutely will invite them and their father to dinner," she said when—for the third time—Mr. Anson expressed his hope to meet all of the Townsends.

"Excellent," Mr. Anson said. "Do you have their address? Could you send a note in the morning? The sooner this can be arranged the better I will like it."

"I must wait for them to contact me," Caroline said. "I did not get their address but they walked me home so they know how to get in touch."

"Let's hope it is soon," Mr. Anson said. He turned to Jack. "You were charged with finding another concert. Did you?"

"There are two later this week," Jack replied. "I just need to know which one to get tickets for."

"We shall get tickets for both concerts," Mr. Anson said. "The two of us will go tomorrow morning and I will make sure we have enough tickets for everyone. Be ready to leave at eight."

"Of course, Mr. Anson," Jack replied.

Mr. Anson nodded and turned back to Caroline. "Is there a chance that you will create a team with the Townsends? I would recommend you do if at all possible."

"They are a threesome," Caroline said. "Along with their older brother."

"Ah, that's unfortunate. Their father has a formidable reputation."

"We," Mrs. Anson said. "That is, Mrs. Smith and I, have discussed how lovely it would be if Jack and Caroline teamed up with Iona and Sean. It is completely your decision, of course."

"Caroline and I have talked about it," Jack said. "But we feel Father would want us to be cautious and not make a commitment too soon."

"Quite right," Mr. Anson agreed. "We will take the Smiths into account when we acquire tickets for the concerts. Mrs. Anson." He turned to his wife. "We must be ready for a dinner party of up to eleven, if the oldest Townsend son is in town." He looked at Caroline.

"He lives in town," she said. "But I'm not sure how much time he spends with the rest of the Townsends."

"Don't worry," Mrs. Anson said. "I have already put Mrs. Wooton on notice. I will advise her to expect a few more for dinner, and if the oldest sibling does attend, we will be prepared." She sighed. "How wonderful to be planning another fine dinner party. And Caroline, to think that just a few days ago we worried about not knowing anyone, and here we are, planning a second dinner party, this time for eleven. I dare say some of it is because of the Artifact Society."

"I think you're right," Caroline said. They met Mrs. Smith, Sean, and Iona at the flower exhibition, but Caroline would not have met Harry Townsend if Mrs. Anson hadn't been taking her test to join the Artifact Society.

And the Townsends seemed to be very high on Mr. Anson's list of people he wanted to know better. Caroline was happy to spend more time with Harry and Ella, but knowing that it made her host happy made her feel useful.

Iona was still her favourite person in the whole world, but she rather thought Ella, and to a lesser extent her brother, would end up coming close.

As Mrs. Anson had reminded her, such a short time ago she knew no one in Norbarrow. Now she had multiple acquaintances and plans for more social events.

Her mother was right: she should enjoy everything she could, so she would.

JACK AND MR. Anson had already left by the time Caroline came down for breakfast.

"Are you going to another Artifact Society meeting?" she asked Mrs. Anson as she helped herself to some biscuits.

"Not today," Mrs. Anson said. "I want to wait for Mr. Anson to return with the concert tickets. I don't think Mr. Anson would think it appropriate for you to go alone and I do hope you are not disappointed."

"I am quite able to amuse myself," Caroline said. "I will take a book into the garden since it looks like a very nice day." She'd been thinking about Mr. Anson's comment last night regarding Mr. Townsend: how he'd left a *formidable legacy* for the Endeavour.

The only Townsend she remembered from her Endeavour studies had been the sole survivor of an entire team two Endeavours ago. She would check her books and see if she could find out if Harry and Ella's father was *that* Townsend.

"It's a very useful skill," Mrs. Anson said. "Amusing oneself. A skill that I have developed over the years. Ah, Mrs. Wooton," she said when the housekeeper entered the dining room. "Fresh hot water for the tea would be appreciated. Thank you. And when you have a spare moment, we must discuss the options for the dinner party. I do know it's a challenge when we are not certain of either the date or the number of guests."

Caroline finished her biscuits and, when the hot water had been replenished, poured a second cup of tea. By that time Mrs. Anson had left with Mrs. Wooton to make decisions about the upcoming dinner party.

Caroline felt a twinge of panic when she recalled that she was the one who was to extend the invitation to the Townsends despite not knowing how to contact them. What if Harry and Ella forgot about her, or worse, decided that she wasn't worthy of their time?

How disappointed Mr. Anson would be! She sighed. There was nothing she could do about that at the moment. If two days passed without hearing from them, then she would ask Mrs. Anson how to go about finding where the Townsends were staying.

She finished her tea, grabbed *True Stories of Blackmeadow Abbey* from her room, and made her way out into the garden. She sat down on the bench and opened her book.

She reread the chapter that dealt with the Endeavour twenty-nine years ago. And there on the page was the name of the only surviving member: Patrick Townsend. It could only be Administrator Patrick Townsend, father to Harry and Ella.

In her previous readings, she'd been so consumed by the horror of the three deaths that she'd missed an extraordinary piece of information. Patrick Townsend had left Blackmeadow Abbey with ten artifacts.

It wasn't the record: that was held by a team four Endeavours ago who found twelve. But it was certainly the most a single competitor had ever acquired.

There wasn't a lot of information about how Townsend's teammates died, just some speculation by the author that implied Mr. Townsend was in some way to blame.

Caroline had to wonder if this was what Harry had alluded to when he'd said that the book contained embellishments. Surely Harry knew the truth about his father's teammates and that the truth had little to do with what the book inferred.

Mr. Townsend was an Administrator: he would not have such a prestigious position if he'd been the cause of three deaths during the very event he now helped manage.

But ten artifacts! That was impressive.

"Caroline," Jack said from the path. "I'm back with the tickets. And we have received an invitation for this afternoon." He waved a note. "This just arrived from the Smiths."

"Oh." She closed her book. "That is excellent." She'd been hoping for word from Harry and Ella, and not just because she knew Mr. Anson would be asking, but any outing increased the chance of running into the Townsends. At the very least it would distract her from worrying. "What are they planning?"

"A drive around town," Jack said. "In a carrier. Mrs. Smith has hired one for the whole afternoon. They will pick us up at two."

"Goodness, that is impressive," Caroline replied. She smiled. Her second carrier ride in as many weeks. She had better write home tonight because soon she would simply have too much exciting news for a single letter.

# 7

It's the red one," Caroline breathed. She and Jack stood on the front steps as the red carrier stopped in front of the house. "I saw it pass by the night we arrived in town. It's lovely."

"It's an unusual colour," Jack said. "The trademark of a very specific Builder. Sean, Iona." Jack waved as the siblings stepped out of the carrier, followed by Mrs. Smith.

"Isn't it smashing?" Sean said. "It's the best one they had for hire."

"I am not surprised," Jack replied. "I believe I know who the Builder is and they have a reputation for quality. Mrs. Smith, how kind of you to invite us along today."

"It's an exciting time," Mrs. Smith said. "So, I thought I would help make it memorable. Is Mrs. Anson inside? I thought that she and I could take a ride later while you four go off and enjoy yourselves right now."

"She's waiting for you," Caroline said. "Shall I fetch her?"

"No, I'll find her." Mrs. Smith turned to Sean. "You are to be back in two hours. That should give you plenty of time to see the city."

"Yes, Mother," Sean said. "Well, everyone, we have no time to waste."

Caroline got in first, followed by Iona. Despite patting the seat next to her, her friend sat down across from her. Jack settled in beside Iona, leaving a place for Sean at Caroline's side.

Sean had to give instructions to the driver, but then he climbed into the compartment. He pulled the lever and the carrier set off.

"I've told the driver to take us everywhere anyone of note will be," Sean said. "I want to be seen."

"We all want to be seen," Iona agreed. "Don't we?" She turned to Jack, who nodded.

Caroline nodded as well, even though she wasn't sure she wanted to be seen, and certainly not by *everyone of note.* Whoever that might be.

The carrier turned a corner onto a street Caroline was not familiar with. A few moments later they were on a bridge. She craned her neck to see out the window. The Haven River was below her, the water sparkling in the sun.

"I haven't been to this side of the river," Caroline said, pulling her head back inside. "What's over here?"

"The largest estates, for one," Iona said. "You can see some of the grounds from the street." She shrugged. "Mother brought us here for a walk. She's ever so interested in the gardens."

"Of course," Caroline replied. "That's why she suggested we meet at the flower exhibition."

"Exactly," Sean said. "Although I must admit I am far more interested in the private carriers in front of some of these houses than I am in the grounds."

"Look," Jack said. "Isn't that Harry Townsend and his sister?"

Jack was peering out the window opposite to hers. Caroline did her best to see past Sean but since he had also turned to look, her view was blocked.

"I can't see," Caroline said. "Was it them?" Should she ask Sean to stop the carrier? Would it seem too forward to stop them on the street and invite them to dinner and a concert?

Then they were past them and the moment was gone.

"I'm certain it was them," Jack said. "They were with another young man—perhaps it's their older brother."

"Do you think they have a house around here?" Caroline was looking at her brother when she asked, but Sean answered.

"Why else would they be walking here?"

"I suppose." Caroline wondered if the Townsends were simply out for a walk, as the Smiths had done in this exact neighbourhood. And then she wondered why Sean hadn't voiced that possibility.

She tried to catch her brother's eye but he was talking to Iona, their heads bent so close together that all she could hear were whispers.

"There's a park up here," Sean said. "With a grand promenade. Everyone who is anyone walks along here. I shall have the driver stop when we get there."

"I would love to see the park," Caroline said, when really, she was worried that she wasn't dressed for a promenade. She looked over at Iona, who was wearing a lovely yellow muslin day dress, then back at herself and her perfectly serviceable, yet uninspiring navy wool.

Not that she had much to choose from. Life in the country meant there were very few events that required fine clothes, and limited access to fancy fabric.

Sean pulled the knob and the carrier slowed and then stopped. "Come on," he said. "Let's stretch our legs and show off."

Sean helped Caroline out of the carrier while Jack did the same for Iona. Before Caroline could catch up to her friend, Iona and Jack were already steps ahead.

Sean fell in step beside her and she felt it would be rude to rush ahead. But she so wanted to spend some time with Iona. How could they be sitting in the same carrier and yet not speak more than a few words together?

"Ah, there's a gent who knows how to wear a hat," Sean said, nodding towards a man a few steps away.

Caroline nodded, but she didn't find Sean's observation very appealing, although he seemed to take her nod for interest.

The path they walked along followed the river, and while Caroline's eyes were drawn to the swans and geese, Sean kept up a steady accounting of what was worn—and how well—by every single person they encountered.

They finally reached a lovely fountain. Jack and Iona had stopped, and Caroline immediately took Iona's arm and pulled her gently forward.

"I do hope Jack is not boring you," Caroline said. "I know how he can go on about Builders and their enhancements to artifacts."

"I find your brother's conversation very interesting," Iona

said. "He is very knowledgeable and seems to have a real passion for the subject." She glanced over at Caroline. "He's also charming."

"Jack? Charming?" Thinking her friend was making fun of her brother, Caroline almost laughed.

"He's very charming to me," Iona said. "Is he not usually?"

"Not to me," Caroline said. "But I am his sister. Is Sean charming to you?" She didn't really think it was a good comparison, because she did not find Sean Smith the least bit charming.

"Sean is not at all charming to me." Iona laughed. "So perhaps it's something that is true of all brothers and sisters."

"I would say that brothers aren't even always nice to their sisters," Caroline said. "So, you are probably right."

Jack and Sean caught up to them.

"We have more places to visit," Sean said. "I suggest we head back to the carrier."

Once again, Sean walked beside Caroline while Jack and Iona huddled together.

In an effort to listen to as few of Sean's observations regarding other strollers, Caroline set a brisk pace. She quickly entered and settled in the compartment of the carrier, determined to have Iona sit beside her.

Sean was having a word with the driver and Jack and Iona were still a few steps away, when she saw the Townsends.

She fumbled with the door, trying to get out without being so crass as to shout at them, then thankfully, she saw them stop to talk to Jack and Iona.

Caroline finally managed to get out of the carrier and join them.

"Ah, Caroline," Jack said. "I was just telling Harry and Ella, along with their brother Cedric, about the Ansons' invitation."

"They are very interested in you joining us," Caroline said. "There is a concert as well, so dinner will not be a grand event."

"I much prefer less grand events," Harry said. "Caroline, this is my brother, Cedric Townsend, Miss Caroline Morris."

"The one who belongs to the Artifact Society," Cedric said. "Father has told me about them. Amateurs."

"Indeed," Caroline said. "*Interested amateurs.* Although I'm not sure I can think of any professionals who deal with artifacts. Other than Builders, of course." Cedric Townsend was certainly handsome and fashionable, but Caroline wondered if his apparent arrogance was a result of his disappointment at not competing in the last Endeavour. She would hate Becca to become like that.

Harry grinned, but Cedric scowled. "Administrators could also be considered professionals," Cedric said.

"I disagree," Harry said. "Administrators are professionals, but with regard to the Endeavour, and Blackmeadow Abbey, not artifacts. Mrs. Anson's knowledge of artifacts might even surprise Father."

"Perhaps they can discuss that over dinner?" Ella said. "Father does like a challenge."

"Yes," Cedric said. "But if you are wrong and he is bored, it will be on you." He turned to Jack. "What day is this concert?"

Jack gave them the two dates and started to describe the concerts while Caroline stepped over to Ella.

"I do hope you can come," she said. "I had a lovely time at the flower exhibition with the two of you. And Mr. Anson is terribly interested in making your father's acquaintance. He has hopes of joining him on the Administration."

"Does he?" Ella replied.

"Yes. He competed the same year as your father," Caroline said. "He was one of the few who actually entered Blackmeadow Abbey."

"I will let my father know," Ella replied. "Perhaps if your Mrs. Anson is as knowledgeable as you say, it will help his cause. Many people want to be Administrators."

"It's a very important role," Caroline replied.

"Not to mention, prestigious," Ella replied.

"Of course," Caroline said. She was about to add that she didn't think Mr. Anson wanted it for the prestige when Sean joined them.

"The driver is waiting," Sean said. "We need to go soon if we are to maintain our schedule."

"Then we won't keep you," Harry said. "We have the dates and will send word once we've discussed it with Father. I warn you that he is very busy these days so there is no guarantee he can make it."

"You are all invited whether Mr. Townsend can attend or not," Caroline said.

"I am sure the rest of us will accept," Harry replied. "Even if Father can't make it. Thank you."

They said their goodbyes, and Sean corralled Jack on the way back to the carrier, leaving Caroline in the company of Iona. Finally.

"They are a very striking family, the Townsends," Iona said. "Especially Cedric."

"I suppose," Caroline said. "I want you to know that you are to be included in the invitation. Mr. and Mrs. Anson wanted to extend the invitation to Mr. Townsend first in order to give him an option for the date."

"Oh, that's lovely. I did wonder. I can certainly see how you need to make allowances for an Administrator, especially in the lead-up to the Endeavour. I do hope the other three Townsends can make it even if their father cannot." Iona linked arms with Caroline.

"I do too." Caroline smiled as she climbed up into the carrier compartment. When Iona sat beside her, she didn't think she'd ever been so happy.

Her dear friend was beside her, and she and her brother had delivered the invitation to the Townsends. She wasn't sure if Mr. Anson or Mrs. Anson would be more delighted: Mr. Anson because he had a chance to make such a great connection, or Mrs. Anson because an Administrator might interrogate her about artifacts.

She would take great joy in informing her hosts.

She smiled and settled back into her seat. Even the fact that Iona spent the rest of the journey leaning across to talk to Jack couldn't spoil her mood.

The Ansons were bound to be proud of her, and so would Father and Mother.

MRS. ANSON AND Mrs. Smith were waiting when they arrived back at the house.

"You are late," Mrs. Smith said as soon as Sean set foot in the parlour.

"It was our fault, Mrs. Smith," Caroline said before Sean could reply. "Mr. and Mrs. Anson tasked me and Jack with inviting the Townsends for dinner and a concert. We couldn't pass up the opportunity when we came across them in a park."

"Oh." Mrs. Anson sat up straight. "Were you able to extend our invitation?" She turned to Mrs. Smith. "I beg you to forgive their lateness. This is for the dinner party I was telling you about. Did the Townsends accept?"

"They promised to discuss the dates with their father," Caroline said. "And let us know if he can attend. If he is too busy, I told them that they are all welcome anyway: all three, including their older brother Cedric, who we just met."

"Oh yes, of course," Mrs. Anson replied. "We have the concert tickets so there is no issue there. Did they seem hopeful that Mr. Townsend would agree?"

"Ella seemed to think that Mr. Townsend might be interested in discussing artifacts with you," Caroline said.

"Cedric agreed with her," Jack added. "So perhaps there is enough to draw a busy man out for an evening."

"Goodness," Mrs. Smith said. "I absolutely will forgive them for taking extra time. Imagine, dinner with an Administrator. Now, Mrs. Anson, shall we take that ride?"

"Certainly," Mrs. Anson said. "It will be a chance for me to relax before my time is required for organizing the dinner party. I will also need to prepare for a discussion about artifacts. How wonderful that will be."

The two women left, and Jack and Sean went outside, leaving Caroline alone with Iona.

"It's rather remarkable that we happened upon the exact people you needed to see," Iona said. "All because we hired a carrier."

"It is remarkable," Caroline agreed. "It feels like fate."

"But Caroline," Iona said. "It may have been Jack who extended the invitation initially, but it was you who made it enticing. I truly believe that if you had left it to Jack the Townsends would have declined."

"Oh, I don't think so," Caroline said.

"Since their father is an Administrator they must receive dozens of invitations," Iona said. "Yet, they seemed delighted with yours. Harry Townsend practically promised to attend even if his father could not."

"I do enjoy both his and Ella's company," Caroline said. Was Iona somehow jealous that she'd spent time with the Townsends? "But I am ever so happy that you will be attending the concert as well."

"It's bound to be quite an occasion," Iona said. She stood up. "I think we should find out what our brothers are up to. Trouble, no doubt."

Caroline led the way to the garden, determined to put her friend at ease. She liked Ella Townsend and her brother very much, but Iona was destined to be her lifelong friend.

AT DINNER THAT night, Caroline basked in the glow of approval from both of her hosts. She met Jack's grin across the table.

"Jack made the initial invitation," Caroline said. "So, he deserves the credit."

"And he shall get it," Mr. Anson said. "As will you. Even if Mr. Townsend isn't able to attend, he will know who I am since I will host his children. It's as good a connection as I have made so far. Thank you to both of you."

Caroline sighed with pleasure and relief. Despite Mrs. Anson's approval, she'd been worried that extending the invitation to Harry, Ella, and Cedric without their father might have been taking too many liberties. She was, after all, a guest of the Ansons.

"Never fear, dear," Mrs. Anson said. "I will spend some time with the Artifact Society making sure I am up to date on current insights and knowledge."

"Mr. Townsend has to accept our invitation first," Mr. Anson said.

"I have no doubt he will," Mrs. Anson said. "What a fine party it will be."

MRS. ANSON WAS correct: the very next morning a letter arrived from Administrator Patrick Townsend accepting dinner and a concert on behalf of him and his three adult children.

It was for the first of the suggested dates, and Mrs. Anson declared that she would have no time for anything except dealing with dinner and brushing up on her artifact knowledge. If

Caroline decided to attend the Artifact Society meetings with her, she would have to understand that she would be left on her own while Mrs. Anson conducted her research.

With her duties as Mrs. Anson's companion reduced, Caroline had extra time to fill. When Jack told her that he was meeting Sean and Iona, she quickly agreed to join them.

"I am so happy that we have given Mr. Anson a reason to be glad he brought us," Caroline said as they set out for Administration Hall. Jack had told her that Sean and Iona would be in the square at noon.

"It allows us more time to find teammates," Jack replied. "Although I really think Sean and Iona are well suited."

"Father would want us to be absolutely certain," Caroline said. She expected that they would end up teaming up with Sean and Iona, but now she wasn't completely sure it was a good idea. She adored Iona but there was something about Sean that didn't sit well with her. He seemed very . . . superficial. She rather doubted he would be very interested in researching how to find lost artifacts.

"Another week will satisfy Father," Jack said. "Mrs. Anson would be delighted, which would reassure Mother."

"Probably." She wanted to say that neither Mrs. Anson nor Mother would have to trust Sean Smith in potentially dangerous situations, but she held her tongue. Today and the dinner party would allow her more time to observe Sean Smith. If after that she still had doubts, she would raise them with her brother. They were making a very important decision that would affect the rest of their lives. They had to get it right.

RATHER THAN BE disappointed when Jack and Iona once again paired off leaving her with Sean, Caroline saw it as an opportunity to interrogate Sean.

"What are you studying at Linley Academy?" Caroline asked.

"The same as Jack, I assume," Sean replied. "The Classics, Latin, some mathematics—although I am not overly fond of that. I plan on going into law when I am finished."

"Do you like it? Jack loves the college, although I am not certain the formal studies are what he loves."

"Ah yes, his obsession with Builder enhancements." Sean

laughed. "Does he hope to become a Builder?"

Surprised, Caroline stumbled. "Could he? I didn't think that was even possible? Why not hope to become a Natural?"

"Naturals are born with magic," Sean replied. "To my knowledge, Builders are not born Builders."

"The children of Builders become Builders," Caroline said. "Don't they?"

"Usually, yes," Sean said. "Although we have a Builder's son at Linley and he is not following in his father's footsteps. He wants to be ordained."

"I suppose Builders need clergy the same as the rest of us." At no time, despite his obvious interest—and yes, obsession—with Builder enhancements, had Jack ever mentioned wanting to become a Builder. She should ask him.

"They do," Sean agreed. "So perhaps that is where he will end up."

"Is he competing in the Endeavour?"

"No. Most Builders don't," Sean said. "But I also heard that he had no artifact to submit, so even if he wanted to compete, he couldn't." He grinned. "It makes less competition for the rest of us."

"I suppose." Caroline took a deep breath. She was supposed to be learning about Sean but she was learning more about her brother. "Are you afraid of the Endeavour?" she asked, more to get the conversation back to Sean than because she wanted to know his answer.

"Of course not! This is the most exciting event in my life, in *our* lives. I can't wait to set foot in Blackmeadow Abbey and come out with artifacts that will make my fortune."

"I'm a little afraid," Caroline said, even though Sean hadn't asked. "Every Endeavour a few contestants are hurt, and sometimes they even die. It can be very dangerous."

"I'm not worried," Sean said. "Not to speak ill of the dead, but I think that those who perished must have made mistakes."

"Mr. Townsend was the only survivor from his team," Caroline said. "Do you think he and his team made mistakes?"

"I'm sure of it."

Caroline hid a frown. She hadn't been able to find out what had happened to Mr. Townsend's team, but the reports she'd read about others who had died did not mention *mistakes*. "So how do you keep from making mistakes?" she asked.

"You designate a single person as the decision maker," Sean said. "That way there are no arguments about what to do. A single person who directs all actions. That's how the army works."

"I guess it is," Caroline said. She didn't even have to ask: the way Sean was talking made her certain that *he* would be the person making all of the decisions. She would let Jack know that there was no way she would allow Sean Smith to make life and death decisions for her.

She squared her shoulders. She knew she had a lot to contribute to an Endeavour team even if Sean didn't. She'd talk to Jack as soon as possible. They needed to start searching for new people to team up with. People who weren't Sean Smith.

For the rest of the walk, even though Caroline did her best to ignore Sean, she couldn't help but notice just how much he talked about wealth and connections.

She realized that even his comments on how people dressed were rooted in the cost of items or whether they were this year's fashion. She was surprised that she hadn't noticed this yesterday, but she realized he had done the same thing then, too. Now hiring the red carrier seemed very much part of his attention to outward displays of wealth.

Then she had to wonder why he was even bothering with her since her clothing was so old and plain that there was no season when they would have ever been fashionable in Norbarrow.

She watched Iona and Jack, who were a few steps ahead of them. Iona had linked arms with her brother and leaned in to speak into his ear. Caroline couldn't hear what was said, but she heard the trilling laugh of her friend. Jack seemed flustered but he didn't look away from his companion.

Was Sean's interest in her more about Iona's interest in Jack? She'd thought that Iona wanted to be *her* friend but for some time now Iona'd hardly been parted from Jack.

"You said that your younger sister missed the age cut-off," Sean said. "Has she taken it badly?"

"Very badly," Caroline replied. "It was always Father's plan that the three of us would compete together. Now poor Becca will be one of the older competitors for her Endeavour."

"Like Cedric Townsend."

"Yes," Caroline replied. "It must be a difficult thing."

"Cedric will be competing with his brother and sister," Sean said. "So that's a silver lining of sorts."

"Of sorts." So far Becca didn't see competing with their younger brother as a silver lining.

"Your father must have set aside an artifact for your sister," Sean said. "If she was expected to compete in this Endeavour."

"Of course," Caroline replied. "It's locked up at home with mine and Jack's. I suppose she'll get hers back once this year's contest is over."

"I see."

Something about the way Sean said that made her pause. What exactly did he see? "And yours and Iona's?" she asked.

"Mine and Iona's? Oh, you mean our artifacts. Yes, they are safely locked away, like yours." He smiled, but she didn't think he was happy. "You can't be too safe with artifacts right now."

"No, you can't," she replied. "Look, there's a bench. I could do with a rest. Jack," she called. "Iona. Can we sit down, please?"

She wanted a few minutes to think about her conversation with Sean. It wasn't the first time she'd been asked about Becca's artifact by a Smith: Iona had asked her about it. But what did that mean?

# 8

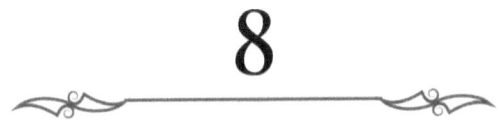

Caroline didn't have a chance to discuss Sean's behaviour or comments with her brother until early the next day. Since the dinner and concert were later in the evening, Mrs. Anson had much to do and had even breakfasted early. Jack was alone in the dining room when Caroline entered.

"Are you excited about tonight?" he asked as she helped herself to some fruit rolls and tea. "I've been to dinner parties larger than this one but I'm sure it's a first for you."

"It is," Caroline said. "And I am excited. So many new people to talk to and then my second concert. I have written to Mother already but Becca will get my letter with news of tonight."

"Poor Becca," Jack said. "I feel very sorry for her. It must be hard to miss the Endeavour by just a year."

"Yes. Harry mentioned his brother Cedric was also just a year too young to compete in the last Endeavour," Caroline said. "It didn't sound as though Cedric had ever quite gotten over his disappointment. I hope Becca does better than that." She looked over at her brother. "At least she has an artifact ready for when she does compete."

"Yes," Jack said. "Although Iona thinks it's a waste to hold onto an artifact for so many years. She thinks it would be better to put it to use now."

"Does she? But then what would Becca use to enter the Endeavour?"

"An artifact that we find," Jack said. "If we find any extras."

"What if we don't find any? Or, what if we only find useful ones? Ones that we don't want to give up?"

"Then either we or Father could buy Becca one when the time comes," Jack said. "If the ones we find are useful we would most likely be able to make money from them."

"It doesn't matter," Caroline replied. "Since Father will never allow it."

"That's what I told Iona."

"When did you two talk about artifacts?" Caroline asked. "Because Sean asked me about ours yesterday."

"We've discussed them a few times," Jack replied. "Iona is very interested in artifacts."

"Is she?" Not once had Iona commented on the Artifact Society or broached the subject of artifacts with her other than when discussing the need for one in order to compete. "I wonder why she hasn't mentioned that to me."

"She's intimidated by you and Mrs. Anson," Jack said. "Because you are members of the Artifact Society. She would be embarrassed by how little she knows and does not want you to think less of her."

"I would not think less of her for knowing little," Caroline said. "Mrs. Anson does not think less of me because I don't know as much as she does. That's how one learns, by interacting with people with more knowledge. Isn't that what school does for you?"

"Iona is not in school," Jack said with a laugh. "And neither are you. She asked me not to even tell you she was interested in artifacts because she feels that her knowledge is so inferior. Please, don't mention this to her."

"All right." Caroline sipped her tea. It had cooled so she added more from the pot to her cup.

"I'm heading out for a walk," Jack said, rising from the table. "In case anyone is looking for me."

Puzzled, Caroline finished her tea. She'd thought she and Iona were such great friends so it pained her to think that such a kind, sweet person felt self-conscious around her.

Now she worried how Iona would feel tonight at dinner when Mrs. Anson and Mr. Townsend were likely to have an expert conversation about the very topic Iona felt inadequate in.

Walking to the concert with Iona would allow her to broach the subject.

Caroline couldn't possibly let her very dear friend feel intimidated by her in any way. She would not allow it no matter what she'd promised her brother.

"Mrs. Anson," Caroline said. "You look wonderful. Your dress is lovely." Caroline resisted the urge to inspect her own, rather dowdy, brown silk and compare it to her hostess's emerald green.

"Thank you," Mrs. Anson said. "I bought it a few years ago and had it updated when Mr. Anson decided to petition for a seat on the Administration. Now come along. We should be in the parlour when the guests start arriving."

Caroline followed Mrs. Anson to the parlour. Jack was already there, looking bored. She took the seat beside him on the settee.

"I'm saving that spot for Iona," Jack said.

"Iona might prefer to sit with me," Caroline replied. "Besides, I think you should spend more time talking to Sean. I have informed an opinion of him as a potential teammate and you need to do the same."

"I already know we should be on a team with them," Jack said. "Sean and especially Iona will be outstanding teammates. I rather think that we will all be lifelong friends after this. We just need to wait long enough to satisfy Father before we make it official."

"Official?" Caroline's voice raised on the last syllable. "It's not even unofficial. Jack Morris, you better not have promised anything to Sean and Iona Smith, because I have *not* agreed to anything."

Caroline wasn't sure how much of what she said Jack even heard because the doorbell had chimed and Jack's eyes had fixed on the doorway. Now Mrs. Wooton stood just outside the parlour, introducing the Smiths.

Jack made a beeline for Iona, leaving Caroline sitting alone on the settee. Rather than wait for Sean to plunk himself down beside her, she rose and went to stand next to Mrs. Anson.

"Mr. Anson will be with us directly," Mrs. Anson said. "Refreshments will be served as soon as our other guests arrive."

The doorbell chimed again and Mrs. Anson jumped a little.

"Caroline," she whispered. "Would you be a dear and let Mr. Anson know that Mr. Townsend and his family have arrived?"

Caroline stepped into the hallway and headed to the study. She knocked on the door before opening it. Mr. Anson looked up from a paper he was reading.

"The Smiths are here and the Townsends have just arrived."

"Excellent." Mr. Anson set the paper to one side, stood up, and smoothed his coat before striding across the room.

Caroline backed away from the door to allow him room to exit, then she followed him along the hall, back to the parlour.

She paused just outside the crowded room when Mr. Anson made his entrance and stayed back as he greeted Mr. Townsend, Cedric, Harry, and Ella and then the Smiths.

By the time there was room for her to enter the parlour, their guests had all been seated. Jack was beside Iona, of course, but she had her head bent towards Cedric Townsend. Sean was motioning to her but she saw Harry and Ella by the window and joined them.

"I hope you have not been overlooked?" Caroline asked the pair. "Since your father and brother have not met everyone before."

"We are fine," Ella said. "But it was very kind of you to ask." She paused and leaned closer. "Father usually hates these types of things but he did appreciate what you told me about your Mr. Anson. He's promised to be on his best behaviour."

"I do hope he doesn't find us a bore," Caroline. "And that Mrs. Anson is at least an *interesting* amateur."

Harry laughed. "I find your attitude refreshing. Cedric didn't know what to make of you when you agreed with his assessment of the Artifact Society. Like Father, he thinks it's an insult."

"Things could still go very wrong." Caroline glanced over at Mr. Townsend, who had been cornered by Mr. and Mrs. Anson.

"Then it's a good thing that dinner is short and the rest of the evening is a place where conversation is not encouraged," Ella said with a grin.

The hired serving man brought around small glasses of cordial. Caroline sipped at hers, deliberately keeping her eyes away from Sean. She was certain that the least bit of encouragement would bring him to her side.

"Iona Smith seems to be fascinated with Cedric," Ella remarked.

Caroline chanced a peek: Iona was leaning close to Cedric, whispering in his ear. Jack seemed very put out until Sean sidled over to him and started a conversation.

"Is he fascinating?" Caroline asked. "That she should be so taken by him?" Jack was listening to Sean but she thought his frown was directed at Cedric.

"He likes to think he is," Harry said. He lowered his voice. "The rest of us think he's a pompous bore."

"She certainly seems to be making Cedric feel exceptional," Ella said. "Which means he will have a very high opinion of her since it reinforces his own opinion of himself."

"Do you think that's what she's doing?" Caroline asked. She adored Iona, but was that because Iona made her believe that *she* was exceptional?

"Yes," Harry said. "Because of Father we've all been exposed to people who will use all of their charms to gain access to him. I think Iona Smith is doing just that."

"Oh dear," Caroline said. "What you must think of Mr. and Mrs. Anson." Mr. Anson had been very clear that he wanted to host Mr. Townsend because he felt that he could help him gain a seat on the Administration.

"Father appreciates being told up front what someone wants," Ella said. "Which is why he accepted Mr. Anson's invitation."

"Father admires ambition and ambitious people," Harry added. "What he hates is someone who lies and tries to trick him in some way."

Mrs. Wooton hovered in the parlour doorway and then Mrs. Anson called them all to dinner.

Caroline hadn't been part of the planning so she wasn't aware how the seating had been arranged, but she did note Mrs. Anson's frown when Iona sat down beside Cedric.

She understood the frown when the only available seat had a card with Iona's name on it. Mrs. Anson had wanted *her* seated beside Cedric: she could only guess that it would put her in a position closer to Mr. Townsend and the Ansons so she could participate in any artifact discussion.

Caroline sat down and laid the card flat. She was more than

happy to be seated beside Harry and Mrs. Smith, who was at the end. Across from her was Jack, and then Ella. Poor Ella would be subjected to Sean's conversation but Caroline was too far away to have to give him much attention.

Dinner went well for both Mr. and Mrs. Anson, from what Caroline could tell. After the main course, Mrs. Anson seemed to be answering questions from Mr. Townsend.

"Did you father just smile?" Caroline asked Harry. "I have not seen one yet so I must ask."

Harry grinned. "It's a rare occurrence but yes, that was a smile. I believe Mrs. Anson has charmed him."

"I doubt that very much," Caroline replied. "Mrs. Anson would not set out to charm anyone, even at her husband's request." Caroline liked Mrs. Anson very much, but she would never call her charming. "Dare I think that Mrs. Anson's knowledge of artifacts has impressed your father?"

"If that is the case, then well done, Mrs. Anson," Harry said. "Father is notoriously hard to impress, as all of his children can attest."

"Well done, Mrs. Anson," Caroline repeated under her breath.

The next course was served and Mrs. Smith engaged her in conversation, and then it was time to leave for the concert.

Caroline had planned on seeking out Iona for the walk to the concert hall. She saw Jack trying to engage Iona, who ignored him and set off with Cedric. A sullen-looking Jack dropped back to walk with Sean.

Caroline overheard her brother complaining about Iona not having any time for him but she didn't hear Sean's response since Ella caught up with her.

"Harry thinks Mrs. Anson has impressed your father," Caroline said to Ella.

"I think so too," Ella replied. "She must know a great deal about artifacts."

"She does. When she joined the Artifact Society, she told me her test wasn't nearly as difficult as she expected it to be."

"Did you take the same test?"

"Oh, no," Caroline replied. "I am not an artifact expert. They were kind enough to test me on Endeavours. I had to be a member in order to accompany Mrs. Anson and they were very accommodating."

"They sound like a lovely group," Ella said. "Father has misunderstood them, I think."

"The members I have spoken to are nice," Caroline said. "But perhaps there are others who think they are more than a leisure pursuit."

"Father always implied they wanted some sort of official recognition as an Administration-endorsed group which, according to him, would require more work from an already overworked organization."

Caroline laughed. "I think what they were looking for was an actual room where they could hold their meetings. Right now, they are allowed to meet in a hallway." She smiled and met Ella's eyes. "One they have to share with a drawing club which can be quite chaotic."

"Perhaps Mrs. Anson will convince Father to give them a room," Ella said. "He may even decide that he likes Mr. and Mrs. Anson enough to promote Mr. Anson's application to the rest of the Administration."

"Do you think there's even the slightest chance of that?" Caroline hadn't thought past having Mr. Townsend come for dinner and the concert. If she had even the smallest bearing on helping Mr. Anson achieve his goal of becoming an Administrator, she would feel like she'd been able to repay him for bringing her and Jack to Norbarrow.

"Father wouldn't have come if there hadn't been at least a slight chance," Ella said. "But he gets great pleasure in having people fail his tests. I have hope that this time his pleasure will be in someone passing."

As she took her seat in the theatre, Caroline couldn't stop smiling. Mr. Anson had a real chance of becoming an Administrator and honestly, that's all anyone could hope for. A chance to prove your worth. If you then came up lacking, well, it meant you hadn't worked hard enough, or didn't have the correct temperament, or connections or any number of things but at least you had been considered.

Even the presence of Sean beside her could not dampen her spirits. Despite Mr. and Mrs. Anson focusing on Mr. Townsend, she'd noticed that when the Ansons had to direct others to their assigned seats, Sean had sidled up to Mr. Townsend and engaged him in conversation. Caroline had no idea what they could be discussing so intently, but it did mean that there was less time for Sean to speak to her before the concert started.

"It was unfortunate that we did not sit together at dinner," Sean said. "We have so much to talk about."

"We do? I hope you understand that this evening is about Mr. and Mrs. Anson." Caroline did not want to know what Sean thought they had to discuss because she was afraid that he wanted to talk about competing in the Endeavour as teammates. She wasn't going to agree to anything no matter what Jack might have promised but neither did she want to make a fuss in public, when Mr. Anson had a chance to make his case for being an Administrator.

"Oh, of course," Sean said. "I will tell Mrs. Anson that dinner was superb. As are our seats for the concert."

"They are very good seats, aren't they?" She was no judge, but they were much closer to the performers than they had been for the previous concert.

The lights dimmed and the musicians filed onto the stage.

Sean leaned over and whispered in her ear. "I hope we have a chance to talk after the concert."

Then the concert started and mercifully, Sean stopped talking, and Caroline was able to concentrate on enjoying the music.

But when her mind wandered, she vowed to make sure she *didn't* talk to Sean later. She even went so far as to devise ways to get out of it: a sudden illness, perhaps a migraine. The problem was that anything she came up with might reflect badly on Mr. and Mrs. Anson.

In the end, Mr. Townsend saved her from Sean. When they were leaving the concert, he beckoned her forward before Sean had a chance to engage her.

"Mrs. Anson tells me that you are very nearly as knowledgeable about Endeavours as she is about artifacts," he said when she joined him.

"She is too generous," Caroline replied. "I am fascinated by them and always eager to learn more."

"An eagerness to learn is a very good quality," Mr. Townsend said. "As is realizing that there is more to learn. There is *always* more to learn. Do you think your studies will help you when you compete in your own Endeavour?"

"I believe that they will," Caroline said. "For one, I know how dangerous Endeavours can be so nothing about the competition should be taken lightly."

"I know too well of the dangers," Mr. Townsend said.

"Oh, of course. I am sorry, I mean." Worried that she would start babbling, Caroline paused and took a breath. "As a student of the history of Endeavours, of course I am aware that you know the dangers better than anyone else alive," she finished carefully.

They were almost out of the theatre now: she could see the street lights through the double doors.

Mr. Townsend met her eyes and nodded. "Exactly," he said. He looked past her. "Mr. Anson, walk with me, will you?"

Mrs. Anson linked her arm through Caroline's as Mr. Anson fell into step beside Mr. Townsend.

"All in all, a very productive evening," she said to Caroline. "If Mr. Anson does not get Mr. Townsend's endorsement it will not be because of anything we did wrong. And if he does?" she winked at her. "I rather think it will be in part because I impressed him with my knowledge of artifacts."

"I have no doubt of that," Caroline said.

At the corner, they said goodnight to Mrs. Smith, Sean, and Iona, who pouted when she was separated from Cedric. Jack caught up to her. Mrs. Anson was chatting with Ella, who she claimed had the loveliest dress of all the ladies in their party tonight.

"What did Mr. Townsend want with you?" Jack asked her.

"He wondered at a comment Mrs. Anson made about my knowledge of Endeavours," she replied. "I hope it means he was impressed enough that Mr. Anson has a chance at becoming an Administrator."

"It won't help us if he does."

"Jack, we owe them for bringing us here," Caroline said. "I am happy to be able to help them when they had no expectation that we would be able to. Besides, if he does become an Administrator, it might benefit Becca and Miles. Don't you think that would be wonderful for them?"

"I suppose," Jack said. He sighed. "I'm sorry, tonight did not go as I had hoped. You're right that I should be happy if we've been a small part in helping Mr. and Mrs. Anson."

"You're forgiven." She almost asked him about Iona: she was the reason Jack's plans hadn't worked out, but that might bring up what she thought Sean had wanted to discuss. Namely, joining forces as an Endeavour team.

Caroline wasn't ready to have another talk with Jack about that, not when she knew it would end up as an argument.

WHEN SHE ENTERED the dining room the next morning, Caroline was surprised to find Mr. Anson at breakfast with both Jack and Mrs. Anson.

Once she had filled her plate and tea cup, Mr. Anson cleared his throat.

"I want to thank you, Jack and Caroline," Mr. Anson said, beaming. "As well as my wonderful and intelligent wife for exemplary behaviour last evening. And of course, I especially wish to thank Caroline because without her chance meeting with Harry Townsend, I would not have become acquainted with Administrator Townsend." He smiled. "I have been invited to meet with the rest of the Administration. There are no guarantees, of course, and I am not the only person petitioning for one of the three open positions, but Mr. Townsend assures me that I am a very good candidate."

"Isn't that wonderful news?" Mrs. Anson said. "I am so proud of all of you for making such a good impression on Mr. Townsend."

"Congratulations," Caroline said. "I am so happy that all of your efforts have paid off."

"Yes," Jack said. "Very well done, Mr. Anson. Let us know if we can help in any other way."

"I think from here it is up to me," Mr. Anson said. "If I am accepted, I believe that there is a reception for family which you will certainly be invited to, but I dare not get ahead of myself."

"When do you meet with the full Administration?" Caroline asked.

"Mr. Townsend will send me word," Mr. Anson replied. "But not for a few days. Until then I will spend my time studying the rules that govern the Endeavour."

"I'm sure we will all see to it that you are not disturbed," Mrs. Anson said. "We three will find ways to amuse ourselves away from the house."

"Thank you," Mr. Anson said. "If I'm needed, I will be in the study."

Once he had left the room, Caroline turned to Mrs. Anson. "Will we attend the Artifact Society meeting today?"

"We should and leave Mr. Anson in peace," Mrs. Anson said. "Jack, perhaps you have a task that will take you out of the house?"

"I will walk with you to the Administration building," Jack said. "I still have the river cruise to organize. Should I plan that for tomorrow? There are Builder-enhanced boats for hire that I want to get a look at."

"Oh," Mrs. Anson said. "I almost forgot about that. We need to make sure the Smiths are available since I want to reciprocate for their carrier ride. We could make a picnic of it."

"That sounds lovely," Caroline said, when in truth she didn't want to spend more time with Sean. Although she did want Jack to get to know him better. Perhaps then he would understand her reluctance to team up with the Smiths.

"I will send them a message at once," Mrs. Anson said. She went off in search of writing supplies, leaving Caroline and Jack alone.

"Are you sure you will be all right while we attend the Artifact Society meeting?" she asked.

"I will investigate our boating and picnic outing," Jack said. "We can arrange to meet for lunch if it makes you feel better."

"Yes, that would be good."

MRS. ANSON'S NEWS of her husband's upcoming meeting was the focus of the discussion at the Artifact Society. Even Miss Foster agreed that Mrs. Anson's membership and knowledge of artifacts had more than likely helped her husband's cause.

"Perhaps the Administrators will see fit to allow us the use of a room," Miss Foster said. "Now that one of our own will be joining their ranks."

"Mr. Anson has not yet been asked to join. We don't want to

get ahead of ourselves," Mrs. Anson replied, echoing her husband's comment at breakfast.

"Of course not," Miss Foster said. "But even getting an interview with the entire Administration is a major accomplishment. I am sure Mr. Anson will do well."

"As am I," Mrs. Anson replied.

Caroline headed down the hall, away from the meeting.

Now that Mr. Anson's objective had been met, her thoughts were turning to her and Jack's need for an Endeavour team.

She did not want to join forces with Sean and Iona Smith. But if not them, then who? Time was not on their side. There were just six more weeks before the teams had to be formed and artifacts handed in. Six weeks for her and Jack to meet potential teammates and determine who they could trust.

Because she was certain that she did not trust either Sean or Iona, no matter how much she had adored Iona when she first met her.

And Iona's behaviour last night! She had ignored Jack and fawned over Cedric Townsend. Caroline hadn't liked the attention Jack had showered on Iona, but she'd thought that his feelings were reciprocated.

She sighed. She would be happy to join Ella and Harry if that was a possibility, but they only needed one more for their team. And while she trusted the two of them, she hadn't spoken to Cedric at all, not when Iona had commanded all of his attention. And in front of Cedric's father! Her behaviour had been shameful, really.

Caroline found herself out on the mezzanine, very near to where she'd met Harry Townsend. Could she meet someone else looking to create a team for the Endeavour? Or in four weeks would she and Jack need to put their names on the list of people searching for teammates? Would that process provide them with better potential teammates than Sean and Iona?

She and Jack really needed to discuss their options.

Mrs. Anson came looking for her and then the two of them went in search of Jack at the tea shop.

When they arrived, they found Jack with Sean, who was delivering the Smith family's reply to Mrs. Anson's invitation.

"My mother sends her regards," Sean said. "And her thanks for a wonderful evening. She and I can commit to an outing tomorrow, but Iona was not at home when your message arrived and neither Mother nor I can speak for her."

"It was a wonderful evening, wasn't it?" Mrs. Anson said. "And good practice for me if Mr. Anson is accepted on the Administration. I dare say I will both give and attend more dinner parties if that happens. Goodness, we might need to purchase a home in Norbarrow rather than just hiring one for a few months. I think with Mrs. Smith and your acceptance we can safely plan our event. Jack, I know you haven't booked anything yet, but can we decide where and when the Smiths can meet us?"

While Mrs. Anson and Jack discussed the plan for tomorrow, Sean leaned towards Caroline.

"Did you enjoy last night?" he asked. "I didn't get much of a chance to talk to you. I thought the dinner conversation was informative: Mrs. Anson truly impressed Mr. Townsend."

"I wasn't close enough to hear," Caroline said. "But I'm sure you're correct. Mrs. Anson is very well informed. My favourite part of the evening was the concert. I think I will miss live performances the most when I return to my quiet life in Gaynesford. I imagine you are now spoiled and the student performances at Linley will fall short."

"If Mr. Anson becomes an Administrator, life in Gaynesford might not be quite so quiet," Sean said. "As for me, I will be done with school soon. Perhaps I will move to Norbarrow and be able to attend all the concerts I care to." He glanced past her to Jack. "Much depends on how successful I am in the Endeavour."

"Yes, of course." Caroline desperately wanted to change to subject: she did not want to discuss the Endeavour with Sean. She did not want him to suggest they be a team. "Have you been in a Builder-enhanced boat before? I am not as excited as my brother, but I am quite keen to see how it works."

"I have not," Sean replied. "But I'm not sure they are that much different from regular boats, except that there is a pilot rather than sailors."

"Will we picnic on the boat itself or do you think the operator will find us a place to land? Would we need to wade through water?" Now she was worried about what she would wear.

"We'll only tie up at docks," Jack said. "So, there will be no need to get wet. And yes, there is a plan to eat on dry land."

"It sounds lovely," Mrs. Anson said. "Jack is going to confirm the boat this afternoon while I discuss the picnic with Mrs. Wooton. Caroline, we must head back to the house. I have much to do."

"I look forward to seeing you all tomorrow," Sean said.

"Same here," Caroline said. She followed Mrs. Anson out of the tea shop, leaving Jack and Sean together. Hopefully, her brother would spend some time really talking to him. Although Jack would probably just ask where Iona was. Asking would be rude, but she didn't think Jack would care if Sean thought him rude.

# 9

They arrived back at the house to the news that Ella Townsend had been by to call on Caroline. Mrs. Wooton handed her a note that Ella had written when advised that Caroline would be out for most of the day.

The note was short: just a simple request to arrange a meeting, along with the address of the Townsends' house in the city.

"You must send her a message," Mrs. Anson said. "And make plans. If I knew how big the boat Jack is hiring was, I would say to invite them all to come with us."

"I shall ask them if they can wait until we know more," Caroline said. "Tomorrow is, after all, reciprocating the Smiths' carrier ride, so they are the priority guests. Unless you think they would feel it forward if we invited the Townsends?"

"Mrs. Smith would be delighted at the larger party. I'm equally certain that Mr. Anson would be pleased that we are all getting along, even though I am sure that he is far too busy preparing for his meeting with Mr. Townsend and the rest of the Administration to join us. Let me know what reply you get to your note. Now, Mrs. Wooton, I am terribly sorry for so many last-minute events, but we need to put together a picnic for six to nine people. And it must be ready first thing in the morning."

Mrs. Anson and Mrs. Wooton headed for the kitchen, leaving Caroline with the note from Ella.

She would reply right away, of course. She would tell Ella of their plans for boating and a picnic, and say how very sorry she was that she could not immediately extend an invitation to Ella and her brothers. But if Caroline found out that the boat could accommodate all of them, and the Townsends were available, she could send an invitation in the morning. She ended it with a request for a reply as soon as possible. If no reply was forthcoming, then perhaps Ella and Caroline could schedule a visit for the following day.

Note completed, she found Wooton and asked him to have it delivered immediately. Once that was done, Caroline went out into the garden.

The past few days had been a whirlwind and she needed to sit and think about everything that had happened. And the many things that still needed to.

AFTER LUNCH MRS. Anson had some free time, so to keep out of her husband's way, Caroline accompanied her to investigate some of the nearby shops.

Mrs. Anson bought a new shawl at one shop and spent a good deal of time discussing a new dress at another. The shopkeeper showed them the latest styles in sleeves and lace, which made Mrs. Anson wonder if she was too old for such new styles.

"I'm just not sure it would be appropriate for the wife of an Administrator," she said to Caroline as they left the shop. "I feel like I should wait and see what the other wives are wearing first, but if Mr. Anson does get the position, I won't meet any of them until the reception, which is when I would want to be wearing a new gown." She sighed. "I suppose I must resign myself to waiting: Mr. Anson would not be happy if I wore an inappropriate gown to his reception."

"You have two very fine gowns," Caroline replied. "And the new shawl is elegant in an understated way."

"Yes," Mrs. Anson said. "You have identified it completely. Understated elegance, that is what I must strive for. Thank you, Caroline, you always make such good observations. Oh, look. There is Mrs. Smith. Mrs. Smith," she called out.

Up ahead, Mrs. Smith paused and turned around.

"Mrs. Anson, Caroline, how lovely," Mrs. Smith said, joining them. "What a grand scheme you have planned for tomorrow. A river cruise on a Builder-enhanced boat. Let's hope it is as nice a day tomorrow as it is today."

"Let's hope," Mrs. Anson replied. "We anticipate increasing our party to include Harry, Ella, and Cedric Townsend if the boat is large enough. I do hope that will suit you?"

"The more the merrier," Mrs. Smith said. "Have you been to the shops?"

"We have," Mrs. Anson said. She launched into a description of her shopping trip.

Caroline wandered over to a nearby shop window and stared at the hats on display. Her attention was caught by someone waving at her from inside.

"Ella!" Caroline exclaimed. Mrs. Anson was still talking to Mrs. Smith so Caroline entered the store.

"I received your message," Ella said. "I have not had a chance to speak to my brother Cedric." She rolled her eyes. "He is out with your friend Iona Smith. But Harry and I are available tomorrow if there is room."

"Wonderful." At least it was wonderful that Ella and Harry were available. Jack would not think it wonderful that Iona was with Cedric. "I won't know if we can all be accommodated until Jack gets back from making the arrangements. I am terribly sorry that I can't extend the invitation immediately. I know it's very bad manners."

"Last-minute plans are like that," Ella said. "And it means I don't know what my day will hold tomorrow, so right now it is full of possibilities." She linked her arm through Caroline's. "Come, I should greet Mrs. Anson. Is that Mrs. Smith with her as well?"

"It is," Caroline replied. "We just now met her after wandering into a few shops. But are you finished your shopping?"

"I was browsing only," Ella said. "Harry was meeting with a friend and I was at loose ends. But now that you are here, perhaps we can have tea?"

"I'm sure Mrs. Anson would agree to that."

Mrs. Anson did agree to tea, as did Mrs. Smith.

Talk centred around plans for the next day, with neither Ella nor Mrs. Smith commenting on Cedric and Iona's current get-together.

Mrs. Smith begged off first, saying that she had to confer with her housekeeper about the evening meal.

Mrs. Anson and Caroline walked Ella across the bridge and home to a fine estate. With a promise to send a formal invitation as soon as she could, Caroline said goodbye to her friend.

"Ella Townsend is a very charming young lady," Mrs. Anson said as they turned for home. "Not once did she make any of us feel embarrassed for not being able to commit to their invitation. I appreciate that very much. It could have been awkward. I do hope the boat is big enough for all of us. I will be terribly disappointed if we can't invite them, especially after she was so understanding."

"I hope we can invite them as well," Caroline said, although she was worried for her brother. What would Jack do if Iona ignored him and focused all of her attention on Cedric?

HAPPILY, THE BOAT Jack hired was large enough for the bigger party.

"Caroline," Mrs. Anson said. "You must send a message to the Townsends immediately. Wooton," she called. "Wooton. We have a message that must delivered right away. Caroline, is your note done?"

"I need a minute," Caroline said. She'd assumed that the morning would be soon enough, but perhaps she should have anticipated this and prepared a note. Although she would have had to prepare two notes: one with an invitation and one sending regrets.

Since she didn't want to cause Mrs. Anson any grief with a delay, her note was brief. As it was, Wooton was waiting in the hall while she signed and folded it.

As soon as she handed it to him, she worried that the note was too short; that it was too abrupt. The door closed as Wooton left the house and it was too late to change anything. If Ella was somehow offended, Caroline would have to make it up to her tomorrow.

"Lovely," Mrs. Anson said. "I am really starting to enjoy entertaining."

ELLA'S REPLY CAME just as they were sitting down to dinner.

"What does she say?" Mrs. Anson asked. "If it's not too personal, could you read it out loud?"

"Dear Caroline," she read. "It is with great pleasure that I accept Mrs. Anson's invitation on behalf of myself and my brothers Cedric and Harry. We will meet you at the dock at the appointed time. Warmest regards, Ella Townsend."

"They're all coming," Mrs. Anson said. "How lovely."

For the rest of the meal, Mrs. Anson went over every detail of the outing. She had Jack describe the boat—her brother only sounded excited when he was explaining the Builder-enhanced features—before she launched into a description of her discussions with Mrs. Wooton about the choices and preparation for the picnic lunch.

Mr. Anson commented that he was very glad that the Townsends could make it, and that he would appreciate having a quiet house for the whole day. His meeting with the Administration was set for the following day and he would spend the day studying.

Jack seemed out of sorts, so once they were finished eating, Caroline followed him to the parlour.

"Are you excited about tomorrow?" she asked. "It's your first time on a Builder-enhanced boat, isn't it?"

"That part will be fine," Jack said as he flopped into a chair. "But I don't like that Cedric Townsend was invited. And worse, that he's accepted."

Caroline sat down beside her brother. "Ella said that Cedric and Iona met today," she said gently. "Perhaps you should just ignore them tomorrow."

"I don't want to ignore her," Jack said. "I want him to leave her alone."

"Who she spends her time with is her choice," Caroline said.

"She'd spend time with me if we promised to team up for the Endeavour."

"No!" Caroline couldn't help her response.

Jack glared at her. "Why not? We need to create a team soon, so why not pair up with Sean and Iona?"

"I don't trust Sean," Caroline replied. "I can't put my finger on exactly why, which is why I've been asking you to spend more time with him. And Iona is proving to be such a fickle creature that I'm not sure I trust her either. You know how dangerous the Endeavour can be. I will not compete with people I don't trust." She'd been so sure that she and Iona had developed a great friendship that would last their whole lives, and here she was declaring to her brother that she didn't trust her. She was sad and angry that the early promise of a lifelong friend now seemed nothing but an illusion. Or worse, that she might have been taken advantage of.

"Then perhaps I'll work with Sean and Iona and you can find your own team."

"You would do that?" Caroline sat back in her chair and studied her brother's face. He was angry and hurt, but would he compete in the Endeavour without her? "I would rather not compete than compete with people I don't trust," she said finally. "Although that would break Father's heart."

"Then it's settled," Jack said. "I will team up with Sean and Iona and you can do whatever you want." Jack got to his feet. "I'll arrange it with them tomorrow. You'll see, it will work out great for me." He stomped out of the room, leaving Caroline sitting there, shocked and sad.

She blew out a deep breath. She knew she wouldn't change her mind: she really would rather not compete than compete with people she didn't trust. She could only hope that Sean and Iona Smith didn't put her brother at risk.

She went up to her room, her previous excitement at tomorrow's outing dimmed.

CAROLINE WOKE UP feeling like a huge weight had been lifted from her. Rather than being sad and distressed about her conversation with Jack and the decisions they had each made, she was relieved.

There was no more worry about trying to convince her brother that her reservations about the Smiths were justified; no stress about teaming up with people she didn't trust.

And even better, she decided that there was absolutely no reason for her to be more than polite to Iona and Sean, which left her free to spend her time with Ella and Harry, both of whom she admired greatly.

Jack sulked all during breakfast and didn't perk up until they arrived at the dock and the Builder-enhanced boat.

The Townsends were already there, and Mrs. Anson greeted them cheerfully, as did Caroline. Jack was already speaking to the boat's pilot, and Cedric wandered over to listen in but came back as soon as the Smiths arrived.

As Caroline had expected, Iona immediately attached herself to Cedric.

"It's a very fine day," Ella said.

"Yes," Caroline said. "I am so glad you were able to make it on such short notice. And I apologize if my invitation was abrupt. Mrs. Anson was very keen that I write it right away and I fear I was not very gracious."

Ella smiled. "Your note was fine. It was very good to get it all sorted out last night." She leaned in closer. "Cedric wasn't sure he wanted to join us until I assured him that Iona Smith would be here."

"They do seem quite taken with each other. Oh look, we're being asked to board."

ONCE ABOARD THE boat, Ella, Harry, and Caroline wandered to the side that looked out over the river while Iona and Cedric found a spot in the prow. Mrs. Anson and Mrs. Smith parked themselves on a bench near the stern, and Jack and Sean hovered near the open door to the pilot's cabin.

"There is another concert," Caroline said. "Mr. Anson bought tickets to two with different dates, in case you and your father weren't available for one. It's tomorrow night. Would you like to attend?" If she wasn't going to compete in the Endeavour, Caroline was determined to enjoy every single event she could while she was in Norbarrow. "I'm not proposing dinner. We could meet at the concert hall before the start."

"I would love to," Ella said. "And a simple night out would be agreeable. Harry?"

"You can count me in," Harry said. "Who else? Should we invite Cedric?"

"Yes," Caroline said. "I will speak to Mrs. Anson. I'm sure the Smiths will all be invited." She smiled at Ella. "Cedric will no doubt agree to come when he hears that."

"I'm sure he will," Ella replied, shaking her head. "He seems quite besotted." She turned to her brother. "Can you tell me what he sees in her?"

"Please do," Caroline said. "Jack is quite jealous so I would like to know what charms a man sees in her."

"She's very pretty," Harry said. "And she gives those she talks to her complete attention. Some people like that kind of devotion."

"I see," Caroline said. And she did. Iona's full attention had been directed at her, early on, and she, too, had been besotted. "Iona can be very charming."

"Yes," Harry said. "She is a pretty, charming young woman who takes an interest in you to the exclusion of everyone else."

"Even ignoring those she previously took an exclusive interest in. What is she looking for, do you think?" She couldn't imagine always needing to fawn over someone new.

"That is a very good question," Harry said. "What is Iona Smith looking for?"

WHEN THEY WERE truly on their way, Caroline went in search of Mrs. Anson, who was sitting alone on the bench while Mrs. Smith took in the sights behind them from the back of the boat.

"I asked Ella and Harry about going to the concert tomorrow night," she said to her host. "I suggested we keep it simple and meet at the concert hall. I hope you don't mind that I didn't discuss it with you first." She paused. "But I know we have that other set of tickets and I do so want to go."

"I forgot about the tickets," Mrs. Anson said. "I think it's a splendid idea. I will ask everyone who went to the last concert. And since his meeting will be over, I dare say Mr. Anson will want to attend too. And don't fret about not discussing it with me first. If you hadn't brought it up, we might have missed a chance to get a party together. Oh, Mrs. Smith, Caroline has had the most brilliant idea." Mrs. Anson joined Mrs. Smith while Caroline returned to Ella and Harry.

"Mrs. Anson will do the rest as far as the concert is concerned," Caroline said, and Harry laughed.

"You do rather well with her, don't you?" he asked.

"I like her," Caroline said. "She is very inquisitive and likes to try new things." She sent him a sidelong glance. "My sister Becca thinks she talks too much, but you've met Mr. Anson. If Mrs. Anson didn't say anything there would hardly be a word spoken between them for days."

"Being inquisitive and liking to try new things are admirable qualities," Harry replied.

"You sound just like Father," Ella said.

"What an insult," Harry said, but he grinned. "I suppose that is something he would say. It doesn't mean it's wrong."

"That is one of the most infuriating things about our father," Ella said to Caroline. "He's usually right, even when you hate that he is."

For the next hour they talked about what they saw on the shore, or the boats they passed, or the people fishing along the banks of the river.

Up ahead an island came into view. A dock on it jutted out into the river and the boat turned towards it.

"We are landing for our picnic," Mrs. Anson called out. "Jack, come and help carry our picnic ashore."

CAROLINE AND ELLA wandered around the small park area while the young men, following Mrs. Anson's directions, set up the tables and chairs for the picnic.

"Have you and your brother found teammates for the Endeavour yet?" Ella asked. "I don't mean to pry so you don't have to answer if you don't want to."

"It's not a secret that we need to form a team," Caroline said. "Jack wants us to pair up with Iona and Sean." She sighed. "Mostly because of Iona. He thinks if we are teammates, she will pay attention to him again, instead of Cedric."

"That would solve your team problem," Ella replied.

"And create new ones. I don't trust either of them and I told Jack that." She shrugged. "I would rather not compete than compete with people I don't trust. Jack is furious with me."

"He doesn't show it," Ella said.

"That's because he's obsessed with Iona Smith. Once he discovers what she's really like—assuming he ever does—he will be angry at her instead of me. But I fear that by then it will too late for us to assemble a team." She linked arms with Ella. "So, since I will likely not compete in the Endeavour, I plan to enjoy every event, small or large, that I can."

"That would be a shame," Ella said. "If you don't compete."

"My mother didn't get to compete," Caroline said. "Not everyone does. At least this way I won't be giving up my artifact and I can keep it for the future." She grinned. "Or maybe Jack will figure out that my artifact is useful after all and missing the Endeavour won't matter. That is the point of competing, after all."

"It is," Ella agreed. "It's good to remember that. Look. Your Mrs. Anson is waving at us. I think the picnic is ready."

NOT EVEN SEAN'S presence at her side could spoil Caroline's pleasure. She'd been on picnics before, of course, but never one on an island.

"They've never built a bridge to it?" she asked Sean, who seemed to know a lot about the small island—Stub Island, he'd called it—where they'd landed.

"There's not much point," Sean replied. "There's nothing here, not even enough land to graze a few sheep and that would not pay for a bridge."

"Now I'm worried that we're trespassing," Caroline said. "Who owns it?"

"The boating company. Jack said that's why he chose to hire this company, which luckily meant a larger boat that could accommodate us all."

"That *was* lucky." Caroline did like that Mrs. Anson had Mrs. Smith as a companion, and Sean seemed to be on his best behaviour. But she didn't think Iona had spoken to anyone other than Cedric Townsend since boarding the boat. She could have at least engaged with Mrs. Anson, who was the hostess.

"It's like it was meant to be," Sean said. "It's fate."

"I'm not sure I believe in fate," Caroline said. Harry was across the table from her and she caught his eye. "How about you, Harry? Sean thinks it was fate that we all came on this picnic today. Do you believe in fate?"

"I believe in coincidences," Harry said. "But so far fate has not been a factor in my life."

"But you don't disbelieve in fate," Sean said. "You acknowledge that it might exist."

"I am no mystic," Harry replied. "But magic exists, so yes, it's possible that fate, which I would classify as a type of magic, might exist."

"I'll accept that as an answer," Sean said. "And we can both be right."

Sean and Harry both laughed but Caroline had to wonder if Sean always had to be right. Just another reason why he would be a terrible Endeavour teammate, she supposed.

She glanced along the table: Ella was seated beside Jack, but her brother was staring across the table at Iona and Cedric, a scowl on his face. If she had been sitting closer, she would have tried to kick him under the table.

His infatuation would make people uncomfortable if they noticed. Then she saw Cedric raise his glass to her brother and Jack's scowl deepened. Someone *had* noticed, but it didn't seem like it had made *them* uncomfortable. She had to wonder what Cedric's intention was since he very clearly knew that Jack was angry. Or was that it? Did he simply want to make Jack jealous?

Thankfully, Mrs. Anson told them that it was time to clear up the picnic and board the boat for their return journey.

After that there was a flurry of activity as the picnic was disassembled.

Ella found her and they watched Mrs. Anson direct Harry, Jack, and Sean as they packed and loaded everything onto the boat. Cedric was the only man who didn't help; instead, he and Iona waited near the dock, their heads bent together.

"I still think Iona wants something from your brother," Caroline said. "But what is Cedric getting out of this relationship? Is it just attention?"

"Cedric is an unmarried man of a certain age, with a prominent father," Ella replied. "He can get attention from any number of young ladies." She rolled her eyes. "And their mothers. But he is competitive."

"I would think getting Iona's attention was not that great a challenge."

"It's not about Iona," Ella said.

"You mean Jack?" Caroline replied. "I wondered if he wanted to make my brother jealous but how on earth is Jack competition for Cedric?"

"I don't think it's just about Jack," Ella replied. "Jack has an interest in Builder-enhanced artifacts that may give him an advantage in the Endeavour, and you," she met her gaze, "have enough knowledge of Endeavour history to impress my father."

"He sees Jack and me as a threat?" Caroline was tempted to laugh, except Ella was serious. "How? Teams don't compete against each other, they compete against Blackmeadow Abbey."

"As our father's oldest son, Cedric considers emerging from the Endeavour as anything less than the clear winner, with the most artifacts, as a loss. He thinks that you and your brother have the skills and knowledge to best him."

"That's ridiculous," Caroline said. "I'm more worried about getting out alive than anything. And what does that have to do with Iona?" Then she knew. "Cedric doesn't trust Iona and Sean either. He thinks that if he makes Jack jealous, my brother will do exactly what he told me he wants to do: team up with them, creating a team Cedric wouldn't consider a threat."

"Yes," Ella agreed. "I believe that's Cedric's plan."

"Well, if I don't compete, he'll get his wish. I will not be a threat."

"That's not why I told you this," Ella said. "Cedric forgets that women make their own decisions, but if you don't compete in the Endeavour, he wins this little battle."

"I don't care," Caroline said. "He's fighting for something that doesn't matter to me. If I were to compete in the Endeavour, my main goal would be making sure my team survives. How many artifacts we can bring out would be secondary." She sighed. That was the worry she had with Sean and Iona. If she was on their team, she would do nothing except try to make sure they all survived. She was not at all convinced that the Smiths would have the same concern for her and Jack.

"I agree with your goal," Ella said.

"It looks like we're ready to leave," Caroline said. "I'll apologize to Mrs. Anson for not helping."

"Oh dear, should I apologize as well? I didn't think to offer."

"She would have been offended if you had," Caroline said with a laugh. "Just as she would have refused my help. But apologizing now lets her be magnanimous and tell me all about the challenges she overcame." She grinned. "It also lets her rehearse what she will say to Mr. Anson when she gets home."

"She's lucky to have you," Ella said, linking arms.

"I'm glad you think so," Caroline said. "Because I am lucky to have Mrs. Anson."

# 10

Jack spent the trip back the same way he'd spent the trip out: talking to the operator of the boat. Sean kept trying to get Caroline alone, and she worried that he wanted to ask her about Endeavour teams, so she stayed close to Ella and Harry. Mrs. Anson and Mrs. Smith joined them, leaving Iona and Cedric alone in the bow.

"Is everyone clear on where to meet?" Mrs. Anson said. "We don't want to be late for the concert. I dare say that anyone not there on time will miss out. Mr. Anson does not tolerate tardiness."

"Another outing," Mrs. Smith said. "What a social whirl we've all been having these past few weeks. And all because of a chance encounter between former teammates at a tea shop." She patted Mrs. Anson's arm. "I couldn't have asked for anything better."

"Neither could I," Sean added. "We've all become such good friends that I am certain we will keep in touch."

"Yes," Mrs. Anson said. "I know Mrs. Smith and I will write. And visit, I hope. If Mr. Anson becomes an Administrator, no doubt we will be spending more time in Norbarrow. Is that how it is for your father, Harry?"

"It is," Harry said. "Although Ella and I mostly stay close to home and Cedric has his own lodgings in town."

"And where is home?" Mrs. Smith asked. "I don't believe I know."

"We're rather in the country, I'm afraid," Ella said. "There is only a small hamlet close by."

"What's the nearest landmark?" Sean asked. "So we know which part of the country you are in?"

"Blackmeadow Abbey is the nearest landmark of note," Harry said. "Everything else for miles is forest and farmland, other than the small hamlet of Wellsdon."

"You live near the Abbey?" Caroline asked. "Have you seen it?"

"Often," Harry replied. "The main road goes past it, although at a safe distance. Only Administrators are allowed to get close and even they only plan to visit when they think the Abbey is ready for the Endeavour."

"It sounds fascinating," Sean said. "My curiosity would get the better of me. I'm not sure I'd be able to stay away."

"Then you'd be taking an incredible risk," Caroline said. "If the stories are true, more than one curious person has perished by getting too close to Blackmeadow Abbey at the wrong time."

"Surely those are just stories," Sean said. "And no one has really died."

"They have," Harry said. "My father has been part of quite a few rescue and recovery efforts."

"It's incredibly dangerous," Ella said. "There have been a few times when they've had to wait years to recover a body because the magic of the Abbey was just too unstable."

"How terrible," Caroline said. "That someone else's foolishness puts people like your father at risk."

"I dare say people put others at risk during the Endeavour," Mrs. Anson said. "I trust that none of you will be so reckless when it's your turn to compete."

"I would never risk someone's life," Caroline said. Ella and Harry agreed with her but she noted that Sean didn't say anything. Mrs. Smith and her son exchanged looks, which made Caroline doubt her as well. It was a very good thing that she was not going to compete on the same team as Sean Smith.

Caroline wandered away from the group. She could see the top of the Administration building now, so they were getting close to their embarkation point. They rounded a curve in the river and the bridge came into view.

"I need to talk to you," Jack said as he joined her.

"All right."

"I'm going to tell Iona and Sean that we'll team up with them."

"No. I told you, I would rather not compete than be on the same team as Sean Smith. And you can't make me."

"Father can," Jack said, anger in his voice. "I'll write him as soon as we get off this stupid boat. He needs to come to Norbarrow with our artifacts anyway, so I'll ask him to come early. He'll make you agree to this, you know he will."

"He can't make me agree," Caroline said. "And when he comes to Norbarrow, he'll meet Sean and Iona and will understand why I will *never* team up with them. Are you really going to tell him that you want to partner with people I don't trust because you're mooning over one of them? She won't stay around, you know. She'll find someone else who she thinks she can get what she wants from and forget all about you."

"You don't know that!"

Jack was furious now, and she thought it was because he knew that she was right about Iona. Iona Smith hadn't even said a word to him all day, and yet here he was, trying to figure out how to get her to pay attention to him.

Caroline sighed and shook her head. "I hope you don't end up competing with them, for your sake. You're my brother and I want you to be happy, but more importantly, I want you to be safe."

"You don't want me to be happy," Jack snapped and stomped away.

Caroline sighed again, wondering if she should write to Father, detailing her concerns about Jack and the Smiths. She shook her head. She'd give it a week and see what came of Jack's complaint. She almost wished Father *would* come to Norbarrow right now. Someone needed to talk some sense into Jack and it looked like it wouldn't be her.

"There you are," Ella said, stopping beside her. "I saw Jack leave so I know you had a fight. I won't pry other than to ask if you're all right. I know what it's like to argue with an older brother."

"You argue with Harry?" Caroline asked, grateful for the distraction. "I find that hard to believe."

"We haven't always gotten along as well as we do now," Ella

said. She smiled. "And I have two older brothers who have been known to close ranks against me."

"That doesn't sound at all fair," Caroline said. She knew that Ella's mother was dead, but she hadn't really thought what that meant: that she was the lone woman in a household of men.

"No, it doesn't," Ella agreed. "But I have learned to hold my own." She met Caroline's eyes. "As I think you are learning to do."

"I suppose that *is* what I'm doing," Caroline replied. Just a few weeks ago she would never have dreamed of opposing her brother the way she had just now. Nor would she have been prepared to stand up against Father. She had changed since coming to Norbarrow, and she had to admit, she rather liked the ways she'd changed. But Jack didn't appreciate it and she worried that the rest of her family would feel the same as he did. Especially Father.

JACK IGNORED HER for the rest of the day, which suited Caroline.

Dinner was a simple meal, and immediately afterwards, Caroline excused herself and headed for her room. She spent an hour re-reading *True Stories of Blackmeadow Abbey*, but she still could not determine which parts of it had been embellished. It did maker her wonder what the truth was regarding Administrator Townsend's Endeavour. Perhaps if she got to know Ella a little better, she would ask her. After all, it was one of the most dramatic Endeavour competitions in history. A team of four enters, only one survives and that one brings out the largest collection of artifacts ever retrieved by a single competitor.

The real story had to be more tragic—and terrifying—then how the book described it. Mr. Townsend couldn't have done something wrong, could he? There were very thorough investigations when contestants were injured or died: could the investigators have missed something? Or, as the sole survivor, had Mr. Townsend been able to lie and make up a story?

She shook her head and put her book down. She didn't think Mr. Townsend would be the type to lie and cheat and yes, murder, to acquire a few extra artifacts.

Because if all four had lived, they would have each received two-and-a-half artifacts. That was a very substantial result for any Endeavour. Why taint the rest of your life for a few more artifacts?

Caroline wasn't even sure any of Mr. Townsend's artifacts were worth much.

She got ready for bed and once she'd slid in between the covers, she vowed to talk to Mrs. Anson in the morning. She was the expert on artifacts: she'd be able to tell Caroline if Mr. Anson's Endeavour had resulted in any huge successes.

AS EXPECTED, MR. Anson had already left the house for his meeting with the Administration by the time Caroline arrived for breakfast. She had not expected Jack to be absent as well.

"Wooton didn't have any more information, my dear," Mrs. Anson said when Caroline asked where her brother was. "Just that Jack had eaten with Mr. Anson and left the house just after my husband did. I dare say it's a shocking hour for a social visit."

"It is," Caroline agreed. She sighed and picked a roll from the plate. She had a terrible suspicion that Jack had gone to ask—no, that he'd gone to *beg*—Iona Smith to throw over Cedric Townsend and focus her attention on him. And that he would promise to be on their team for the Endeavour in order to secure her agreement.

She sighed again. She couldn't control her brother's actions; she could only control her own. She would not, however, honour any promise he made on her behalf. Jack did not speak for her, and for that matter, neither did her father.

"Are you tired today?" Mrs. Anson asked. "I was hoping you would join me at the Artifact Society. I need to stay occupied or I will worry about Mr. Anson's meeting."

"I would love to," Caroline said. She smiled widely at her hostess. Her and Jack's disagreement should in no way impact Mr. and Mrs. Anson. "Let me have some tea and I will be ready to leave."

"Excellent. I just have to see Mrs. Wooton and arrange for a light supper before we go to the concert. Good news on that front too," Mrs. Anson said. "Mr. Anson will be joining us. And since he will be seeing him today, he promised to extend the invitation to Mr. Townsend. Isn't that marvellous? Our whole party together again."

"It is wonderful," Caroline replied, but Mrs. Anson had already left the room. Caroline quickly poured herself some tea, finished her rolls, and returned to her room for a shawl.

By the time she came back downstairs, Mrs. Anson was waiting for her.

They set off on the now familiar walk side by side.

"Would you think it impertinent of me to ask you about Mr. Townsend's artifacts?" Caroline asked. They were halfway to the Administration building, and she thought that if they got too much closer, someone overhearing them might know who they were talking about.

"Impertinent? Of course not," Mrs. Anson replied. "Anything to do with artifacts is a serious matter of knowledge. What would you like to know?"

"Mr. Townsend came away from his Endeavour with ten artifacts," Caroline said.

"Ten artifacts and three dead teammates," Mrs. Anson added. "He divided those ten up with their families. I believe that two teammates were siblings so their family received five and one family only asked to replace the one that was lost. Mr. Townsend was left with four."

"Oh, that's very different than what I read." This must be one of the embellishments Harry had spoken off. *True Stories of Blackmeadow Abbey* most definitely implied that Mr. Townsend had kept all ten artifacts for himself.

"I don't have to tell you how important it is to learn the truth," Mrs. Anson said. "That's why I am such a student of artifacts and I assume it drives your interest in Endeavours."

"It does," Caroline agreed. Wanting to know the truth was why she was asking Mrs. Anson these questions. "Are any of the artifacts Mr. Townsend brought out of the Abbey important? I mean, are they useful, do they have value?"

"Oh certainly," Mrs. Anson said. "Unfortunately for Mr. Townsend, the ones he gave away turned out to be the most valuable."

"Oh. He must regret giving them away then."

"I doubt that," Mrs. Anson replied. "Mr. Townsend doesn't strike me as man who would begrudge good fortune to the families of friends he saw die. I wouldn't be surprised if it even helps him deal with the guilt he must feel. Imagine being the only survivor of a group you considered your best, most trusted friends in the world. It makes me thankful that I didn't compete and have to go through something like that." She turned to Caroline. "I hope this isn't putting you off your own Endeavour."

"It's making me think," she replied. "About what I want out of my experience: about what's most important to me."

"Good," Mrs. Anson said. "That's as it should be. Oh look, there's Miss Foster. Miss Foster!"

Mrs. Anson and Miss Foster chatted the rest of the way to the meeting, leaving Caroline to think about how Mr. Townsend must have felt when he was the only one of his team to leave the Abbey alive.

And how she would feel if anything happened to Jack because of Sean and Iona.

She still wasn't going to team up with them: she was under no illusions that she would be able to save anybody, including herself, if things went badly.

But she would try to talk Jack out of it: she had a very bad feeling about the whole affair.

JUST BEFORE DINNER Caroline found Jack sitting on a bench in the garden.

"Did you see the Smiths today?" she asked as she sat down beside him.

"I did. Iona is looking forward to seeing me tonight," Jack said. "She promised to sit beside me. You're welcome to sit on her other side."

"Oh, that's very nice of her," Caroline said. Iona had ignored her for days, so what did she want? "You told her that I will not be part of their team?"

"No," Jack replied. "I said nothing of the kind because Father will make you be on our team. I told Sean and Iona that the four of us would compete together."

"I won't do it," Caroline said. She was angry, but mostly she was sad. Sad that her brother couldn't see how he was being manipulated and sad that he didn't think she had the ability to make her own choices. "Have you sent a note to Father?"

"Yes, and when he arrives, you'll see that he agrees with me."

"I don't know why you want to force me to be on your team," Caroline said. "It doesn't sound promising to be fighting even before we've handed in our artifacts."

"Mrs. Smith thinks that two brother and sister pairs means we'll have good fortune," Jack said. "I think she's right. Besides, if you back out now, you'll be disappointing them all."

"I won't be doing anything, including backing out," Caroline said. "Since I never agreed to be on this team in the first place."

"You have to. I promised."

Caroline stood up. "*You* don't speak for me, Jack. So no, I *don't* have to." Angry, she left him and went inside.

Dinner was called and Jack said not a word to Caroline through the entire meal. Mrs. Anson filled the silence, of course, so Caroline didn't think their hosts sensed the tension between brother and sister.

After dinner it was time to leave for the concert. Mr. Anson and Jack led the way, and Caroline was more than happy to walk with Mrs. Anson, who had learned from Miss Foster that tonight's performers were great favourites.

The Townsends were already waiting outside the concert hall when they arrived.

"I have some news," Mr. Townsend said when they'd greeted each other. "The formal announcement will come tomorrow, but since I was seeing you tonight and I must leave tomorrow on Endeavour business, I have been given leave, Mr. Anson, to let you know that you have been accepted as an Administrator. Congratulations." Mr. Townsend clapped Mr. Anson on the back.

"How wonderful," Mrs. Anson said to her beaming husband. "My dear, how absolutely wonderful."

"Well done, Mr. Anson," Caroline said.

Ella linked arms with her and grinned. "Father has been so impressed with all of you," she said. She leaned in closer. "There's more."

"Thank you, Administrator Townsend," Mr. Anson said. "I appreciate your confidence, as well as your help navigating the application process. I will always be in your debt."

"I was more than happy to aid such an outstanding applicant," Mr. Townsend said. "I have no doubt that you will be an asset to the Administration for years to come. There will be a swearing in ceremony as well as a reception, but that will happen just after the Endeavour participant's artifacts have been placed in Blackmeadow Abbey. We should all be back in time for that."

"All?" Caroline leaned over to Ella and asked, "Are you leaving with your father?"

"Harry and I are," Ella replied. "Cedric will stay here, of course, until it's time to hand in our artifacts and register as a team."

"I shall miss you," Caroline said. She sighed. She was not looking forward to being at the mercy of her brother and Sean and Iona Smith.

"You might not have to," Ella said.

"Mr. and Mrs. Anson," Mr. Townsend said. "I will ask one more favour. For years Ella has been lonely for female companionship at our home in the country, and she has been quite impressed with Miss Caroline Morris." He smiled at Caroline. "As have I. I was wondering if you could spare her as a companion and allow her to visit with Ella for a few weeks at our home. Unless, of course, the young woman would prefer to stay here in Norbarrow and enjoy the festivities."

"I would love to visit," Caroline said. "If Mrs. Anson can spare me." Even Father wouldn't stop her from visiting the home of an Administrator, especially when he'd been instrumental in Mr. Anson's successful petition.

"Of course, you must go," Mrs. Anson replied. "This is the time in your life to try every new experience that comes your way. But did you say you were leaving in the morning?"

"I leave in the morning," Mr. Townsend replied. "Ella and Harry can leave whenever Caroline is ready."

"Are you really happy to visit?" Ella asked. "I know that in some ways it's not convenient. I mean, you don't have a team for the Endeavour yet, do you?"

"And I'm not likely to," Caroline said. She smiled sadly. "I will tell you all about it another time, but this is exactly what I want to do."

The Smiths arrived and Mrs. Anson filled them in on the news while Mr. Anson and Mr. Townsend huddled together.

Iona did attach herself to Jack, but at hearing of Caroline's imminent departure, she frowned and strode towards her.

"You're leaving us?" Iona asked. "But we have so much to discuss and prepare for." She turned to Ella. "Jack and Caroline are teaming up with Sean and me for the Endeavour."

"I am sorry," Caroline said. "But my brother has misspoken. I have not committed to any team, including one with you and Sean. My brother is free to make his choice, and it sounds like he has, but he does not speak for me in this."

"But he promised!" Iona said, frowning. "You can't go back on a promise."

"His promise, not mine. I have reminded him that I make my own decisions. I am truly sorry for any confusion my brother has caused."

"He promised," Iona repeated. Her frown deepened. "Jack even said that your father would approve. Are you going against your father's wishes?"

"My father has not even been informed," Caroline said. "So, I'm not sure how Jack knows what his wishes would be. I assure you that Jack no more speaks for our father than he speaks for me."

"You should be complaining to Jack," Ella said. "Not to Caroline. Perhaps your and Sean's relationship is different, but both of my brothers know better than to commit me to anything without getting my agreement first."

"I will complain to Jack," Iona said. "And I'll tell Mother, who will no doubt tell Mrs. Anson, who I'm sure will see this as an affront to her generosity towards you." Iona turned and marched back to Jack.

"I assume that this is part of what you referred to earlier," Ella said. "When you said you were not likely to have a team for the Endeavour."

"Yes. I will not be bullied into competing with people I don't trust," Caroline said. "And this behaviour will not make me change my mind. Jack will be angry at me, but Mrs. Anson will surprise them."

"Will she?" Ella asked. "Even if it goes against the wishes of her old friend Mrs. Smith?"

Caroline watched as Iona and Jack had a tense conversation. Jack glared at her and she smiled. Her smile widened when Iona stepped away from Jack and sidled up to Cedric.

"I think Mrs. Anson will surprise her old friend most of all."

CAROLINE SAT BETWEEN Harry and Ella, and it felt as though she was using them to shield her from Jack and Sean, who kept whispering and frowning at her.

Iona, of course, was concentrating all of her attention on Cedric, who seemed very aware of the situation since he kept sending smug looks in Jack's direction.

If the musicians were better than the previous ones, Caroline couldn't say. Sadly, the quarrel with her brother made it impossible for her to really enjoy the concert.

Afterwards, Ella and Harry walked outside with her.

"I am sorry if I ruined tonight's concert for you in any way," she said when the three of them stopped a few paces from the rest of their group.

"You didn't," Harry said. "And none of it was your fault. It sounds like Jack overstepped his brotherly authority."

"You really wouldn't commit Ella to something?" Caroline asked.

"He wouldn't dare," Ella said.

"I wouldn't," Harry replied. "And especially not for something this important. Does he usually do things like this?"

"No," Caroline said. "But Iona has some kind of hold on him and he won't listen to reason." She sighed. Normally Jack was the best of brothers: somehow Iona Smith had changed that. "I still don't know what she wants."

"Whatever it is," Ella said. "Now she thinks she has a better chance of getting it from Cedric."

"Yes," Harry agreed. "So, what do both Jack and Cedric have that Iona wants?"

"I have no idea," Caroline said. "Oh, look. I think Mrs. Smith is going to complain to Mrs. Anson about me. Jack won't like this at all."

Sure enough, a frowning Mrs. Smith left Sean and Jack and made her way to Mrs. Anson. Sean smirked at Caroline but Jack was still frowning.

Mrs. Smith pulled Mrs. Anson to one side and leaned towards her. Mrs. Anson patted Mrs. Smith's arm and smiled, but her old friend's frown only deepened. Mrs. Smith sent an angry look towards Caroline, who resisted the urge to smile.

"You were correct. Mrs. Anson is not giving Mrs. Smith the answer she wants," Ella said. "Or expected. She is not happy."

"Mrs. Anson and I have had conversations about the Endeavour," Caroline said. "Where I am quite certain Jack has not. I have a much better idea of what Mrs. Anson considers important, or right, or fair, than he does."

A visibly furious Mrs. Smith stepped away from Mrs. Anson and gestured to her children. Sean hurried to her side but Iona was too focused on Cedric to notice.

"Iona," Mrs. Smith called out sharply. "We are leaving."

Pouting, Iona stepped away from Cedric and joined her brother and mother. Without even saying goodbye, the three of them set off down the street.

"Caroline," Mrs. Anson called. "A word please. Jack, you as well."

"This won't go well for Jack," Caroline said to her companions. "Shall I try to be packed for tomorrow or the day after?" She leaned in close. "I won't regret not spending another night under the same roof as my brother."

"Tomorrow afternoon, then," Harry said. "Say around two? We will be travelling by carrier and it is only a five-hour trip."

"Excellent, I'll see you then." She nodded and went to where Mrs. Anson and a glowering Jack were waiting.

"My dears," Mrs. Anson said, but she was looking directly at Jack. "Please do not involve me in matters that are not my concern. Your choice of teammates for the Endeavour is a deeply personal one: one that cannot be forced, and one that must be based on trust."

"But Father—" Jack started to say, but Mrs. Anson held up her hand.

"Your father will agree with me," Mrs. Anson said. "Eventually. Now Jack, has Caroline been clear about not committing to the Smiths?"

"Yes, Mrs. Anson, but her reason doesn't make sense."

"She doesn't need to even give you a reason, she just needs to tell you what her decision is. And she did, yet you tried to browbeat her into changing her mind, even to the extent that Mrs. Smith was recruited to help. I am very disappointed in you."

She turned to Caroline. "I am curious why, although it won't affect my thoughts on this matter."

"I don't trust either Sean or Iona," Caroline said.

"That's the very best reason to not be on a team with them," Mrs. Anson said. "Now, it looks like the Townsends are taking their leave. Let us be gracious and say goodnight, shall we?"

Jack had enough awareness to seem embarrassed by Mrs. Anson's last remark, which Caroline knew was a dig at the departed Smith family.

After they said goodbye to the Townsends, Mrs. Anson made a point of walking home with her husband, saying that now that he would be an Administrator they had much to discuss.

"You can walk with me," Caroline said to her brother. "I'm not angry at you."

"You knew what she would say," Jack said as he joined her.

"I did," she agreed. "Mrs. Anson and I discuss quite a few things. I am sorry that you and Sean felt that you had to involve Mrs. Smith."

"She was furious," Jack replied. "She kept saying that Mrs. Anson would be very angry and that they'd planned for us to team up from the moment they'd become reacquainted."

"Which obviously was not true even though Mrs. Anson said that they discussed it," Caroline said. "You might want to ask yourself why the Smiths seem determined to partner with us. And why, when it was apparent that wouldn't happen, Iona immediately left you for Cedric."

"They need a team," Jack said. "Like us."

"But the Townsends are a team of three," Caroline said. "There is no room for her brother even if they do accept Iona onto their team. She wants something that she thinks—no, that their whole family thinks—both you and Cedric have. But what?"

"You don't think it's about me?" Jack asked. "Or Cedric?"

"I wonder that you do. Or why you even bother with Iona if she clearly prefers Cedric."

"Because Sean tells me that she prefers me," Jack replied, but Caroline thought she heard a tinge of doubt in his voice. "But you think the whole family is part of this, so I can't trust what Sean tells me."

"Mrs. Smith has very possibly ruined her friendship with Mrs.

Anson, who will be the wife of an Administrator," Caroline said. "She is risking losing a highly desirable social connection and I can't see her doing that over me. Sean may very well be telling you the truth: that Iona does prefer you. Which means she—and the rest of her family—think they now have a better chance of getting what they want from Cedric. But what?"

Jack sighed. "I don't want you to be right, but I can see what you mean."

"I don't want to be right either," Caroline said.

The rest of the walk home was silent, and she really hoped her brother was thinking about what the Smiths' actions said about them. She liked to think she didn't hate anyone but she was starting to hate the Smiths—every one of them—because they were manipulating Jack; using his emotions to try to get what they wanted.

And there, she came back to that. They wanted something. Until she knew what, she feared that nothing about this entire situation would make sense.

## II

**M**rs. Anson was alone at breakfast when Caroline entered the dining room.

"Mr. Anson has taken Jack with him today," Mrs. Anson said as Caroline selected two rolls from the serving plate. "He has a few people to thank, now that he has the Administrator role. And I told him that Jack has been left to his own devices far too much." She poured tea for both of them. "I blame myself for introducing the Smiths to the two of you. I did not expect it to cause a wedge between you."

"Jack and I talked," Caroline said. "He doesn't want me to be right about the Smiths but he understands my reasons for distrust."

"Good. I will talk to him later myself," Mrs. Anson said. "And make sure he understands that I have noticed Iona's behaviour and find it puzzling in the very least. Until last night I had thought her very much attached to Cedric Townsend, but early in the evening she paid a great deal of attention to Jack."

"Until she learned that I was not going to compete with them," Caroline said. "That's when she turned her charms and attention and focus on Cedric. While Sean had Jack's ear."

"And then his mother's," Mrs. Anson said. "Not to worry, my dear. I will find out what they are scheming about."

"You think they are up to something?" It was good to know that Mrs. Anson felt the same way she did.

"I do," Mrs. Anson said. "Why else would all three Smiths be so angry that you chose not to compete with them? I could see Sean and to a lesser extent Iona, being upset. But for Mrs. Smith to accost me and tell me that I had to *force you*—her words—to join their team, well, I was shocked. All that did was make me believe that your reasons were entirely valid. I never! Forcing someone to team up for such a dangerous competition is a terrible idea."

"I think so too," Caroline said. "I hope you find out what they are after. And please, do your best to have Jack reconsider his promise to join their team. I fear for his safety if he goes into Blackmeadow Abbey with them."

"I will do my best," Mrs. Anson said. "Now, shall I ask Mrs. Wooton to help you pack? I worry that all this turmoil has taken some of the joy away from your trip, and we must do our best to change that. You must be excited. Another carrier ride—how fortunate you are."

"I am indeed," Caroline said, easily giving in to Mrs. Anson's change of topic. She was relieved on Jack's account too. Caroline had full confidence that Mrs. Anson would discover what the Smiths were up to and what it was they wanted, because she was certain that there was more to it than simply creating a team for the Endeavour.

Hopefully that meant Jack would not compete with Sean and Iona. He would hate it if he didn't compete at all, but she would hate it even more if something happened to him during the competition.

She just didn't trust any of the Smiths.

THE CARRIER PULLED up in front of the house just after two.

Ella and Harry both jumped out but Caroline was already on the front steps by the time they reached her.

"Wooton will be out with your cases," Mrs. Anson said as she stepped out of the house. "It looks like a very fine day for travelling. Not that the weather would make a big difference when you are in a carrier."

"I will be able to stick my head out and watch the scenery," Caroline said. "I hope you won't mind if I am silly about the journey. I've only ever travelled here to Norbarrow and I love seeing new places."

"You'll get a glimpse of Blackmeadow Abbey," Harry said. "We'll be passing by just after the sun sets."

"Will it be too dark to see it?" Caroline asked, trying to hide her disappointment.

"After dark is the best time to see it," Ella said. "Now that the magic has waned it's less bright, but the Abbey glows."

"Really? I have never heard that before." Caroline thought she knew what to expect regarding Blackmeadow Abbey, that was partly why she did so much research, and yet, here was something new.

"Competitors always enter in the day," Harry said. "But the glow of the magic at night is one of the things Administrators, like Father, monitor to determine when it's time for the Endeavour."

"That's why it's not a well-known fact," Ella said. "If people knew what signs to look for, they might decide for themselves when it was safe to enter to search for lost artifacts."

"Which is dangerous for them and for our father," Harry said. "Since we're so close, he's the first one who is contacted to help with rescues."

"I hope no one will be so foolish or desperate to enter unauthorized this year," Mrs. Anson said. "Oh, here's Wooton." She stepped aside so Wooton, who carried both of Caroline's cases, had room to pass her on the steps.

Caroline turned to her host. "I can't thank you enough, Mrs. Anson, and Mr. Anson too, for letting Jack and me stay with you. It's been fantastic for me and I hope not too much trouble for you."

"You know I always enjoy spending time with you, Caroline," Mrs. Anson said. "And now that we are both members of the Artifact Society, we might want to start our own chapter. Wouldn't that bring a little of Norbarrow sophistication to Gaynesford?"

"I would love that," Caroline said. "I will write and keep you up-to-date on my news."

"I will do the same," Mrs. Anson said. "I think I shall even get at least one letter to you out of Jack. And do not worry on that score. I am very determined."

"Thank you." Caroline knew that Mrs. Anson was referring to Jack not teaming up with Sean and Iona, rather than his letter writing.

"It's been lovely meeting both you and your husband," Harry said. "And we will see you at the reception for the new Administrators."

"I look forward to seeing some friendly faces," Mrs. Anson said. "As I am quite certain that I will know no one else."

"Then goodbye until then," Ella said. "We seem to be ready."

Caroline hugged Mrs. Anson. "Thank you so much for everything." Then she followed Ella and Harry to the carrier.

Once inside, Ella pulled the lever and they set off.

"I can't tell you how excited I am," Caroline said. "And I wasn't joking about sticking my head out of the window. I didn't dare do that on my way here. Mr. Anson would not have approved."

"I have a feeling your Mrs. Anson might have joined you," Harry said.

Caroline grinned. "I think she might have."

THE CITY GAVE way to rolling farmland and after half an hour of watching that, Caroline pulled away from the window and leaned back on the upholstered bench.

"Tired of the scenery already?" Harry asked.

"It looks very much like what I see from my bedroom window at home," Caroline replied. "Farmland and farm animals, although at home I see more sheep than cows."

"It's much the same until we get to the Abbey," Ella said. "I often fall asleep during the trip."

"It's certainly a smooth enough ride for that," Caroline said. "But I think my younger brother Miles would be horrified if I told him I slept through a carrier ride. He's ten and is almost as fascinated by Builder enhancements as Jack is."

"I did notice that Jack spent a lot of time talking to the boat operator during our river cruise," Harry said. "I thought he was just angry . . ." he trailed off.

"Angry that Iona was attached to your brother instead of him?" Caroline said. "He was, but if Iona had been fawning over him, Jack would have had a dilemma. I doubt even he could tell you which would win out between Iona or learning about a

Builder-enhanced boat."

"So, he's interested in artifacts?" Ella asked. "Like Mrs. Anson?"

Caroline laughed. "I'm not sure *anyone* is interested in artifacts like Mrs. Anson. Not even the Artifact Society has a member as knowledgeable. Well, they do now that she is a member. No, Jack likes the Builder enhancements of artifacts. How they multiply an artifact's magical ability so that one single artifact can power numerous objects like carriers and boats."

"Do you think he wants to become a Builder?" Harry asked.

"He hasn't said that to me," Caroline replied. "And I've been meaning to talk to him about it, but yes, I think he would, if he could. We don't know any Builders, so I suppose his best chance would be to find a powerful artifact and leverage that somehow."

"He knows an Administrator now," Harry said. "He might be able to meet a Builder willing to take him on as an apprentice."

"How often do they take on an apprentice who isn't born into a Builder family?" Caroline asked. "Would they expect Mr. Anson to do them a favour in return? I'm not sure Jack and Mr. Anson are that close." Mr. Townsend would use his influence to help his own children but she didn't think Jack could count on Mr. Anson doing the same for a family friend.

"I see what you mean," Harry replied. "So, it's back to finding an artifact."

"And a lost artifact at that," Caroline said. "Which means he has to compete in the Endeavour. But I won't be on a team with Sean and Iona and I fear for my brother's safety if he does." She sighed. She hadn't expected life to be so complicated.

"Would either of you add your names to the list of spares?" Ella asked.

"I doubt I would," Caroline replied. "I realize that I need to trust my teammates and I'm not sure there would be enough time to sort that out." The list would go up in a few weeks, leaving two weeks to meet and assess potential teammates before teams had to be decided and names submitted.

"But Jack might," Harry said. "If he sees the Endeavour as the best chance to secure his future."

"Yes." Caroline sighed. "Would competing with strangers be better than competing with Iona and Sean? I'm not sure."

"I am," Ella said. "You *know* that Iona and Sean can't be trusted. There are lots of reasons why someone doesn't have a team and none of them are because they can't be trusted. Take you and Jack. You simply don't know enough people."

"If I could find teammates like me and Jack I would gladly compete," Caroline agreed. "Jack may have fallen for Iona's charms, but away from her, I would trust him with my life."

"Which is what you need for an Endeavour teammate," Harry said.

AS SHE'D WARNED, Ella fell asleep beside her. Across from them, Harry pulled out writing supplies and set to work on a note or letter. Caroline opened her book, even though she wasn't sure how true anything in it was.

How jaded she'd become in just a few short weeks. When she'd first put her hands on *True Stories of Blackmeadow Abbey*, she'd been excited to own what she'd thought was the ultimate account of Endeavour competitions. Now all she could think about when she read it was, which parts were false or made up? And did the author, Mr. Samuel Jones, believe what he'd written or had he knowingly lied and fabricated and embellished?

She liked to think he'd written his book with good intentions but now she knew not everyone acted that way. The Smiths had a hidden agenda so it stood to reason that Samuel Jones might, too.

She sighed and Harry glanced up at her.

"Something wrong?" he asked.

"Just this book," she replied. "I wish I knew what parts weren't actually true, but without knowing the real story, I can't know what the author has made up." She closed the book. "But learning the truth is why I bought the book in the first place."

"I see." Harry frowned and looked over at his sister. "Father never talks about his Endeavour, but I can tell you one thing about it that Mr. Jones got terribly wrong. Magic killed his teammates. Father said that they were on their way out when a blast of magic rolled over them. It knocked him out and when he recovered his senses, the others were dead. Father spent hours bringing them all out of the Abbey, including the artifacts they'd died recovering."

"How terrible," Caroline said. "Mrs. Anson told me that he made sure their families all received their share of artifacts."

"Father says that's the only reason he bothered bringing them," Harry said. "He didn't want their deaths compounded by the loss of artifacts."

"That must have been difficult."

"I don't think he will ever get over it," Harry said. "Or stop blaming himself for surviving, even though he didn't do anything wrong."

"And no rhyme nor reason for why he was spared," Caroline said.

"Father thinks there *is* a reason," Harry said. "Our family histories indicate that there are Naturals amongst our ancestors, but of course it was so many generations ago that the magic has been diluted over the years. Father believes that the magical blast spared him because he carries a minute amount of Natural blood. And that we three, me, Cedric, and Ella will also be safeguarded against similar magics." He paused. "You can't tell Father that I told you, and please don't tell anyone else, not even Mrs. Anson."

"I won't," Caroline said. "I promise." It felt like too big a secret to pass on anyway.

"We're getting close to the Abbey," Harry said. "It's time to wake up Ella."

CAROLINE WAS PRACTICALLY standing in the compartment trying to get the best view.

"There's a fence," she said, turning her head so Harry and Ella could hear her. "I didn't realize there was a fence."

"And some spells placed there by Naturals," Ella said. "Although Father thinks they are so old that they are fading. He says the Administration hasn't been able to convince any Naturals to recast them. He claims that's why so many people are able to get inside the fenced area, which is dangerous even when the magic of the Abbey is waning, like it is now."

"Has he met any Naturals?"

"I think a couple," Ella said. "They really don't like the rest of us though, and I believe they only met him because of the way he survived the Endeavour."

"Oh look!" Caroline stared across the fence and wooded area.

The sky was shimmering in soft pinks and blues and greens. "It's beautiful."

"It is," Ella agreed. She was beside Caroline now, the soft glow casting shadows on her face. "I don't travel much so I haven't seen it nearly as many times as Harry has. It always amazes me. That slight hill means you can't see the Abbey from the road so I've never seen the actual building."

"And that's magic?" Caroline asked. "The lights, they're caused by magic?"

"Yes. The whole place is imbued with it from that long ago battle," Ella said. "I always think about the enormous amount of magic that must have been unleashed here for it to remain this strong even after so many decades."

"The two most powerful Naturals who ever lived," Caroline said. "It's too bad they couldn't get along. Think what wonderfully useful things they could have done with all that magic?"

"I wouldn't hold my breath waiting for Naturals to do good deeds," Ella said. "After he met with one, Father said it was a good thing they kept to themselves. He has a high opinion of Builders, but Naturals are far too self-obsessed."

"Which I suppose would make them dangerous," Caroline said. It was unlikely she would ever meet a Natural, but there was always the possibility that a fight amongst them would cause another Blackmeadow Abbey: another ruin full of dangerous magic.

It was still an incredibly beautiful sight.

A few minutes later they rounded a small hill, although she could still see the glow in the sky.

Half an hour after that, the carrier turned off the road onto a bumpier laneway.

"We're here," Harry said. "Welcome to Farview. It's a bit of a ruin, but it's home."

IT WAS TOO dark for Caroline to see if it was indeed a ruin. Lights lit the front door and the wide stairs that led up to it. A man waited at the bottom of the stairs and she saw Mr. Townsend exit the house and stand on the top step.

"That's Jessop," Ella said. "Our butler. If you need anything, he's the one to ask. Father makes the rules but Jessop enforces them."

"Do you have many servants?" They had a cook at home, and a woman from the village came in once a week to clean the house and do laundry, but other than with the Ansons in Norbarrow, she hadn't dealt with a lot of house servants.

"More than half a dozen," Harry said. "But some of them take care of the grounds and horses. Father wages a constant battle against nature. He claims that it creeps up on us in the night."

"Could it be affected by the Abbey?" Caroline asked. "It's not that far away." She suppressed a shudder. She wasn't sure she would want to grow up so close to so much dangerous, wild, uncontrolled magic. "It might be carried here on the wind."

"Father says no," Harry said. "Come on, he doesn't like to be kept waiting."

Caroline followed Ella out of the carrier. The butler—Jessop—was already pulling suitcases off the back of the carrier. When everyone was out of the compartment and the suitcases were all unloaded, the carrier drove off along the driveway. Surprised by the light on the back of the vehicle, Caroline watched it until it was out of sight.

"Miss Morris, welcome to Farview," Mr. Townsend said, echoing his son's earlier welcome. "I hope you enjoy your stay. Jessop will sort out the luggage and show you to your room but for now, I have arranged a light meal and some tea. This way."

He led the way into the house and Caroline stepped past Harry and Ella and followed her host into the house.

"I really appreciate your hospitality," Caroline said. "And please, if I do anything to disrupt your household, let me know. I am not a very experienced house guest. My stay in Norbarrow with Mr. and Mrs. Anson was my very first time."

"I'm sure if you conduct yourself here as you did with the Ansons we will all get along just fine," Mr. Townsend said. "This is the dining room." He stepped aside to let her enter. "We take lunch and dinner here. There is a sunroom that I prefer to use for breakfast. I'm sure Ella will show you how to get to it."

The dining room was huge; a table that could probably seat more than twenty stretched down the centre of the room. The far end was set with three place settings and a buffet held a few covered dishes.

"I ate earlier," Mr. Townsend said.

Ella and Harry slipped past their father to join her in the dining room.

"I'll leave you to it," Mr. Townsend said. "As I'm sure you understand, I am very busy right now, so you three will be on your own for much of your visit, I'm afraid. Good night." He closed the door, leaving Caroline, Harry, and Ella staring at it.

"One of Father's famous exits," Harry said. "If he's around enough while you're here, you'll get used to them. Come on, I think I smell onion pie." He headed to the buffet and lifted the lid of one of the serving dishes. "I'm right." He sliced the pie and set a piece of it on a plate.

"Harry is usually right about food," Ella said. She linked arms with Caroline and pulled her towards the buffet. "But often wrong about other things."

"I'm right about the important things," Harry said. He sat down at the table and waited while Ella served food onto a plate for Caroline.

"No, you sit at the end," Ella said. "When Father is here that's where he sits, of course. But you're our honoured guest."

"All right." Caroline gingerly sat down at the end of the table. Even with just the three of them it felt odd. Her father always sat at one end and Mother at the other. If Father was absent his seat went empty. She looked down along the length of the table to the door. It was a little unsettling, being able to see everything in the room at once.

"What are your plans for tomorrow, Ella?" Harry asked.

"I thought I'd start with a tour of the house," she replied. "Unless Caroline needs to rest after our journey."

"Goodness," Caroline said. "The carrier ride was not tiring at all. I am very much looking forward to seeing the whole house and grounds." She ate a small bite of pie. "I have never been to such a fine estate so I am very curious about everything."

"Yes," Harry said, smiling. "You are indeed very curious about everything, which makes you a very enjoyable companion. No doubt your insights will allow us to see our home in a different light."

"I expect that too," Ella said. "We shall start right after

breakfast. Will you join us then, Harry?"

"In the morning, probably," Harry said. "No doubt Father has a list of chores he needs me to attend to." He turned to Caroline. "Cedric has been very clear that Farview does not interest him, so Father is making sure that someone in the family knows how to manage it."

"Are you happy about that?" Caroline asked.

"I am," Harry replied. "I'm not nearly as ambitious as Father, or Cedric, who very might well want to become an Administrator once he has a successful Endeavour behind him. A quiet life in the country would suit me very well."

"I believe Jack feels the same way about our holdings as Cedric does about this estate," Caroline said. "But I'm not sure he has spoken to our father about it."

"Because he wants to be a Builder, not a farmer, right?" Ella asked.

"Yes. I suppose after the Endeavour he'll know what his options are," Caroline said. "I rather envy that these first-born sons get to choose what they want to do with their lives."

"I do too," Ella replied.

"Ella, you get a choice," Harry said.

"I can choose to marry and leave Farview, or I can choose not to marry and hope whichever brother inherits allows me to live here with his bride and children. In both cases I am beholden to a man. That's not much of a choice."

"What would you want to do otherwise?" Harry asked.

"I would want to teach," Caroline said. "Or maybe write books. At the very least I would love to continue my education, perhaps even attend Linley Academy. There is so much I don't know and I want to learn about it all."

"I recognize the look in your eyes, brother," Ella said. "Do not mock someone for wanting to know more when you have no idea what it's like to not have the opportunity to even dream of it."

"I'm sorry," Harry said. "You're right. I was going to say something that I thought would be smart, but that would most likely have been hurtful. I do have more options than either of you, even though they are dependent on Cedric's choices."

"I suppose all of us are dependent on the Endeavour," Caroline said. "On whether we even compete or not, and if so, whether we will consider it a success when it is over."

"And what is success to you?" Harry asked.

"Coming through it in one piece," Caroline said. "And having fond memories of the whole experience. Which so far, I will have even if I don't compete."

"What, no expectations of finding multiple artifacts?" Harry asked. "Of having the chance to make your fortune?"

"I have read far too extensively about Endeavours to assume that would happen," Caroline said. "I'm sure my brother has dreams of finding a way to secure his future, but I am much more practical. The most I can hope for, besides me and anyone I team up with coming through it safely, would be to exit with a single artifact to replace the one handed in to compete."

"There is still a chance to find a lost artifact," Harry said. "Would that not be worth the risk?"

"Whose risk?" Caroline asked. "I am sure that there are those who would risk their lives and those of their teammates for such a prize, but I would not risk others."

"The Smiths," Ella said with a nod. "You think that Sean and Iona would risk others for their gain."

"Yes," Caroline agreed. "I hope that I have talked Jack out of competing with them, because I believe they would show little regard for his life—and mine if I had agreed—in order to secure artifacts for themselves."

"That's a very serious accusation," Harry said.

"One I don't make lightly," Caroline said. "I have no proof, so please do not repeat it to anyone. Mrs. Anson agrees that there is something going on with the Smiths, and will let me know what she finds out."

"I have confidence in Mrs. Anson," Ella said. "I am quite sure that if there is something to be found, she will uncover it."

"I think so too." Caroline was happy to have the conversation veer towards a lighter subject so she launched into a detailed description of Mrs. Anson's activities at the Artifact Society.

When she was done, Jessop arrived with news that the bags had all been delivered to their rooms. Caroline followed him upstairs to a fine bedroom at least twice the size of the one she shared with Becca.

She yawned as she prepared for bed but once she slid under

the covers, she couldn't stop thinking about the magic of Blackmeadow Abbey. She rose and went to peer out the window but whether she was looking in the wrong direction or the light from the magic didn't reach this far, all she saw was darkness.

Back in bed, it took her a long time to fall asleep.

# 12

The next morning, once she made her way downstairs, Caroline followed the sounds of conversation to the breakfast room.

It was bright and sunny with windows on three sides. Ella jumped up when she saw her.

"I asked Jessop to see if you were awake," she said. "But he swore that there was not a sound from your room. I am sorry you had to find your own way here. Let me get you some tea."

"I've been awake for some time," Caroline said. "But I was reading. No doubt I was far too quiet for Jessop to hear me. And I would love some tea." She sat down in the only unoccupied chair with a place setting. Ella handed her a cup of tea and Harry passed her a plate of rolls.

"This is a delightful room," Caroline said.

"It was Mother's favourite," Ella replied. "She would spend hours in here. She said it was the best light for her needlework."

"I imagine it would be," Caroline replied. "Did she do a lot of needlework? I hate it, although my sister Becca is a fine sewer."

"I think Mother found it relaxing," Ella said. "When I was small, I would watch her for what seemed like hours." She grinned. "Like you, I was never fond of it. Too fussy for me."

"Ella prefers gardening and looking after the horses," Harry said. "Anything that allows her to get muddy and ruin her clothes."

"I don't ruin them on purpose," Ella said. "Except for that horrible green muslin that made my skin look grey. That deserved to be ruined."

"We don't have much of a garden at home," Caroline said. "Just a few roses." She took two rolls from the plate and put a dab of butter beside them.

"I grow herbs," Ella said. "Along with some medicinal plants."

"Watch out for the poisonous ones," Harry said. "They're in their own fenced plot so no one confuses them with the herbs."

"Before you think I'm planning to murder anyone," Ella said, "some of the medicinal plants can be dangerous in large quantities. They're fenced off so horses and deer can't get at them."

"Show them to me so I know to stay away," Caroline said. "Are you so very far from a doctor that you need to be able to treat yourselves?"

"They're mostly used on the horses," Harry said. "There's no way I would allow my sister to experiment on me."

"I know what I'm doing," Ella said. "And if you were ever sick enough, you'd be grateful for my help."

"I probably would," Harry agreed. "If I thought I was already dying and you could only kill me faster, I would likely take a chance. Otherwise, I would wait for a real doctor."

"I'd accept your help," Caroline replied. "I trust that you are extremely competent."

"Thank you," Ella said. "I'm not sure I want to let my untrusting brother come along on our tour."

"I can't anyway," Harry said. "Father made an appointment for me this morning in Wellsdon." He stood up. "Knowing Father, I'm probably already late for it. Have fun. I might not see you until dinner."

Once Harry had left, Caroline pushed her empty plate away. "I'm ready if you are."

CAROLINE WAS A little surprised that there really was a ruin. An entire wing of the house was blackened, and a wall had collapsed.

"There was a fire here six years ago," Ella said. She paused. "It's where my mother died. She was able to get out of the music room, but she'd breathed in too much smoke. Father was away at the time so it was just me and Harry."

"That must have been horrible," Caroline said. She thought she could still smell the smoke but that would be impossible, wouldn't it?

"It was." Ella gave her a sad smile. "The doctor from Wellsdon was here within an hour but there wasn't much he could do except keep her comfortable. She died before Father could make it home. Some days I'm not sure he doesn't pretend she's still here."

"Is that why the building hasn't been repaired?" Surely the Townsends could afford to have their house restored?

"None of us wants to go in there," Ella said. "I think we should tear it down rather than build it back again, but what I think doesn't count for much around here, especially with regards to the estate."

"If you tore it down you could put in a nice commemorative garden," Caroline mused. "Maybe add some plants or flowers that were special to your mother."

"That's what I think," Ella said. "It would replace the horrible memories with lovely ones. Anything would be better than coming outside and being reminded of how she died. Come on, my garden is over here."

Caroline followed Ella through some trees into a large open meadow. Half of the ground was covered in raised garden beds. Off in the far corner was a fenced area that must be where the more dangerous plants grew.

Ella walked along a row of green plants, naming them as she went. Caroline only recognized the names of herbs; the rest were a mystery. At the end of the row, they stopped at the fence.

"You know all the names so I assume that you must know how to use them," Caroline said.

"Of course," Ella said. "I don't plant anything until I know all about it. Some of the ones here are far too dangerous to grow if you don't know how to handle them. See that one." She pointed over the fence to a plant with spiky purple flowers. "That's Pennyroyal. In small quantities the oil can be diluted and rubbed on the chest to soothe a cough. But if it's too strong it can cause blisters. And no one should ever ingest it. Most of these plants are very useful for treating minor ills."

"Is that what you would do with your life if you had a choice?" Caroline asked. "Be a doctor?"

"I would be more useful than a doctor," Ella said. "At least more useful than the one who treated my mother. Half of the plants here would have given her more relief, and a better chance to live, than what he'd offered."

"That's why you grow medicinal plants."

"Yes, although even Harry hasn't bothered to understand me enough to realize that."

"They don't have the constraints on their lives that we do," Caroline said. She sighed. "My mother's advice to me when I left with the Ansons was to enjoy every single experience that I could. She didn't have to explain what she meant—that I would probably never have another chance to visit a city like Norbarrow and attend receptions and dinner parties and concerts. That these memories would have to last me the rest of my life."

"Yes," Ella said. "Exactly."

They sighed in unison and then Caroline pasted a smile she didn't feel on her face. "So, that's the garden. I saw some stables so there must be horses."

OVER THE NEXT few days Caroline and Ella fell into a routine.

After breakfast—which never included Mr. Townsend but did include Harry—they spent the morning in Ella's garden, weeding or harvesting plants.

Caroline learned so much that she was determined to plant her own medicinal garden back at home. When the men were out, they ate lunch in the breakfast room, enjoying the bright views outside.

In the afternoons they walked the grounds, usually ending up sitting under a huge willow tree that grew alongside a small creek.

Dinner was served in the formal dining room and they never knew until they arrived who would be there. Usually just Harry made it but one night a distracted Mr. Townsend had attended. He'd asked Caroline a few questions about how she was enjoying her stay before heading to his study with a warning that he would be leaving for Norbarrow the next day.

After dinner, Ella, Caroline, and Harry played card games or read before retiring for the night to start all over again the next day.

The sixth day after she'd arrived, Caroline came down to breakfast to find a letter for her.

"It's from Mrs. Anson," she said to Ella, who was already seated. "I must read it right now." She ripped the letter open, unfolded it, and sat down.

It was a good thing she was sitting, because Mrs. Anson's first sentence made her gasp.

"I hope not bad news," Ella said.

"Shocking news," Caroline replied. "But not unexpected when I think about it." She looked up at Ella. "Iona Smith does not have an artifact. Since Mrs. Smith never had the chance to retrieve an artifact during her Endeavour, Mrs. Anson said that she was having a hard time figuring out which specific artifacts Sean and Iona owned. So, she asked Mrs. Smith. Well, the reply did not make sense to Mrs. Anson. Here, let me read what she wrote. *The claim was of an artifact that I know has been lost, although even that description wasn't very clear. How Mrs. Smith ever thought to fool me, an expert on artifacts, I will never know, but eventually, in tears, she admitted that they only had one artifact and that it was always going to be Sean's. If Iona wants to compete, she must secure an artifact for herself.*" Caroline met Ella's eyes. "They have been lying all this time."

"But wasn't Mrs. Smith angry that you would not agree to form a team with her two children?" Ella asked. "Why would she do that if she knew that only one could compete?"

"Sean and Iona each had discussions with both Jack and me about our sister Becca's artifact," Caroline said. "Jack even told me that Iona thought saving it for Becca was a waste. Would they have hoped we would give it to them?"

"What's happened?" Harry asked, entering the room. "Or is it a secret?"

"It's not a secret," Caroline said. "Mrs. Anson writes that Iona Smith has never had an artifact. That they only have one for Sean."

"I see," Harry said, nodding.

"What do you see?" Ella asked. After a brief pause, she raised her eyebrows. "Of course! There are so many rumours about the ten artifacts Father brought out of the Abbey, perhaps once they felt that your sister's artifact was out of reach, they decided that Cedric was a better option for securing one."

"That's why she was so interested in him," Caroline said. "After being so attached to Jack." She was so thankful that she'd decided not to compete with them. "What do you think would have happened if Jack and I had teamed up with them?"

"They probably wouldn't have told you until the very last minute," Harry said "when it was too late to join another team and you had to either supply an artifact for Iona or be disqualified from competing in the Endeavour."

"What's worse, the Administration would have banned your team if they found out you'd been blackmailed," Ella said. "If you decided to supply the artifact in order to compete you wouldn't have been able to tell anyone what horrible people they are."

"It's also possible they hoped to steal one of your artifacts," Harry said. "Making it a family decision to use your sister's for either you or Jack. If they could hide the fact that they were using one of yours until it was handed in, it would be too late to do anything about it."

"I was asked more than once *where* my artifact was," Caroline said. "I can't believe they were so deceitful. Especially since Mr. and Mrs. Anson were generous enough to invite them for dinner twice."

"They sound rather desperate," Ella said. "They must not have the funds to purchase a second artifact. But this was not the way to go about things. Did Mrs. Anson send news of your brother?"

Caroline picked up the letter again: she hadn't actually read it to the end. "Just that he will be sending me a letter himself, apologizing for his part in the scheme."

"His unwitting part," Harry said. "Iona, with the help of her family, tricked him."

"I could also say something about a brother who behaved badly in this affair," Ella said. "I am convinced that Cedric knew something was going on and did nothing because it suited him."

"Cedric didn't make any promises or lie to my brother," Caroline said. "But he wasn't helpful, either." She remembered the smirks he'd directed at Jack when Iona had chosen him instead of her brother.

"Cedric bears some responsibility," Harry said. "I think he was deliberately misleading Iona even as she thought she was tricking him. All to Jack's disadvantage."

"I wish he had simply warned Jack of his concerns," Caroline replied. The entire Smith family's behaviour had been terrible, but if Harry was correct, Cedric Townsend hadn't behaved much better. She wondered that Harry and Ella, who seemed very truthful and trustworthy, were happy to be on the same Endeavour team as their older brother.

"Well," Harry said. "That's enough intrigue for me. Father left instructions and a list of tasks to complete before he returns." He sighed and stood up. "Whoever thinks that running an estate is a quiet life has not ever had to do it."

"Poor Harry," Ella said when he'd gone. "I think any occupation would be too much work. Come on, I think it might rain today and there are things to be done in the garden before that."

JACK'S LETTER ARRIVED the next day.

It was full of remorse and apologies for his thoughtless infatuation with Iona Smith and his gratitude that Caroline had seen through the Smiths early enough to save them both from disaster.

He'd had it out with Sean, who had admitted that their plan was to wait until the time for selecting teams had expired. Then all three Smiths would pressure the Morris family to supply an artifact—which they knew existed—for Iona, with the threat that otherwise none of them would be able to compete.

It was Caroline's willingness to forego the Endeavour that had ruined their plan, and Jack claimed he would forever be in her debt for that. To take Becca's artifact from her, after she had just missed the cut-off age, would have been unthinkably cruel and could have made their sister an enemy for life.

Jack ended his letter stating his intent to add his name to the list of competitors without teams, and he would add Caroline's as well, either along with him, or separately if she decided she could not trust him enough to be on the same team as him.

"What will you do?" Ella asked after Caroline read her the letter.

"I don't know," she replied. "I have not changed my mind

about competing only with people I trust, so I likely will not compete at all."

"You could compete with us," Ella said. "We still need a fourth." She leaned closer. "Father thinks very highly of you, and Harry told me he said that if you were not already teamed with your brother, he would consider you for our team."

"He thinks I am a good candidate?" Caroline rather doubted Mr. Townsend, or Cedric either, would take her, at only seventeen, over someone older and more experienced.

"He would not have invited you to Farview if he didn't," Ella said. "Please, I have no authority to tell you this, so you cannot mention it even to Harry, but think about it. I will consider how to approach Father, if it's something that you would contemplate."

"I'll think about it," Caroline said.

"Good," Ella said. "That's all I can ask. If you are not offered the spot, I hope that you will not hold it against me."

"Of course not," Caroline said. "This visit has been wonderful, and I hope that we are to be lifelong friends no matter what happens with the Endeavour." She really doubted Mr. Townsend would invite her to compete with his family, nor was she certain she wanted to compete without Jack. In fact, she would write to him and ask him to include her on the list of spare competitors, if he thought that two would have a better chance of securing a team than he would alone.

As she'd promised herself, Caroline wrote to Jack that night. In the morning she dropped the letter off with Jessop, who said that he would put it in the post straight away.

She and Ella were in the garden when Jessop appeared. Thinking that there had been some issue with posting her letter, she hurried over to him.

"Mr. Townsend sent word via the speaker that his instructions are to be carried out immediately," Jessop said to Ella. "A carrier has been ordered to take Miss Morris home."

"But why?" Ella said. "What reason did he give for this abruptness?"

Caroline was confused, especially since Ella had told her that Mr. Townsend considered her a suitable teammate for his children.

"He did not say, miss," Jessop replied. He turned to Caroline. "Mr. Townsend wishes me to inform you that your visit is over. At this moment your bags are being packed. A carrier will be here in an hour and you will depart Farview at that time. You will be driven to your home in Gaynesford. A message has already been sent to your family, telling them to expect you."

"Can I not be delivered to the Ansons in Norbarrow?" Caroline asked. "My brother is still there and it is much closer than home."

"Those were not my instructions," Jessop replied. "Please see that you are ready in one hour."

Caroline looked at Ella. "Have I done something wrong?"

"No," Ella replied. "That I cannot believe, although it's possible the scandal with the Smiths has reached Father's ear. Why that would taint you, I have no idea."

"Well, I am not travelling past Norbarrow without seeing the Ansons no matter what Jessop's instructions are. I will jump out of the carrier if I have to." She linked arms with Ella. "It is not you I am perturbed by. Are we not destined to be lifelong friends?"

"How gracious of you to say that," Ella said. "After such ungracious treatment by my father."

Caroline shrugged. "You and I both know that fathers give orders that daughters have no choice but to follow. I cannot hold you responsible for this." She grinned. "Besides, I have been instructed by my mother to experience as much as I can. I can now say that I have had an invitation to visit rescinded. Even Mother has not experienced that."

"I am glad that you are able to joke about this," Ella said. "I am mortified. Come on, Jessop will report any deviation from the plan to Father. There is no need to add to his anger, because he must be angry to dispatch you with such short notice."

CAROLINE WAS READY to leave when the carrier drove up to the house. Ella stood with her as her two cases were loaded onto it. Then there was nothing to do but say goodbye.

"I am sorry I can't say goodbye to Harry," Caroline said. "You will tell him, won't you? I wish you both well, along with Cedric and whoever your fourth teammate is."

"Maybe we'll see you at an Endeavour event?" Ella said. "Or perhaps we will meet at the reception for new Administrators?"

"I can't guarantee anything," Caroline replied. "Although I would love to see you again."

She hugged Ella tightly before stepping away. Under Jessop's watchful eye she entered the carrier's compartment and closed the door.

At some signal from outside, the carrier started moving. Caroline leaned out of the window until they rounded a curve and she could no longer see Ella. She sat back and brushed a tear from her eye.

She had done nothing wrong, she was certain of that, but knowing that didn't stop her from being upset and angry at the treatment she'd suffered. She thought that perhaps Cedric Townsend had told his father about the Smiths' scheme. It was very possible that Cedric, who certainly seemed to be a man who liked to cause trouble, had embellished the story.

But she was certain of one thing: she *would* be delivered to her brother and the Ansons in Norbarrow.

She pulled the knob in the compartment the way she'd seen others pull it and the carrier slowed and stopped.

"Is something wrong?" a man asked through a speaker.

"I must go to Norbarrow," Caroline said. "I will give you the address."

"That is not what I have been instructed and paid to do," came the reply.

"Your instructions do not come from any relation of mine," Caroline replied. "My closest family member to me right now is my brother, who is in Norbarrow. If you do not let me rejoin him, I will consider myself to be kidnapped. Am I clear?"

There was a pause and then she heard a sigh. "Give me the address."

Satisfied that she'd reasserted at least some control over her life, Caroline settled in for the journey, staring out the window.

Twenty minutes later, she gasped. The green meadow the road ran through gave way to a burnt and blackened landscape. A few yards past that, she recognized the fence.

They were passing Blackmeadow Abbey and the wonder she'd felt seeing it at night, glowing with magic, was replaced with unease at the destruction that was apparent this far from the actual abbey. The landscape was black and dusty and other than some dried grasses just beyond the fence, there was no sign of anything living: no trees, no birds flying overhead. She doubted even insects could survive in such devastation.

Then they were past it, but it took her almost an hour to stop thinking about the sheer power of the magic that had destroyed the land so thoroughly, that nothing grew there even so many decades later.

If she never competed in the Endeavour, she had at least seen Blackmeadow Abbey at both its best and its worst.

## 13

Kidnapped?" Mrs. Anson laughed out loud. "No wonder the driver did as you asked. And quite right you were to come here, too."

Caroline had arrived back at the Ansons' house in Norbarrow just after four. Mr. Anson and Jack were both out, but Mrs. Anson had immediately had Wooton take her cases back to her room.

Now, tea in front of them, Caroline was explaining to her what had happened that day. Although she wasn't planning on telling her what Ella had said about Mr. Townsend considering her as the fourth Townsend teammate.

"I am sorry that I could give you no warning," Caroline said. "Since I received none myself."

"Not to worry," Mrs. Anson said. "I will send a message to your mother telling her that you are once again safe under my care. Wooton?" she called. "Wooton, we must send a message immediately." She turned to Caroline. "Perhaps the message will not arrive too long after Mr. Townsend's telling them to expect you. I would not want your poor parents to worry. I never would have imagined Mr. Townsend would be so abrupt."

"Caroline?" She turned to find Jack staring at her from the hallway. "You're back! I hope my actions have not caused this."

"The Smiths' actions caused this," Mrs. Anson said. "Caroline, beyond what Jack has uncovered and we both have written you about, late last night Mr. Anson received a rather accusatory letter from Mr. Townsend. He claimed that you, Caroline, had misrepresented yourself to Sean Smith—that you had lied to him about coming from a Natural bloodline in order to make you and your brother look like better teammates. Mr. Townsend hates liars and quite rightly does not want his daughter to be friends with one, but you are not a liar. Well, this morning Mr. Anson sent him a sternly worded reply correcting him on that account."

"I told Sean no such thing," Caroline said.

"Of course, you didn't," Mrs. Anson replied. "You would never lie about something like that. Mr. Anson was quite annoyed that Mr. Townsend would even think to trust anything that Mr. Sean Smith told him. I confronted Sean and his mother earlier today. It seems that Sean has been behaving worse than even Mrs. Smith knew because he admitted telling Mr. Townsend that he was going to team up with a brother and sister who had Natural blood." Mrs. Anson paused. "Mr. Townsend concluded that he meant the two of you. So Caroline, Mr. Townsend's own mistake was partly to blame. But none of it is the fault of either of you." She ended by crossing her arms, and Caroline knew that Mr. Townsend would get a piece of Mrs. Anson's mind the next time they met, no matter who was there or where it was. She rather hoped she got to watch.

Wooton arrived and Mrs. Anson left with him to craft a message to Mother and Father.

Jack sat down across from her.

"I am sorry for ruining everything," he said. "Right now, I can't even tell you what I found so fascinating about Iona. Now that I know how much she led me on, I am quite ashamed. I will do everything in my power to salvage your Endeavour."

Caroline smiled. "It has been eventful and we haven't even joined a team yet, never mind competed. Do you think we dare do more?"

Jack nodded. "The Endeavour presents a possibility I can't pass up."

"Of finding an artifact that can gain you an apprenticeship as a Builder," Caroline said, nodding.

"You know about that?" Jack asked. "It's an almost impossible dream but I have to at least try."

"I will help in any way I can," Caroline said. "Whether it's as a teammate or by stepping back so you can join a team that has three members."

"I won't join a team without you," Jack said. "You deserve a chance to compete, especially since you averted what would have been a disaster for both of us."

"All right. But we can only compete with people I feel we can trust."

"Yes," Jack agreed. "You have shown that you are much better at judging people than I am, so I agree."

Mrs. Anson returned to the parlour. "Well, the message has been sent. I also asked your father to either bring or send your artifacts. It's only a few weeks before they must be handed in and we can't chance any last-minute delays." She sat down on the sofa. "Now, we need to plan how we're going to find you suitable teammates. As the wife of an almost Administrator, I believe I may have some influence."

THREE DAYS LATER, a message arrived from Father. He would be arriving in a week with their artifacts, and he dearly hoped that Jack and Caroline had teammates for him to meet, despite their ordeal.

"The list goes up first thing tomorrow," Jack said to her after dinner. "We should go down and see who is on it."

"Mrs. Anson has made us an appointment for the morning," Caroline said. "With the children of an Administrator. We'll have to go in the afternoon."

"Won't all the best options be taken by then?"

"*We're* someone's best option," Caroline reminded him. "And we're not even putting our names on the list. Even Mr. Anson agrees that this is the best plan."

"I know." Jack sighed. "I just want it all sorted out, one way or another."

"Me too," Caroline said. Now that she'd made the decision to compete, she knew that she would be very disappointed if she didn't. "I'm going up to bed. Good night."

BLEARY-EYED, CAROLINE went down the stairs. She hadn't slept well at all, and now she was worried that she wouldn't make a good impression for the potential teammates Mrs. Anson had invited over.

"Caroline," Mrs. Anson said when she entered the dining room. "There you are. You have just enough time to eat something before our guests are due to arrive. Mr. Anson," she called. "It's almost time."

Caroline managed to eat half a roll before her nerves set in. The doorbell rang and she stood up and nervously smoothed her skirt.

"Are you coming?" Jack asked from the doorway. She nodded and followed him but the sound of a familiar voice stopped her.

What on earth was Mr. Townsend doing here?

"Caroline, Jack," Mr. Anson said. "Come here, please. Mr. Townsend has something he wants to say to you." He ushered them all into the parlour.

Caroline found a chair and Jack stood beside her. Mr. Townsend stepped into the centre of the room and cleared his throat.

"I owe you both, and especially you, Miss Morris, an apology," Mr. Townsend said, shocking Caroline. "My behaviour towards you was most unkind and rude. I have no excuse for my appalling manners, especially since I know better than most the kinds of rumours and lies people are capable of spreading. Will the two of you accept my apology?"

"I will," Jack said. "Since my stupidity was a cause of some of the misunderstandings. Caroline, what do you say?"

"I will accept it as well," Caroline said. "As a student of Endeavour history, I have read that emotions can run high, but now I know what that feels like. I hold no hard feelings and in fact hope that you will approve if Ella and I remain friends."

"Of course," Mr. Townsend said. "My daughter said that you would be forgiving but I feared that I had given you far too many reasons not to be." He turned and nodded to Mr. Anson, who motioned to Wooton.

A moment later Ella poked her head in through the hallway door.

"Ella!" Caroline rushed to her friend and they hugged. "I am so happy to see you. And Harry is here as well." She paused and searched out Mrs. Anson, who was beaming. "Are these the children of an Administrator we are to meet with? Yes? But what about Cedric?"

"After his part in all of this," Harry said. "Ella and I told Father that we could no longer trust Cedric enough to compete with him."

"He could have stopped much of this by warning Jack," Ella said. "Not doing so for his own amusement was not to be tolerated."

"You need to trust your teammates," Mr. Townsend said. "It could be a matter of life and death, as I tragically know from personal experience."

"Will you team up with us?" Ella asked.

"I will," Caroline replied. "Jack will have to make his own decision and he might need more time."

"Then let's spend some time together," Harry said. "Did you have any plans for today?"

"Other than meet potential teammates?" Jack replied. "No. I say we go out to the garden and talk."

"YOU REALLY KICKED Cedric off your team?" Caroline asked Ella once they were outside. "How did he take it?"

"It turns out he had some friends he could compete with," Ella said. "One of their members was recruited by a team with an actual Builder, and he said that he couldn't pass up that opportunity so Cedric took his place."

"Well, it's all worked out wonderfully," Caroline said. "I'm sure Jack will eventually agree."

"I already have," Jack said. "I told you I would trust your judgement and I meant it. I can only hope to prove as dependable and trustworthy as the three of you."

"Father will be pleased," Caroline said. She turned to Ella. "He's arriving in a week and will want to meet you both. You're staying in town?"

"Yes. Our father will be back and forth between here and the Abbey but we are here until the Endeavour."

"Same here," Caroline smiled. "So, we can attend some of the parties and concerts, can't we?" They also needed to make some decisions about targeting lost artifacts, but that could wait for another day.

"Of course," Ella replied. "We especially need to attend the

164     Jane Glatt

reception introducing Mr. Anson as an Administrator."

"Yes, we do," Caroline said. "It's a good thing we're all friends again. I'm not sure what Mrs. Anson would have said to your father even at such an important event for her husband."

"I will not underestimate Mrs. Anson again," Jack said. "I think we're all happy we won't have to witness that."

THE FOLLOWING WEEK was busy. Every single night there was a new event: a reception for already formed teams, followed by two concerts, and then a night of fireworks.

Mrs. Anson was delighted that the Artifact Society had been granted a room for their meetings and spent most of her mornings at Administration Hall with her fellow society members. She was quite convinced that it was because she was now the wife of an Administrator, even though Mr. Anson said it was Mr. Townsend's request and that he had nothing to do with it.

Caroline's group formally submitted their names as a team at Administration Hall, which then allowed them access to the records room.

After that, afternoons were spent there, reading every first-hand account of Endeavours that they could find. They'd agreed as a team that they would concentrate on searching for lost artifacts and were hoping to find clues in previous competitor's reports on how to do that.

As well, they were trying to understand the dangers they faced and then figure out what items to bring inside to minimize the risks. Each competitor was allowed a single item to help in their search so deciding what to bring was extremely important.

Jack called Caroline's idea to make a map based on the descriptions from the competitor accounts brilliant, and soon they had a rough layout of Blackmeadow Abbey.

"I'm not even sure the Administrators have a map," Harry said. "Father has never mentioned one."

The four of them were at a table, the map spread out in front of them.

"Maybe that's because it's impossible to make an accurate one," Caroline said. They'd discovered that the Abbey seemed to change: hallways and doors that existed in one Endeavour were not where a previous account put them. There were a few things that were constant: the main entrance and a door at the back that led outside. There also seemed to be a very large room that many competitors found, although each Endeavour they seemed to get there by different routes.

"It's better than nothing," Jack said. "At the very least it's good to know that things like hallways and doors can move around while competitors are inside."

"I agree," Ella said. "We can only go forward, so we need to be careful and stay together. We haven't read any reports of teams being separated, but we don't want to be the first."

Caroline nodded, as did Harry and Jack.

"I think we should do our very best to find that main room." Caroline jabbed a finger at the square that was at the centre of the map. "There's bound to be a few artifacts in there."

"That's a good plan," Harry said. "It seems that most years only a half dozen teams find it, so I would expect it holds some lost artifacts."

Caroline met Jack's eyes. That was his hope: to find a lost artifact that was imbued with years' worth of magic. She mostly just wanted them all to survive.

"Then it's agreed," Jack said. "We find the room and don't reverse our path unless there is no way forward."

"Good."

A clock chimed and Caroline sat up. "We should get back to the Ansons'," she said. "Father was due an hour ago."

Jack rolled up the map and they all hurried from the records room to the stairs. There were a couple of other teams spending time reading the records, but not as many as Caroline had expected.

They were embarking on one of the most important events in their lives: she just couldn't understand why everyone wasn't trying to learn everything they could about Endeavours and Blackmeadow Abbey.

"THERE YOU ALL are," Mrs. Anson said when they returned to the house. She was in the hallway, outside of the parlour. "Your father has arrived and is in the parlour. I'm just going to ask Mrs. Wooton for some tea."

Caroline followed Jack into the parlour, with Ella and Harry right behind.

"Father," Jack said. "I hope your trip wasn't too demanding."

"Jack, and Caroline," Father said. "I was just telling Mr. Anson about it. I hired a carrier." He patted his pocket. "I did not want to keep your artifacts in an inn overnight. Until they are safely handed over to the Administrators, I will not rest easy. Mr. Anson, do you have a safe where these can be kept?"

"In my office," Mr. Anson said. "First let me introduce you to Harry and Ella Townsend. Their father, Administrator Townsend, was instrumental in my successful petition for the role."

"Harry and Ella, I am delighted to meet the two of you." Father shook their hands. "I hear that you have been preparing for your competition?"

"We have, sir," Harry said. "We've been reading all of the first-hand accounts in the records room at Administration Hall."

"That sounds useful," Father said. "Jack, what's that you have under your arm?"

"We've made a map," Jack said. "It was Caroline's idea. Perhaps you could look at it later and tell us if it matches up with what you recall from your own Endeavour? We don't feel it appropriate to ask either Mr. Anson or Mr. Townsend, since they are Administrators."

"I would be happy to take a look," Father said.

"Tea is on the way," Mrs. Anson said as she entered the parlour. "Harry and Ella are staying for dinner so there will be plenty of time for everyone to get acquainted."

"Let's get those artifacts locked up," Mr. Anson said. He and Father headed for the office and Caroline steered Ella to two chairs near the window.

"I'm sure Father will like you," Caroline said as they sat down. "So don't worry."

"It's his opinion of *my* father that I'm worried about," Ella replied. "I am certain he was not impressed with how you were treated."

"Then it's a good thing your father isn't due until the Administrator reception in a week," Caroline said. "By that time Father's good impression of you and Harry will make him forget about everything else except what wonderful Endeavour teammates you will be."

Mr. Morris planned to stay just until the artifacts were handed in and Mr. Anson was formally declared an Administrator at the reception that night, then he would return home. The entire Morris family would be back in Norbarrow for the draw that determined when teams entered Blackmeadow Abbey, which was a few days before the start of the Endeavour. The weeks between handing in the artifacts and the draw were filled with more events, although they were directed more towards past competitors than the current ones.

AFTER DINNER FATHER asked to see the map. Mr. Anson promised not to comment when Jack unrolled it, and everyone crowded around the dining room table.

"Hmm," Father said. "I never saw a large room, but this corridor here"—he pointed to the map—"that's the one my team took. From this it looks like we pretty much went straight to the exit by taking this turn here." He put his finger on an intersecting corridor. "We still found ten artifacts because we had such an early starting number."

"The room has been referred to in every Endeavour we've studied," Harry said. "Very few teams find it and the corridors leading to it seem to change. I assume it's because of some lingering spell or magic."

"Yes," Father said. "The magic was what shocked me the most. I could almost taste it. In some places the air crackled like just before a storm." He glanced around the table. "Another team was crying: we heard that very clearly. I never did find out who it was or what happened."

"Even so early?" Caroline asked. "I thought it didn't get bad until later."

"It got worse," Father said. "But it was very unstable even then, which is why so few teams entered the Abbey that year."

"Our father was one of the last to enter," Ella said. "They closed it down as soon as they knew the rest of his team perished."

"Of course," Father replied. "Patrick Townsend. That was such a terrible tragedy. He must be worried about the two of you."

"He is," Harry replied. "But he won't tell us not to compete. We hope that because we've teamed up with the right people and we are preparing as much as we can, it will ease his mind."

"I don't think he'll relax until we're all out safely," Ella said.

"No parents will," Father replied. "What do you say, Mrs. Anson. Are these young people going to succeed?"

"I have no doubt," Mrs. Anson replied. "They all understand the risks and that the most important thing is everyone's safety."

"I agree," Mr. Anson said. "I think their approach to the competition is very level-headed. It sounds like they are doing everything they can to give themselves the best chance possible to succeed."

"Thank you," Harry said. "I believe that my father will agree as well. Now, Ella and I must get home before it's too dark. Mrs. Anson, Mr. Anson, thank you again for your hospitality. Mr. Morris, it was very nice to meet you."

Caroline and Jack escorted the Townsend siblings to the front door.

"I think that went well," Caroline said. "Now we just need our father to meet yours. Shall we meet tomorrow at the records hall?"

"Let's make it in the afternoon," Jack said. "We shouldn't abandon Father so soon after his arrival."

"After noon it is," Ella said. "See you tomorrow."

Jack closed the door and turned to her. "Even Mr. Anson approves of our approach," he said. "That gives me a little more confidence."

"Me too," Caroline agreed. None of the reports any of them had read mentioned that teams had actually prepared for the Endeavour other than attending the receptions and asking questions of Administrators. Was that because so few prepared, or because no one spoke about it?

Surely Mr. Townsend would have told his children if he'd done something to get ready for his own Endeavour; especially since the rest of his team didn't survive.

Caroline and Jack returned to the parlour and the remainder of the evening was spent with Father giving them all the news from home.

THE WEEK WITH Father flew by: the team spent most days in the records room, even though at this point they were re-reading accounts they'd already studied. They made some slight changes to the map but then they all agreed that it was as final as it could be.

Caroline offered to make copies for each of them. The plan was to mark the maps as they went, so even if they were separated, they would know the route they'd taken. It would mean they would be slow once they were inside the Abbey. There wasn't a time limit to get through it but it was thought that the longer you were inside, the more likely you'd be affected by a rogue spell or latent magic, which could be dangerous.

Then Mr. Townsend arrived with Harry and Ella's artifacts and it was time for all of the competitors to hand them in.

"They're here," Caroline said. She took a step away from the front window as the doorbell rang.

A few minutes later, Wooton ushered Mr. Townsend, Harry, and Ella into the parlour.

Mr. Anson made the introductions and Father and Mr. Townsend settled into a conversation.

Ella and Harry joined Caroline and Jack near the window. Harry carried a small, wooden box.

"Is that your artifact?" Jack asked him. "Can I see?"

"Sure." Harry lifted the lid of the box. "It changes things in small ways." He grinned and held up a black button. "I always have to demonstrate." He put the button in the box, closed the lid, waited a few seconds and opened it again.

"It's a rose," Caroline said. "How fun. Does it always turn into a flower?"

"No." Harry closed the lid again, waited, and then opened the box.

Instead of a flower, there was rock.

"It's completely random," Harry said. "Father had Builders investigate it but they couldn't figure out how to make it change things consistently, never mind how to have it produce something useful." He shrugged. "So, it's my ticket to the Endeavour. How about you?"

Jack pulled a shawl from his pocket. "It changes scent," he said, waving it around. "And not all of them are pleasant."

Ella leaned in and sniffed. "It smells like baking bread." Jack waved the shawl again. "Whew, now it smells like a wet dog." She pulled a ring from her finger. "Mine simply resizes for whoever wants to wear it." She put it on her thumb and it fit perfectly but when she took it off and put it on her pinky finger, it also fit perfectly.

"Mine glows in the dark," Caroline said, pulling her necklace out from under her dress. "But not enough to actually see by." She heard laughter and looked over to see Mr. Townsend and her father smiling at each other. "It seems like they're getting along," she said.

"Thank goodness," Ella said. "Oh, Mr. Anson just checked his watch. I think we'll be leaving soon."

Ella was correct and Mr. Anson asked them all to prepare to leave. The artifact hand-in ceremony was due to start in an hour: as Administrators, he and Mr. Townsend had to be there early.

The two Administrators left and Father and Mrs. Anson joined the four teammates.

"Are you getting excited?" Father asked.

"I'm getting nervous," Caroline admitted. "Handing in my artifact makes it feel more real."

"I agree," Harry said. "But that's what all of our preparation is for: so that nerves or fear or any other emotion doesn't take over."

"But we didn't prepare for this," Ella said. "The fact is, handing in our artifacts is the start of our competition."

"I suppose it is," Father said. "I don't really remember much about that part of the Endeavour. Do you, Mrs. Anson?"

"It was a pretty big deal for me," she replied. "Like Caroline, I'd had my artifact for years and even though it wasn't very useful, it had been part of my life. Giving it up made me a little sad."

"Yes, that's how I feel," Ella said. "Sad." She met Caroline's eyes. "And nervous."

"I think it's time to go," Jack said. "We don't want to be late."

They weren't the only ones walking to Administration Hall, and as they got closer, the streets were blocked off to give more room to pedestrians.

There were so many people that Caroline felt overwhelmed. Every team that she saw was accompanied by one or more adults. Men and women wearing Endeavour badges were watching everyone, reminding Caroline that even this close to handing them in, artifacts could still be at risk of being stolen.

Mrs. Anson caught up to her.

"I heard that Sean Smith was picked for a team," she said in her ear. "We might see him today."

"Did you hear that from Mrs. Smith?" Caroline asked.

"No." Mrs. Anson shook her head. "I asked Miss Foster for a favour. She's been keeping an eye on the list of spares. She told me two days ago that his name was on a list and yesterday it had been removed so he must have found enough people to compete with at the last minute."

"I feel sorry for them," Caroline said. "If they are putting their trust in him, they will be disappointed."

"And perhaps at risk," Mrs. Anson said. "I hope that he doesn't cause any harm."

"I do too. Iona is not competing then? She didn't find an artifact?"

"She did not," Mrs. Anson said. "So now all their hopes rest on Sean."

"Which makes him even more desperate—and dangerous." She vowed to make a point of finding out if they would be in the Abbey at the same time as Sean's team. She did not trust him.

They reached the edge of the crowd and Father waved them all over to him.

"This official right here," he said, pointing to a man with an Endeavour symbol on his sleeve, "will help you get to through this crowd to the line of competitors. Mrs. Anson and I will watch from here and I think we'd better say goodbye and good luck. I doubt we'll be able to find each other later."

"We'll meet back at the house," Mrs. Anson said. "Mrs. Wooton is preparing a celebratory meal for us all before we head off to the reception. Of course, Mr. Anson has met all the other Administrators and is already performing his duties, but I will meet them all tonight for the first time."

"Along with their wives," Caroline said. "It's an exciting day for all of us."

"That it is," Mrs. Anson replied.

"We'll see you at the house," Jack said. He grabbed Caroline's arm. "Come on, let's get into the official line up."

They followed the official to the end of the line of competitors. It took an hour for them to get to the front.

"Names of your team members," a uniformed man said. He had them spell their names while a woman scanned a list.

"Verified," the woman said. "Step over to the table and put all of your artifacts on it."

Caroline undid the clasp on her necklace and placed it on the table next to Jack's shawl, Ella's ring, and Harry's box. A man took a polished stick and passed it over the artifacts one at a time.

"Magic is present in all four items and they are authorized as artifacts," he said. "Congratulations, you are now a confirmed Endeavour team. Please present your entire team here three days prior to the start date for the draw for starting positions. If one or more members of your team fail to show up, you will be disqualified and your artifacts will be forfeit. Next!"

Caroline grabbed Ella's arm as the four of them got into yet another surging line. This time everyone was chatting excitedly and she felt her own excitement grow. She was officially an Endeavour competitor, whether she set foot in Blackmeadow Abbey or not. She could write her own account and leave it in the records room, no matter what happened.

"It's going to take hours to get back to the Ansons'," Ella said.

"I don't mind," Caroline said. "It's a once in a lifetime experience. Have you ever been in a crowd of so many people?"

"Never. Oh, look who it is."

Caroline looked up to find Sean Smith staring at her.

"Miss Morris," he said. "Congratulations."

"Same to you," she replied. "I wish you luck."

Sean's smile was sad. "I hope you mean that. I never wanted to harm you or your brother." He glanced away for a moment. "But my family had a plan. It didn't work out but we had to try."

"I have no ill will towards you and do wish you luck," Caroline said, deliberately ignoring the rest of what he'd said. "But I don't recommend you talk to Jack."

"I have to find my team anyway," Sean said, and then he headed in the opposite direction.

"Do you really mean that?" Ella asked. "That you don't have any ill will? I do and he wasn't trying to trick me."

"I meant it," Caroline said. "The Endeavour is not a

competition between different teams, it's about us against the Abbey. But that doesn't mean I want him in the Abbey at the same time as us."

"Well, I hope his team draws the very last entrance position and that we've already found all of the artifacts."

"All of them?" Caroline asked. "Do we need to bring a cart in with us? Come on, Jack and Harry must be ahead of us. I think we're on our own for the walk back to the Ansons'."

# 14

Administration Hall was lit up again, although there wasn't the crowd they'd encountered the night they'd gone to the competitor's reception.

Their credentials were checked at the door, and once inside, Mr. and Mrs. Anson followed Mr. Townsend to a raised dais that had been set up near the stairs.

"It's quite impressive," Father said to Caroline. "Although you've been in so often you must be used to it."

"I'm so focused on my tasks that I fail to notice it," Caroline replied. "So it's good to have nights like this to remind me."

"It's more striking at night," Jack added. "With the lights. We spend most of our time in the records room on the fourth floor, although Mrs. Anson meets with the Artifact Society on the second."

Ella stepped closer. "Father is waving us over. I think it's time to meet the Administrators."

"You've met most of them?" Caroline asked.

"Officially, yes," Harry said, joining them. "But some of them we only met at our father's reception when Ella and I were children. And there are two new Administrators, along with Mr. Anson."

They all got into a line—Caroline was beginning to think that lining up would be one of her most vivid memories of her Endeavour—and one by one they were introduced to each new

Administrator.

After that they huddled in a group and drinks were distributed.

One of the oldest Administrators made a speech welcoming the new members, and then it seemed that the formalities were over. Mr. and Mrs. Anson were in the middle of a group of people congratulating them.

Caroline yawned.

"We can leave now if you want," Father said. "Mr. Anson and I already agreed that we would not need to stay until the end and that there was no reason for us to wait for them."

"I would like that," Caroline replied. "As long as it does not take anything away from Mr. Anson's accomplishment."

"I believe that they will be here for hours," Harry said. "Ella, I will let Father know we are leaving with you, if you wish to leave as well."

"Please," Ella said. Harry left in search of Mr. Townsend.

"Was Cedric invited?" Caroline asked. "I assumed he would be here."

"He was invited," Ella replied. "And I'm sure Father expected him, but now that he has his own team, Cedric has not been around at all."

"We're all set," Harry said when he returned.

"We'll walk you and Ella home," Jack said to him. "Let's go."

FATHER LEFT FOR home the next day and Mr. Anson—as a newly acknowledged member of the Administration—had plenty of engagements to fill the days between now and the draw.

That left Mrs. Anson available so Caroline recruited her to help them prepare.

Mrs. Anson knew more about artifacts than anyone else Caroline could think of. For her part, Mrs. Anson in turn suggested they use any of the Artifact Society members who were interested in helping.

"Mr. Stanford, Mr. Hobson, and of course Miss Foster are willing," Mrs. Anson said. "But unfortunately, my friend Mrs. Digby is not available."

They had met at the top of the stairs of the mezzanine level of Administration Hall, the place where Caroline had first met

Harry. "I can lead the discussion at first, if you would like."

"Mr. Hobson and Mr. Stanford competed in the Endeavour forty-four years ago," Caroline said. "That's the Endeavour where an artifact that allowed people to fly was lost, and that's what they are experts in: lost artifacts."

"Imagine handing in such an important artifact," Harry said.

"Imagine *finding* one like that," Jack added. "You could create a whole new industry based on that single item."

"Miss Foster is more like me," Mrs. Anson said. "A generalist interested in all artifacts, whether they have small magics or large ones. If we're ready, then come this way." She led them down the hall to a small room.

Caroline hadn't been to a meeting since the group had been awarded a room to meet in. It was small; a table and a dozen mismatched chairs took up most of the space, but there was a window at the far end of the room that allowed a slight breeze to circulate.

"Exciting days, Caroline, exciting days," Mr. Hobson said. "Come and introduce your teammates and let's get started."

Caroline introduced everyone and they all found seats around the table.

"We're touched that you thought of us," Miss Foster said. "I have no relatives competing so it's nice to actually be part of the festivities."

"They're not here for festivities," Mr. Stanford said. "They are taking it seriously." His smile softened his words. "But it is nice to be even a small part of their effort. The excitement is contagious."

"It's a little nerve-wracking," Jack said. "Caroline is the Endeavour expert, not me. Before we started studying as a team, I never realized just how often things go wrong."

"They like to tell the good stories," Miss Foster said. "Have you heard about the artifacts that have exploded?"

"There's only one account in the records room," Harry said. "Are you saying it's happened more than once?"

"Every single Endeavour," Miss Foster replied. "Sometimes more than once. Not to worry, there are things you can do to stay safe."

"That's our first priority," Ella said. "Staying safe and making it out in one piece."

"Very wise of you," Mr. Hobson said. "We've come up with a list of the dangers we know about. If it's all right with you, we can go through them one at a time and discuss and answer questions."

"I think we're all fine with that approach," Caroline said. She met the eye of each of her three teammates and everyone nodded. "Ella has offered to take notes for us so please be patient if she needs you to pause while she catches up."

"Certainly," Mrs. Anson said. "I will start by telling you what we know about exploding artifacts."

It took three hours to just skim over the initial dangers that artifacts posed.

"Shall we reconvene tomorrow?" Mrs. Anson asked.

"I would love to if the team is interested," Miss Foster said, and both Mr. Hobson and Mr. Stanford nodded.

"I think we would all be very grateful," Harry said. "I had no idea that even just touching an artifact could be dangerous. I'd like us to try to figure out what items we should bring in order to keep us all safe."

"I'm sure we can come up with a useful list," Mrs. Anson said. "We'll meet here tomorrow after noon."

"I want to thank you all for your time," Caroline said. "What you know is going to help us so much."

"You're one of us," Mr. Hobson said. "We're happy to help. Besides, with the aid of Mrs. Anson and Mr. Townsend, our status has been elevated so much that we have been given a room to meet in. We've been trying the achieve that for years."

"I always think that there's no point in knowledge unless it's shared," Miss Foster said. "I am doing this for the sheer joy of that."

"Until tomorrow then," Mrs. Anson said. She left the room and the teammates filed out after her.

"That was shocking," Harry said when they were once again out near the stairs. "I am so glad you suggested this, Caroline."

"I'm surprised as well," Caroline said. "I knew we would learn a lot, but I had no idea the dangers that artifacts posed within the Abbey." Even *True Stories of Blackmeadow Abbey* only mentioned a few of the issues the Artifact Society had listed.

"It's never a bad idea to learn about things," Mrs. Anson said. "I must meet Mr. Anson. I trust you can all amuse yourselves for the rest of the day?"

"Of course, Mrs. Anson," Jack said. "Thank you for your help with this."

"You're welcome. I'm off."

Once Mrs. Anson had disappeared down the stairs, Jack leaned against the railing.

"This was such a good idea," Jack said. "And Caroline, I apologize for all the times I teased you for reading so much about Endeavours and the hours you spent talking with Mrs. Anson about artifacts."

"Apology accepted," Caroline said. "I'm glad we all agreed that we would study. It would have been frustrating to be the only one to know about the risks we face and not just the rules that must be followed."

"I can't believe we haven't read about other teams preparing like this," Ella said. "Someone must have, but why not give an account? Think of the lives that could be saved if people just knew what to look out for?"

"I suppose we'll have to be the first to write that account," Harry said. "But it won't matter if no one reads it."

"They'll read it if we're successful," Jack said. "In not only coming out safely, but with some useful artifacts. Because I am certain that all of this preparation will help us do that."

"It will help," Caroline said. She didn't add that nothing would help if they didn't actually get to enter Blackmeadow Abbey. And that was literally down to the luck of the draw.

They still had weeks before they would know when they would enter the Abbey.

# 15

It took a full week of meeting with the Artifact Society before the team felt that they had learned as much as they could for now, although they all acknowledged that there was plenty they didn't know.

They spent another two weeks going over the accounts in the records room—sometimes for the third time—to unearth more mentions of dangerous artifacts.

Finally, it was less than a week until the Endeavour started. The Morrises were all coming today and the draw for entry positions was tomorrow.

"I'm too nervous to eat," Ella said. "What if we don't get a good starting position? What if we don't even get to step inside the Abbey?"

"Then we'll still be the most prepared team," Caroline said. They were in the garden of the Ansons' house. Father, Mother, Becca, and Miles were due to arrive within the hour. "That's the only thing we have control over and we've done everything we could think of."

"We've done more than anyone else competing," Harry said. "Even if we don't enter the Abbey, I won't regret the work we've put into it. I think we've become a solid team because of it."

"I still want us to get inside," Jack said. "It would be a shame not to use all this knowledge we've gained."

"If we knew a Natural, we could ask them for a luck spell," Ella said.

"If we knew a Natural, we could have them create a spell to make us the first team to enter," Harry said. "As if one of them would ever bother."

"How is Cedric getting along with his team?" Caroline asked. "You haven't mentioned seeing him."

"We haven't seen him for weeks," Ella said. "Father has though, but he didn't tell us anything. Just as I assume he didn't tell Cedric what we've been doing."

"Father didn't seem very pleased with Cedric," Harry added. "He mentioned—in his disapproving tone of voice—that he'd seen him at an event."

"Mrs. Anson saw the Smiths last night," Caroline said. "She said Sean seemed very sure of himself and Mrs. Smith acted as though nothing had happened, but that Iona was very subdued."

"I'm glad we didn't go to that event," Jack said. "I would rather not meet the Smiths ever again."

"If she had just been truthful about needing an artifact, I'd feel sorry for Iona," Caroline said. "It can't be easy knowing you have no chance to compete."

"I have no sympathy," Jack replied. "Not after they tried to use me and trick the two of us. If we'd agreed to be on their team neither of us would be competing."

"I know," Caroline said. "What they did was terrible, but I do understand that they are desperate." Mrs. Anson had discovered that Mrs. Smith had been left very little by her husband: no doubt they, like many, were hoping that the Endeavour would change their future. She looked over at Jack: her brother had the same hope.

"Caroline! Jack!"

It was Becca. She ran out the back door and launched herself at Caroline.

"We came by carrier," Becca said. She bounced away from Caroline and grabbed Jack's hand. "It was magnificent. I know Caroline's been in one but, Jack, have you? After we stopped for lunch, I asked to sit with the operator and he said yes." She pouted. "At first Father said no but I convinced him it would be fine if Miles sat with us. Hi," Becca stared at Ella and Harry. "You're the teammates, right? I'm Becca. If the Endeavour had been called next year only one of you could have been on *our* team. Do you know which one it would have been?"

"Becca," Caroline warned. "Be nice. And yes, this is Ella Townsend and her brother Harry, Jack and my teammates."

"I read one of Caroline's books," Becca said. "Your father is famous."

"His story is tragic and because of that, well known," Harry said. "But I don't think he would consider himself famous."

"*And* he's an Administrator," Becca said. "Like Mr. Anson. So now I will know two Administrators. That will help me when it's my turn to compete, won't it?"

"It hasn't helped us," Ella said. "I'd say that knowing Mrs. Anson has been a bigger benefit than being the child of an Administrator."

"Mrs. Anson?" Becca laughed. "Really?" She glanced around the group and her smile faded. "How has she been a benefit?"

"Her knowledge of artifacts has been extremely helpful," Harry said. "Because now we know what dangers to watch for. We also have a list of items we'll be taking into the Abbey with us to keep us all safe."

"Are you allowed to take things in?" Becca asked.

"One per person," Jack said. "They can't be magical or Builder enhanced or alive."

"Meaning we can't take Mrs. Anson in with us," Ella said.

"Huh." Becca shrugged. "Anyway, I was sent out to ask you to come in. Mother said if I'm good I can attend the concert tonight but I'm not sure I even want to go."

"You should go," Caroline said. "You'll love it."

"I suppose," Becca said. "I don't have to talk to anyone, do I? I am tired of talking only to Mother, Father, and Miles."

"Once you're at the concert everyone is asked to be quiet," Caroline said.

"Even Miles? It might be worth going just to see that." Becca turned and made her way to the door. "I'll tell them you're coming right in."

"I don't think it's Miles who will have trouble keeping quiet at the concert," Ella said, and Caroline laughed.

FATHER ENDED UP taking Becca and Miles to the concert, along with Mr. and Mrs. Anson. Mr. Townsend arrived to collect Ella and Harry just before they left, leaving Caroline and Jack with their mother.

"I know you've been spending time preparing," Mother said. "But I hope you've still made time to enjoy yourselves. You won't get another chance like this."

"Which is why we've been spending our time preparing," Caroline said and smiled. "Besides, you know I love learning about Endeavours, so having a group where we're all focused on that has been fun for me. I'm not sure about Jack, though."

"It's been surprisingly enjoyable," Jack said. "And interesting. I have to admit, now that we're so close to competing, I am happier than even I thought I'd be that we've done so much research. I am looking forward to competing and although I am still nervous, I feel so well prepared that I'm not dreading entering the Abbey."

"I felt dread," Mother replied. "And was not sad that the Endeavour was called off before it was my turn. Especially when we heard of all of those deaths on Mr. Townsend's team." She paused. "But I see that you are enjoying your experience, so that makes me happy."

"I think we've made some really good lifelong friends," Caroline said. "I hope to see Ella at least a few times a year. Mr. and Mrs. Anson will need to be in Norbarrow for his Administrator duties, so I might be able to travel with them and meet up with Ella when she comes with her father."

"That would be lovely," Mother said. "Perhaps you'll find yourself a nice, young man during your visits."

"Mother," Caroline said, rolling her eyes. "I'm only seventeen. I have years before I'll even be ready to think about that."

"And what will you do for those years?" her mother asked.

"I'd like to go to Linley Academy," Caroline said, and her mother gasped. "Why not? Why can't I get an education?"

"Are women even allowed to attend?"

"There are a few," Jack said. "Mostly older, unmarried women."

"There, you see?" Caroline said. "I wouldn't be the only woman. When the Endeavour is over, I will apply to attend Linley."

"She's smarter and works harder than most of my classmates," Jack said.

Mother sighed. "Your father will not like it, but we can discuss it later. Like me, he will have no desire to live in a house with both you and Becca: her disappointed because she missed the Endeavour and you because you can't attend Linley."

"Thank you," Caroline said. She met Jack's eyes and grinned. She was going to get a real education. She couldn't wait to tell Ella. Maybe she'd want to attend as well and they could share rooms.

Caroline went to bed that night more excited about going to school than the Endeavour, but she woke up nervous about the draw. Today her team would find out their starting place: today they would know if they had a real chance of entering Blackmeadow Abbey.

IN THE END it wasn't very exciting.

The four teammates, along with Mrs. Anson and the Morris family, headed off to Administration Hall. Mr. Anson and Mr. Townsend, in their official capacities, had gone much earlier, of course.

A huge crowd milled around the streets nearby, but only actual competitors were allowed to enter the square. They were then directed to join a long, snaking line that led towards the main doors of the building.

"We should have come earlier," Jack said.

"We all know your opinion on the matter," Caroline replied. "You've told us at least half a dozen times and you were overruled each time." Their starting position would be drawn when they reached the front of the line. Jack thought that they had a better chance of getting an early start if their names were drawn first. The rest of them didn't think it would matter. It was just as likely that all the later starting positions would be drawn first as it was for the opposite. There were one hundred and twenty-three teams competing this year and they were hoping to draw a number no higher than forty. If they had a start position later than that, the chance that they would even enter the Abbey was diminished and their chances of finding any artifacts very low.

Jack sighed. "I hope you're right. Oh. Sean Smith is right at the front. Now I'm glad we're back here."

"Do you recognize anyone he's with?" Caroline asked, trying to find Sean in the crowd.

"No. And I'm glad of that as well. I'm not looking forward to running into him or his teammates at school."

"Hey," Caroline said to Ella. "Guess what? I might be going to Linley Academy. At least Mother isn't completely against it. I think Father would agree if you attended too."

"I've never even thought of doing that," Ella replied. She turned to Harry. "Do you think Father would allow it?"

"If we find some decent artifacts, he won't be able to say no," Harry said. "And for what it's worth, I think it would be a great idea. I can tell Father that it would be a very good place for you to find a husband."

Ella swatted him. "Do not encourage Father like that. You have no idea what it's like to have him see marrying you off as your only option in life."

"I do understand," Harry said. "But if it gives you a chance to get more education, maybe even find a career, it might be worth it."

"My mother made a comment about me finding *a nice, young man*," Caroline said. "If it would help get her and Father's permission, I would absolutely tell them Linley Academy is a good place to find a husband. Even though I have no intention of searching for one when I'm there."

"All right," Ella said. "But I'd prefer retrieving some significant artifacts so we don't have to answer to anyone."

"Isn't that one reason why we spent so much time preparing?" Jack asked.

Despite its length, the line moved quickly. Soon they could see the front. Mr. Townsend seemed to be in charge. At least, when a number was drawn from a box it was handed to him to read.

"Look, there's Cedric," Ella said. She pointed to where her older brother was standing with three other men. "He doesn't seem very happy."

"I'll go talk to him," Harry said and edged forward through the crowd. It took him a few minutes to reach Cedric, who frowned and shook his head at whatever remark Harry had made.

Harry shrugged, turned away from his brother, and then he

grinned.

"A lot of later starting positions have already been drawn," he said when he reached them. "Cedric's team drew number forty-three and he's not happy about it."

"Oh, let's hope we start before him," Ella said. "That would give him one more thing to be unhappy about. I'm still angry at him for not warning Jack about Iona Smith."

"He never apologized?" Caroline asked.

"Maybe to Father," Ella said. "But he didn't act like he was sorry."

"Just sorry that he got caught," Harry said. He turned to Caroline and Jack. "I think missing out on the last Endeavour made him cynical and a little cruel. You should try to stop that from happening to Becca."

"I'll mention it to Mother," Caroline said.

Half an hour later they were next in line.

After checking their names against a list, they were ushered towards a table. Mr. Townsend was standing with the team ahead of them.

A man at the table pulled something from the box in front of him and passed it to Mr. Townsend, who opened his hand to show a white disk with black lettering.

"Number eighty-three," he said, handing the disk to one team member. "Hand this in at the start of your competition."

"Eighty-three," a young man ahead of them said. "We'll never get in."

"We're next," Caroline said, grabbing Ella's arm as they shuffled forward.

The man drew a token, but instead of handing it to Mr. Townsend, he handed it to the woman standing behind him.

"Number twenty-five," she said, holding up the token. She handed that off to Mr. Townsend, who smiled and gave it to Jack. "Congratulations and good luck," he said and then the four of them were ushered away from the desk.

"Twenty-five!" Jack said, holding up the token. "We'll get inside the Abbey for sure."

"Don't lose it," Harry said. "It won't affect our start time but they don't like it when they're lost. Especially if another team tries to use it to start earlier. And yes, that's a very good number."

"It is." Caroline felt cold and hot all at once. It was real! They were going to enter Blackmeadow Abbey. "There has only been one Endeavour where fewer than twenty-five teams entered." That had been the one Mr. Anson and Mr. Townsend had competed in.

"Even better, we start before Cedric," Ella said.

"At forty-three, Cedric's team has a good chance of entering the Abbey," Harry said. "But all of the easily found artifacts will have been discovered by then."

"Which is why we have a plan," Caroline said. She followed Jack as he led the way back through the crowd and out to the street.

Jack stopped abruptly and Caroline almost walked into him.

"Hello Sean, Mrs. Smith," Jack said and paused. "Iona."

"I hope you are all well," Caroline said, stepping ahead of her brother. "Mrs. Anson said that she saw you the other night. I am happy you are enjoying the festivities." Iona seemed to be deliberately ignoring her and instead was peering around at other teams. Caroline wanted to believe it was because she couldn't look her in the eyes, but really, not one of the Smiths seemed in the least bit contrite about the way they had behaved.

"We are," Mrs. Smith said. "But we have not forgotten the reason we're all here. Sean's team has just drawn a very nice starting position: number twenty-nine. Isn't that marvellous? I do hope you all weren't disappointed. I see Ella and Harry Townsend are with you. Sean said that your brother Cedric starts after him."

"Yes," Harry said. "Cedric wished for an earlier start, but the odds are good that he will be able to compete."

"And you?" Mrs. Smith prodded.

"We'll be in the Abbey when Sean enters," Caroline said. "Good luck to you and I'll be sure to tell Mrs. Anson hello." She pushed Jack, who hadn't said a word after his greeting.

Iona hadn't spoken either and that just made Caroline sad. She'd thought they'd been such good friends, when in reality Iona was just looking for someone to take advantage of. Someone unsophisticated and trusting and Caroline refused to blame herself for being those things.

"I'm glad that's over," Ella said.

"I wish we hadn't seen them," Jack replied.

"I'm glad we saw them now," Caroline said. "Rather than seeing Sean for the first time on competition day, which is possible, since we start just a few positions ahead of him."

"There's one hour between team starts," Harry said. "We probably won't see him."

"Not at the start," Caroline said. "But unless we are extraordinarily quick, we'll still be in Blackmeadow Abbey when it's his team's turn to enter. Now, let's find our group and tell them our good news."

THE DAY BEFORE the start of the competition, the first twenty teams were to be taken to Blackmeadow Abbey by carrier.

Caroline and Jack watched them leave from the square: twenty carriers were lined up and competitors milled about, talking excitedly or looking nervous as they said goodbye to their families and friends. A bell rang out and the teams finally climbed into the compartments.

Then the carriers left in one long line.

"One more night before it's our turn to leave," Jack said. "It's time to meet Harry and Ella."

They crossed the square, weaving past the exiting well-wishers to the main doors of Administration Hall. Ella was waiting off to one side of the entrance and waved them over.

"Harry will be a few more minutes," she said. "He decided he needed wheels for his box. The lead lining makes it very heavy."

"He can't wheel it inside," Caroline said. "The rules are very clear that we have to be able to carry our item into the Abbey." There weren't a lot of rules for the Endeavour: the most important one was that that you couldn't make any decisions that might endanger a life. The other key ones were about taking items inside and that teams were not to talk to each other, let alone work together—unless it was matter of helping someone injured. There were never any penalties for that and once a team had even been rewarded. They'd helped a team in distress and had then been awarded the artifacts found by a team who had refused to give aid.

After their discussions with the Artifact Society, they had come up with the items to take inside. Caroline had a pick axe with a telescoping handle for digging out even hard to reach artifacts. Ella was bringing a lamp and extra matches.

Harry's item was a sizeable box that he'd had lined with lead for safely transporting any artifacts they found, and Jack had some extra thick work gloves. The hope was that Harry and Jack's items would ensure that they were safe from dangerous or exploding artifacts.

"He said he'll be able to carry it in," Ella said. "But depending on what we find, it might be too heavy to carry back out."

"I like that optimism," Jack said with a laugh. "According to Mrs. Anson, most artifacts are small: we'd need to recover quite a few of them to warrant the wheels."

"She also said that some of the lost artifacts are larger," Caroline replied. "And that is what we're targeting. Look, there he is."

Harry was crossing the square, heading towards them. He was pulling a large wooden box behind him.

"It's bigger than I thought," Jack said. "I understand the need for wheels."

"I can carry it," Harry said. He grabbed a sturdy looking leather strap and pulled the box off the ground and slung the strap over his shoulder. "Not for very long, but I don't need to carry it far."

"Just until we get into the Abbey," Caroline said. "And there are no rules against resting on the way to the front entrance so we can take our time, if needed."

"You're sure he doesn't have to carry it out as well?" Jack asked.

"Yes," Caroline said. "The rules only state that you must carry your object into the Abbey. There is nothing that says you have to carry it after that, including when you exit. As long as a single competitor can carry it, we should be fine. A team once tried to take a large cart in, but it was disqualified because a single person couldn't carry it. Competitors who require devices like wheeled chairs are exempted from having to carry them, of course, but they still need to be able to carry their object: it can't be towed behind them."

"Then my box is ready," Harry said. "Do we want to take a last look at the archives?"

"I am too nervous and excited to do anything," Caroline said. "Do you think we really won't hear any results before we enter the Abbey?" She could hardly believe they had less than twenty-four hours before they left for Blackmeadow Abbey and what she considered the start of their Endeavour. They would still have to wait for their turn to enter, but they'd be there, on site, while other teams were inside.

"Maybe when we get to the camp," Harry said. "According to Father, they do their best to keep teams that have exited the Abbey from talking to those who haven't yet competed because it could give them an unfair advantage."

"As though starting first isn't an advantage," Jack said. "And yes, I know that the draw is supposed to make it fair."

"Father also said that they can't stop people from talking," Ella said.

"It's not something any team has ever been disqualified for," Caroline said. "I think it's worth trying to see if we can get some information so we can update our maps."

"You're certain the maps won't count as an object?" Ella asked. "We could manage with one map, but then we'd need to decide which object to leave behind."

"We're allowed paper and pencils," Caroline said. "Our paper just happens to be already drawn on."

"I know you said that before," Ella replied. "Sorry to keep asking the same question. I'm just nervous."

"Let's go to the park," Harry said. "Maybe if we talk through every scenario again, we can dispel some of the nerves."

"Good idea," Jack said. He started leading the way across the square.

Caroline sighed and followed. She didn't think going through the scenarios would help her nerves, but it was better than doing nothing.

# 16

Caroline hugged her mother before stepping into the carrier compartment. She settled in beside Harry, across from Ella. Jack was the last one in and he closed the door and sat down.

"Find them all!" Becca yelled from outside the carrier.

"We'll do our best," Jack called, leaning out the window. A bell rang and a moment later, the carrier started to move.

Caroline leaned back and closed her eyes. "I just want to be there!" she said.

"We'll be there for dinner," Harry said.

"Then we'll find out what time we go in tomorrow," Ella said. "I'm so nervous I doubt I'll even be able to eat."

"Do your best," Jack said. "No one thinks straight when they're hungry. And don't forget, we all need to bring water with us tomorrow." He paused. "Sorry, I can't seem to stop saying things we already know."

"It's better than realizing we've missed something important," Harry said.

"Assume that we have," Caroline said. "And then we won't be surprised when we discover exactly what it is."

She settled back and stared out the window. After a few minutes of low conversation, her teammates all quieted.

They'd done what they could—prepared the best they could—and now they just had to wait. Oh, she would still try to talk to someone who had already been in the Abbey: updating their maps would be incredibly useful. But the trip to Blackmeadow Abbey would take hours and until they arrived, there was absolutely nothing to do.

Idly, she wondered what other teams were doing in their carriers: Sean Smith would be in one of the carriers behind them. Was his team discussing plans on how to proceed or were they dreaming about the artifacts they would find and the opportunities they would bring?

Her team had hardly spoken about what came *after* the Endeavour. They were completely focused on what they would do *during* the competition. How to find the large room; how to search for lost artifacts and most importantly, how to make it out safely.

She didn't think she could be happier with how they'd all come together as a team. How hard they'd all researched and discussed and planned for this.

The Endeavour was one of the most important events of their lives: dangerous enough to kill, and yet the potential benefit—the potential of finding an artifact that could change their futures—meant it was a risk worth taking.

They'd done their best to mitigate that risk. She doubted most of the other teams had: doubted that Sean Smith's team had done anything close to what they'd done.

The landscape changed as the hours passed. When she caught a glimpse of some blackened land, she stuck her head out of the window.

"We're here," she said. "I see tents up ahead."

The carrier started to slow and then it stopped. Someone pounded on the compartment door.

"Welcome to Blackmeadow Abbey," a man said. "Find your tent: it has your token number over the door." Then he was gone.

"This is it," Jack said. He opened the compartment door and stood aside while the rest of them got out.

Their bags, including Harry's box, were taken off the back of the carrier and put in a pile. Other teams were scrambling to grab their belongings and rush to the tents but Caroline took a few steps and turned.

There, past the fence, stood the blackened ruins of

Blackmeadow Abbey. They really were here.

The building was impressive despite the obvious signs of disrepair: stones had fallen from the walls and there was a noticeable sag in the peak of the roof. A shiny black path led down to a door that gaped open, the inside a slightly darker black than the outside. She could see a few windows farther back but from the outside there was nothing that looked like the large room.

"Are we ready?" Jack asked.

"Let's let everyone else go first," Caroline said. "I've only seen the Abbey twice and Jack, you've never seen it. Just wait until you see it at night."

Her brother joined her. "I have seen paintings of it," he said. "But it is definitely more impressive in person."

"Look." Caroline pointed. "The carriers have stopped over there. I bet they're taking competitors back to Norbarrow. Let's grab our things and see if we can talk to some of them."

She turned to find that Harry had already loaded all of their bags into the lead-lined box.

"I am so glad I have wheels on this," he said to her. "Let's go."

The carriers had left enough of a track that Harry didn't seem to have any trouble towing their bags. By the time they reached the last carrier, the first ones had already left. A few dozen people were milling around and Caroline stepped closer to them.

"We found five," one young woman was saying to a slightly older man. "The corridors were so confusing that we just kept getting turned around and before we knew it, we were at the exit. We tried to go back but it wouldn't let us."

"That didn't happen to us until after we reached a large room. We took every right turn to get there but once we left that room, the corridor led to the exit. When we turned around, the corridor we'd just taken to get there was gone. There was a wall behind us and the door in front and only one way to go. Out."

The woman spied Caroline and bent her head to her companion, and they walked away.

Caroline returned to Harry, who had stayed with the bags and cart. She pulled out her map and studied it. "I overheard someone say that all right turns took them to the large room," she said, making a note on her map. "And just as we've read, people can't seem to backtrack."

Ella and Jack joined them.

"Someone thought we'd competed," Ella said, grinning. "They told us they went right for two turns and then went left and that took them directly to the exit. They didn't find one single artifact."

Caroline made another note on her map.

"If you're leaving, find yourself a carrier," a man said as he approached them.

Jack held up their token and the man scowled.

"Go find your tent," the man said. "If you haven't competed, you're not supposed to be here."

"Yes, sir," Jack said. "We were just viewing the Abbey." He turned to the others. "I'm hungry anyway."

Their tent was easy to find. Inside, the main area held a table and four chairs, and in each of the two smaller sections at the back, were two cots. A note on the table listed an assigned dining time as well as a map showing the location of the dining tent and latrine.

Caroline unfolded her map of Blackmeadow Abbey on the table and everyone crowded around.

"Based on what I overheard, taking every right-hand turn takes us to the large room," she said. "But I don't know how many turns that is."

"Do we know how many artifacts have been found?" Harry asked.

"The team we talked to said they found none," Ella said.

"I overheard a woman say they found five," Caroline replied. She shrugged. "I'm not sure it even matters to us since we are targeting lost artifacts."

"We already know that anything easily found will already be taken by the time we enter," Jack said. He picked up the note. "It's almost time for us to eat, and I wasn't lying: I'm starving."

Caroline folded up her map and tucked it into her pocket.

They had to line up for dinner, which was served to them on trays. They found a table in the back, and Caroline had just picked up her fork when she saw Sean Smith. He was with three other young men and they were all laughing. He met her eyes for a moment, and he frowned, before his attention returned to his companions.

Caroline shook her head. She hoped he did well, she really did, but what she hoped more than that was that she didn't see him during the competition.

# 17

Caroline's hand shook as she folded up her map. Her stomach was in knots, making her glad that she hadn't attempted to eat very much at breakfast.

"Team twenty-five, are you ready?" Mr. Anson asked. He was tasked with officially authorizing teams to enter the Abbey. The group of them—Caroline, Jack, Harry, and Ella, along with Mr. Anson and another Administrator—stood in front of a gate. Past the gate was the blackened meadow and a rocky path that led to the Abbey.

Jack looked around and Caroline nodded at him.

"We are," Jack said.

"Then good luck. And Harry," Mr. Anson said. "You must carry that box through the door of the Abbey, otherwise your team will be disqualified. We will be watching."

And that was it. Caroline followed her brother. Ella was right behind her and Harry—carrying the lead-lined box—was last. The path was blackened and rough with patches of what seemed like melted rock. As they got closer to Blackmeadow Abbey, a dry wind picked up and dust devils spun black grit along the path in front of them.

A few minutes later they stood in front of the open entrance to the Abbey. Despite the bright sun that shone down on them, barely any light seemed to filter inside.

Jack stopped at the entrance and they all huddled together.

Broken stones that had somehow been chipped from the wall littered the ground, although it was clear directly in front of the door.

A warm wind blew out the door and Caroline covered her eyes to protect them against dust. Once it was past, she nervously stared inside but all she could see was dark.

"I'll get the lamp lit," Ella said. She fumbled with a match but soon the lamp shed a soft glow through the door to the Abbey.

"Are we ready?" Jack asked, echoing Mr. Anson's question.

"Yes," Caroline said, her nerves suddenly gone. "We keep right. That should take us to the big room."

"Then we spend as much time as we want digging around," Harry said. "Let's go. I can't wait to put this box down."

"Jack," Ella said. "You're the lead."

"I'm heading in." Jack stepped through the entrance, followed by Ella, who raised the lamp high to illuminate what was ahead of them.

Caroline looked up when she entered: the ceilings were high and what appeared to be black smoke swirled overhead. The air seemed to crackle with energy so despite the strong smell of old smoke, she guessed that it was magic that eddied above them.

Something thudded to the ground and Harry let out a sigh. "The floors are pretty flat and clear," he said. "I was worried there would be a lot of rocks and debris. The less I have to carry this box the better I'll like it."

"It looks like we take our first right-hand turn up ahead," Jack called out. "Stay close." He led the way forward. Jack and Ella turned the corner, taking the light with them. Caroline followed, Harry and his rumbling box on wheels right behind her.

On the third right-hand turn, when Ella had already gone around the corner with the lamp, something glittering near the floor caught Caroline's eye.

"Wait," she called. "I think there might be an artifact here." She bent down to look. Ella came back around the corner and held the lamp above her head, and Caroline lost sight of the object. "I think I need it to be dark in order to see it."

"Maybe that's why no one else found it," Harry said, peering over her shoulder.

"Should I douse the light or go back around the corner?" Ella asked. "I don't want us to be separated."

"We were both able to turn around and come back," Jack said. "Maybe we weren't far enough down the new hallway. We'll stay close, though. We don't want anyone separated and in here alone."

"That sounds like as a good a plan as any," Harry said. "I'll stay here with Caroline. Hand me the gloves so we can safely put whatever this is in the box."

Jack tossed the gloves to Harry and then he and Ella stepped back around the corner.

As soon the bright light was gone, Caroline could see a faint shimmer in the wall just a few inches above the floor. She pulled out her pick axe and carefully scraped at the top layer of grime.

Something popped off the wall and fell to the floor. "Gloves, please," she said. Harry passed them to her, and she scooped up the item, brushing off all of the grime and dirt.

Stunned, she stood up and held the item out so Harry could see it. "I have never heard of a competitor finding their own artifact before," she said. "Jack, come take a look. I've found the necklace I surrendered."

Jack and Ella returned, bringing the lamp with them.

"It sure looks like it," Jack said, peering down at it. "It always glowed in the dark, so do you think it didn't change?"

"Maybe not," Caroline said. "It's possible that this Endeavour has very weak magic, or the necklace hasn't been in the Abbey long enough." She shrugged. "Or both. Anyway, this is our first artifact. Does anyone mind if I wear it? It feels like a good omen."

"Go ahead," Harry said.

Caroline took the gloves off and handed them to Jack before undoing the clasp and putting the necklace on. It felt right to be wearing it, rather than putting it in the box.

"Are we ready to keep going?" Jack asked.

Ella and the lamp disappeared around a corner, and suddenly, the glow from her necklace flared into a bright light.

"Are you all right?" Harry asked, his face eerily lit.

"I'm fine," Caroline fingered the necklace. "This is new, this amount of light. I guess the Abbey has changed the magic after all."

"What is that?" Harry asked, pointing over her shoulder.

Caroline turned to see a patch of wall a foot above her head, glowing with a bright, white light. She stepped closer to it and the intensity of the light coming from her necklace increased. She unclasped it and held it up, and the light on the wall brightened.

"I think we have found another artifact," Harry called out. "And I think we have an artifact finder."

Jack and Ella came back around the corner, bringing the lamp with them.

"You dig this one out," Caroline said to Harry, handing him the pick axe. "You're the one who spotted it."

"Only because your necklace made it glow," Harry said. He swung the pick axe at the wall. As black flakes were chipped away, the glow of whatever was there became much brighter.

"I think it's some sort of cup," Ella said, shading her eyes from the glare. "Wasn't there one handed in two Endeavours ago?"

"A chalice," Caroline said. "If it is that one, then this is a lost artifact."

A chunk of wall fell to the floor with a thud. "It's gold coloured with a bunch of gems on it," Harry said. "Gloves please, Jack." Harry handed the pick axe back to Caroline and put on the gloves. He reached up and pulled the chalice from a small alcove. It glowed even brighter when it got closer to Caroline's necklace.

"This is going into the box," Harry said. "And that necklace needs to stay out because I think it's going to show us where all the artifacts are."

As soon as the chalice was in the box and the lid was closed, Caroline's necklace dimmed to a gentle glow.

"That's incredible," Jack said.

"It certainly is if it really does show us where artifacts are," Ella said. "Especially lost ones. What's the best way to go forward? With Caroline in front or in the back?"

"I think in the back," Caroline said. "When Ella takes the lamp around a corner, I'll hang back and see if anything glows. But make sure you don't get too far ahead of me. Just because you were able to backtrack once doesn't mean you'll always be able to."

"I'll stay with Caroline," Harry said. "If we do get separated, we can still fill the box with artifacts. But Jack or Ella should dig the next one out."

They all turned the corner, and when Ella raised the lamp, the corridor in front of them stretched off into darkness.

"I don't see the next right-hand turn," Jack said. "Ella, you and I should go back around the corner so Caroline can see if anything glows around here."

Ella turned and stopped. "There's no corner to go around," Ella said. She lifted the lamp and Caroline peered past her down another long corridor.

"Interesting," Jack said. "All right. We always said we'd go forward. I guess we don't have a choice."

"We should stick closer together," Ella said. "And stay in the pairs we already decided on. Here, I'll lower the wick and dim the lamp." She made an adjustment and the light from the lamp turned into an orange glow. "Does that work? I don't want to extinguish the flame. Trying to get it lit again in the dark would not be fun."

"My necklace might give off enough light to light the lamp," Caroline said. "But it's better if we don't have to count on it." She took the necklace off and held it up high: its soft glow reflected off the shiny burnt walls. "Nothing so far." She started walking, the necklace held up in front of her. "Here's the next right," she called after walking a dozen paces. "We just couldn't see it because everything is so black and burned." The wheels of the cart rumbled as Harry joined her.

"I'll stand where I can see down each hallway," Harry said. "Hopefully that will keep us from being separated. You go on ahead."

Caroline nodded and turned the corner. Her eyes widened as the necklace flared to life. "We've found the room already," she called. "Come look." They had been calling it a large room based on competitor accounts but she hadn't been prepared for just how big it was. The ceiling was at least twenty feet above her and she could barely see the far wall. And everywhere she looked, on every wall and scattered across the floor, there were glowing patches of light. There had to be at least a dozen—make that two dozen—patches, and they all had to be artifacts.

"Wow!" Harry joined her. "I don't think the box is big enough."

"This is even better than I could have hoped," Jack said.

"Come on, let's get these artifacts claimed before someone else finds this room."

They were halfway to the closest glowing patch on a section of smooth floor when there was a roar from the hallway. Caroline glanced over her shoulder just as a sudden gust of wind burst through the door into the room. Black mist roiled and swirled up towards the high ceiling. It seemed to crawl the length of the room before dissipating at the far end.

"What was that?" Jack asked.

"Magic," Harry replied. "I felt it."

"Me too," Ella said. "Like an insect crawling along my spine."

"I didn't feel anything," Caroline said. "Jack?" Her brother shook his head. "Is that because you two have Natural blood and we don't?"

"If it is, doesn't seem like it's going to be an advantage for us," Harry said. "Come on. We can't do anything about rogue magic and it looks like we're safer here than in the hallways."

Caroline sucked in a breath as she followed Harry. She did not want to be caught in a hallway by wild magic. She hadn't felt it, not like Ella and Harry, but it seemed dangerous and malevolent to her.

When they reached the glowing spot on the floor, Jack held his hand out, and Caroline handed him the pick axe. He swung it over his head and then slammed it down onto the floor. Shiny black chips flew up and the glow brightened as the artifact was uncovered.

"It's a vase," Jack said, pulling on the gloves. He pulled the tiny vase from the hole in the ground and tipped it. Black sand drained out of it. "I'll put this in the box. Ella"—he handed the pick axe to her—"you're next." He grinned at Caroline. "Mrs. Anson mentioned this one, I think, from three Endeavours ago. Another lost artifact."

Harry lifted the lid of the box and Jack turned and put the artifact in it. Once the lid was down, the light was extinguished.

Caroline followed Ella to the left-hand wall, and a large patch of light.

"Do I just smash it?" Ella asked. "What if I break the artifact?"

"The magic makes them pretty hard to break," Caroline said. "But maybe that's how they explode. Hit the edge of the patch first."

Ella swung the sharp end of the pick axe at the wall and it dug into the shiny black surface. When she pulled the pick out, a large sheet of black slid off the wall and crashed to the floor.

Caroline had to cover her eyes at the sudden brightness.

"Can you tell what it is?" Harry asked. The box he pulled rolled to a stop. "Jack, hand her the gloves. And shade your eyes when I open the box. The more we put in there, the brighter it's getting."

Jack handed Ella the gloves and she put them on before turning back to whatever was in the wall. "It's some sort of wheel," Ella said. She grunted as she tugged at the item. She slipped on the debris from the crumbled wall and almost fell when the artifact suddenly gave way. She brushed off clumps of black dirt and then held up the item. "Does this seem familiar?"

"No," Caroline said. "I don't remember ever hearing about something like that." It wasn't a wheel but it was round. "Is it a platter?"

Ella shrugged. "We'll need to ask Mrs. Anson about it. For now, it goes in the box."

By the time they were halfway across the room, they had uncovered eight artifacts in addition to the necklace and the chalice, and there were still over a dozen more that they could see. They had just put the eighth one in the box and closed the lid when they heard someone yell.

"Quick," Jack said. "Turn the light up. Caroline, hide the necklace."

Caroline tucked the necklace in her pocket as Ella turned the wick to make the lamp shine brighter. Four people stood just inside the entrance to the room.

Caroline's heart sank when she recognized one of them. Sean Smith; the very last person she had wanted to see in Blackmeadow Abbey.

# 18

Caroline stepped closer to the rest of her team as they watched Sean and his team saunter towards them.

"They found the place where we dug out the vase," Caroline whispered.

One of Sean's team members kicked at the hole in the floor. She didn't hear what he said but he sounded angry.

"We'll ask them," Sean said, and the four of them started crossing the floor again. "The Morrises and Townsends have found themselves an artifact or two. Can we see them?"

"No," Caroline said. "That's against the rules, you know that. You're not even supposed to be talking to us, or even in the same space. You're supposed to wait until we leave."

"Who's going to enforce the rules?" one of Sean's teammates said. "You?"

"Yes," Harry said. "My father is an Administrator and he will make sure that anything you find is confiscated."

"They don't do that," the other man sneered. "We get to keep whatever we come out with. What's in the box?"

"They have confiscated artifacts in the past," Caroline said. "At the Endeavour from fifty-nine years ago, one team apparently stole an artifact from another team. Every single artifact that team had found was confiscated, not just the stolen one, and handed to the wronged team. One of those confiscated artifacts was used to create speakers."

"You just made that up."

"Sean knows I didn't, don't you, Sean?" Caroline said. "He knows that I am an expert on the history of Endeavours."

"Yeah, she is," Sean agreed. "And we're not stealing anything. I was hoping we could work together."

"Why would we do that?" Jack asked. "After you tried to trick us into teaming up with you and your sister when all along, Iona didn't even have an artifact."

"Your family had a spare," Sean said with a shrug.

"We don't," Caroline said. "You know that's for our little sister."

"You would just give her a new one," Sean said. "After the Endeavour."

"You still need to wait outside this room until we exit," Ella said. "Not doing so is enough for your artifacts to be confiscated."

"Oh, come on," a second teammate of Sean's said. "Like Sean said, we can work together."

"No," Harry said. "We can't. You know that's against the rules. You need to head back to the hallway and wait there until we are finished in here."

"Make me," the man said.

"No," Sean replied. "They know two Administrators. We'll be disqualified."

"Not if there's no one left alive to complain."

"Are you threatening us?" Caroline asked. She was too angry to be afraid. "Sean, really. You will *never* get away with it, especially since we do know two Administrators. They will discover what you did and not only will any artifacts be confiscated but you will spend the rest of your lives locked up."

Jack grabbed the pick axe out of Caroline's hands. "Even before that, we won't go without a fight. Which one of you is willing to die for this." He raised the pick axe above his head.

"Come on, guys," Sean said. "This is not the way to do this."

"If I don't come out with at least one artifact, I might as well be dead," one man said. Another nodded and now Caroline felt fear.

"Not me," the third teammate said. "I am not fighting anyone. We need to do what they said and go back to the hallway."

"Hey!" Someone was standing in the doorway. "You can't be

in there together!"

"We know," Harry called out. "But this team refuses to leave. And just now they've threatened us. You are our witnesses. What team are you?"

"Number twenty-seven," came the reply. "What's yours?"

"Twenty-five," Harry replied. "And this is team twenty-nine in case you need to report them."

"I might anyway. Hey! Team twenty-nine, you need to come here or we *will* report you."

"Come on, guys," Sean said. "I can't afford to be disqualified. We need to follow the rules."

His teammates grumbled but they all turned and left. Once everyone was out of the room, Caroline sighed.

"We need to do this as quickly as possible." She pulled out the necklace and the buried artifacts glowed brighter in response.

"I'd leave a couple for team twenty-seven if I didn't think Sean Smith and his thugs would get them first," Ella said. She turned the wick down on the lamp and walked towards the nearest buried artifact.

"Do you think that would be allowed?" Jack asked Caroline. "I mean, we wouldn't have to give them an artifact, just identify where one was."

"As long as we don't have a long conversation, I don't think that would be considered working with them," Caroline replied. "But I'm not doing anything to help Sean and his team. They threatened us!"

"I know." Jack sighed. He handed the pick axe to Caroline. "I think it's your turn to find an artifact."

IT TOOK THEM another three hours to dig up all but two of the artifacts.

Ella, her face dirty, held the third last artifact in gloved hands. "I'm getting tired. How many is this?"

"Twenty," Jack said. "With two more to go."

Despite Caroline putting her necklace in her pocket, when the lid to the box was opened, the light that streamed out was almost blinding. Ella put the dirt-covered artifact in the box and Harry slammed the lid shut. There were only two more patches of light left in the room and they were both about halfway up the back wall.

The floor trembled and Caroline almost lost her footing.

"Look out!" Harry pulled her and Ella to the ground behind the box as black mist swept across the floor towards them.

Jack dropped to the ground and huddled behind them as the mist swept over them. For a moment all Caroline could see was black, and then it was gone.

Feeling queasy, Caroline watched the mist skim across the floor to the door.

There were a couple of muffled shouts from the hallway outside the room and then it was quiet.

"Is everyone all right?" Harry asked. Ella nodded.

"I'm a little nauseous," Jack said.

"Me too," Caroline said. "We need to check on whoever is out in the hallway. Even if it is Sean's team."

"And then we should leave," Ella replied. "The next rogue magic spell could be worse, although this time it only affected you and Jack."

"Yes," Caroline replied. "We have twenty artifacts. That's five each, which is an extraordinary number and a record. If team twenty-seven is still there and Sean's team is not, I don't see why we can't mark the remaining two artifacts and leave."

"I agree," Ella said. "I'm tired and dirty, and I would like to help the team that scared off Sean Smith. Besides, we have no idea how many artifacts we might find on our way out. It could still be hours before we leave Blackmeadow Abbey."

Jack took off at a trot. He reached the doorway and stepped into the hall. Sounds of an argument spilled out of the hallway.

Worried about her brother, Caroline was about to head that way when he emerged from the hall and jogged back to them.

"Sean's team just left," he said when he reached them. "One of their members was knocked off his feet by the rogue magic and hit his head when he fell. He's awake but clearly needs medical attention, and the rest of them didn't want to take him out to get it."

"I am not surprised," Caroline said. She'd been right to worry that Sean and Iona wouldn't care about her and Jack's safety.

"Me neither," Jack said. "Not really. Anyway, team twenty-seven threatened to report them if they didn't get him help, so they left. Let's mark these last two artifacts for them. I'd like to leave them something."

"I'll do it," Harry said. He took the pick axe to the back wall and swung it near a glowing patch. Before a chunk of the melted wall even slid to the floor, he was at the second patch of light.

"Done," he said. "Let's get out of here." He handed the pick axe to Caroline and grabbed the strap for the box. He grunted as he started to drag the box across the floor. "This is really heavy now. Two more artifacts and I might not be able to tow it anyway."

When they reached the doorway, Caroline waited until everyone else was out. "We're too tired to really explore the back wall," she said as she passed team twenty-seven. "It might be best if you start there." She nodded and followed Harry, who seemed to be struggling with the box.

"Do you want me to push?" she asked him. "Oh dear." Up ahead was a patch of light in the floor. "We found another one!" she called out. "Shall we get this or leave it? Whose turn is it to dig it out?"

It was her turn. She was exhausted, they all were, but it was one thing to leave artifacts for a team that had helped them and quite another to just leave one behind, potentially undiscovered. Without the necklace they would have walked right past this one, and no doubt others would too.

"I'm going to dig this one up," Caroline said, wielding reaching for the pickaxe. A few minutes later, wide-eyed, Caroline lifted the artifact up.

"Do you recognize it?" Jack asked.

"I do," Caroline said. She raised the candlestick. "It's the artifact that allowed flight! I can't believe we found it!" She also couldn't believe she had been so tired that she'd almost not bothered to dig it up. "In case it still does that, I think you should have it."

"Are you sure that's what it is?" Jack asked. He leaned in for a closer look.

"I'm confident it's that artifact," Caroline said. "But I'm not sure it still holds the power of flight." She rubbed some dirt off the base and metal glinted. "Mr. Stanford was right about it being brass and both he and Mr. Hobson were certain it was a candlestick."

Ella and Harry crowded around.

"It doesn't seem like much," Ella said.

"Exactly," Caroline said. "That's why it ended up back here. Is everyone all right with Jack having this one?"

"It's probably valuable enough for the whole team to share," Jack said. His grin was infectious and Caroline smiled too.

"Then we can share in any profits you earn," Ella said. "I wouldn't even know where to start with something like that, and you would."

"Same here," Harry said. "You already know what you'll do first to test it, don't you?"

"Yes." Jack laughed. "I already know three different tests I want to run on it and who I can ask to do them. All right," he nodded finally, "but we'll share the proceeds."

"Agreed." Caroline put the candlestick in the box and Harry closed it. "Let's go."

They took one last right-hand turn and there, up ahead, was an open doorway. Just past it was the flickering and swirling lights of the Abbey.

"We're here," Jack said. "We made it out."

Caroline peered past him. "I think it's close to midnight. Have we been inside for most of the day?"

"It felt like two days," Ella said. "So I am not surprised."

"You're sure I don't have to carry the box out?" Harry asked. "Because I don't think I could."

"I'm sure," Caroline said. "Hey, all that work and we didn't even use the map." She followed Jack outside and looked up at the dancing lights.

"We did," Jack said. "Just not while we were inside."

Caroline sighed. "And now we're out." She felt her shoulders relax as tension she hadn't even been aware of drained away.

Harry wheeled the box out through the doorway and stopped just past Jack and Caroline. "The official exit table is over there just inside the fence," he said.

Caroline looked where he was pointing. A dozen lamps glowed off in the distance and people were milling around.

"Let's go," Ella said. She held her lamp up. "The path runs in a straight line." She turned to Harry. "And it looks pretty smooth." She set off, and Harry, dragging the box on wheels, followed her.

Caroline linked her arm through Jack's. "Even if that last artifact has nothing to do with flight, I'm sure we found something that will get you started as a Builder."

"The odds are good," Jack said. "And I doubt anyone will say you can't go to Linley Academy."

"The odds are good," she echoed as they made their way to the waiting Administrators.

Caroline was tired and dirty and she was pretty sure she'd broken all of her fingernails, but they'd done it. They'd found a number of lost artifacts and had all come out safely. She was certain that she would not have any regrets about her Endeavour even if nothing they found was valuable.

Even if all they did was write their own Endeavour story for future competitors to read.

# Epilogue

C aroline entered the classroom she'd been able to reserve for their meeting. Jack, Ella, and Harry were already sitting at a table.

"Sorry I'm late," she said. "My teacher wanted to talk to me after class."

"I hope nothing is wrong?" Ella asked.

"No. He wanted to ask if I thought the Artifact Society might be interested in giving a guest lecture."

"Mrs. Anson will love that," Ella said.

"She will." Caroline grinned. She and Ella had been enrolled at Linley Academy for one month now and she could still hardly believe it. They shared a suite of rooms too, and had even had guests over for lunch last week.

"She is something of a celebrity," Harry said. "And no longer an interested amateur."

"She wrote to tell me that the Administration has formally recognized them," Caroline said.

Mrs. Anson and the Artifact Society had become well-known after being asked to identify the artifacts their team had recovered from Blackmeadow Abbey.

Some of the artifacts had been lost for so long that without the Artifact Society's knowledge and research, it might have taken years for them to figure out what magical abilities they should ask Builders to investigate.

As it was, they had four teams of Builders working on powerful artifacts that had great potential both in terms of usefulness and eventual revenues.

That didn't even include the artifact for flight that Jack was working on with the Builder he was apprenticed to.

There had never been an Endeavour team with five major artifact finds before, but they had recovered a total of twenty-one artifacts. It made sense that a number of them would be useful and powerful.

"Shall we start the meeting?" Harry asked.

They'd agreed to share everything, including the less important artifacts. They were meeting now to decide what they wanted to do with the rest of them.

Caroline fingered her necklace. "I will give up my necklace if that's the team decision," she said. It didn't light up in the dark anymore but it did still glow when around magical items. The Administrators were hoping to use it to confirm magical artifacts for the next Endeavour but that was years away, and they couldn't force them to give it up.

"We have sixteen artifacts to divide up," Harry said. "I make no claim to the necklace. Anyone else?"

"You should keep it," Ella said. "If you hadn't found that we never would have been so successful."

"I think we should keep the rest as a group," Jack replied. "But if we do split them up that would be four per person. But since we have no idea who will need what in the future, I'd like to hope that we'll always be able to make fair decisions."

"Since one or more of the lost artifacts will pay off," Caroline said. "I doubt that any of us will need to sell artifacts in order to make ends meet. I would be open to giving a few away for the next Endeavour. We can hold a contest, or maybe a draw."

"I like that idea," Harry said. "It would be nice to give someone that kind of opportunity."

"We should ask the Artifact Society to manage that," Jack said. "They would make sure that whoever received it would deserve it."

"I'd prefer that," Ella said. "A simple draw could reward someone like Sean Smith or his sister Iona."

"A draw for artifacts might mean that there are fewer Sean and Iona Smiths," Caroline said. They hadn't reported the threat by Sean's team to the Administrators and neither had team twenty-seven. They'd recovered the last two artifacts in the big room, which turned out to be lost artifacts.

Sean's teammate's head injury had been relatively mild, but the Administrators had commended them for getting him to safety. It was hard to say for sure if they would have recovered more than three artifacts if they hadn't been forced to leave the competition.

Sean had ended up with one of the artifacts. Mrs. Anson reported that Iona had convinced the rest to blame the injured teammate for their lack of success and take the artifacts for themselves, leaving the injured man with nothing. Caroline was certain that Iona would have argued that Sean deserved an artifact if he'd been the one hurt.

"I like all of those ideas," Harry said. "Other than the five that are being studied, and Caroline's necklace, the artifacts are all safe in the Hall. I vote that we leave them there."

Four hands went up and they all grinned.

"Then let's go find some dinner," Jack said. "My treat."

"Of course, it's your treat," Caroline replied. "You're the only one us who is actually earning a living." They were all being paid by the Builders who were investigating the four artifacts, so they all actually had enough to pay for dinner.

"If you think being an apprentice is earning a living," Jack replied, "you need a better education."

"I am working on that," Caroline replied. She smiled as they all filed out of the room. She was working on that.

# Acknowledgements

I want to thank everyone at Tyche Books, especially my editor and publisher, Margaret Curelas. And a special thank you to Krista D. Ball, whose Twitter tag resulted in this book.

# About the Author

Jane Glatt loves that along with creating original worlds, writing fantasy allows her to indulge her curiosity about an eclectic group of subjects. So far, she's researched synaesthesia, medieval guilds, tidal rivers, cities atop bridges, pirates and privateers, plants used for healing, and the history of spying. For that last one she blames a visit to the International Spy Museum (yes, it's a real place), in Washington, D.C.

For news on Jane's future releases, visit her website http://janeglatt.com/index.html and sign up for her newsletter.

.